THE AUTHOR

Edward Frederic Benson was born at Wellington College, Berkshire in 1867. He was one of an extraordinary family. His father Edward White Benson – first headmaster of Wellington – later became Chancellor of Lincoln Cathedral, Bishop of Truro, and Archbishop of Canterbury. His mother, Mary Sidgwick, was described by Gladstone as 'the cleverest woman in Europe'. Two children died young but the other four, bachelors all, achieved distinction: Arthur Christopher as Master of Magdalene College, Cambridge and a prolific author; Maggie as an amateur egyptologist; Robert Hugh as a Catholic priest and progagandist novelist; and Fred.

Like his brothers and sisters, Fred was a precocious scribbler. He was still a student at Cambridge when he published his first book, *Sketches from Marlborough*. His first novel *Dodo* was published in 1893 to great success. Thereafter Benson devoted himself to writing, playing sports, watching birds, and gadding about. He mixed with the best and brightest of his day: Margot Asquith, Marie Corelli, Ethel Smyth and many other notables found their eccentricities exposed in the shrewd, hilarious world of his fiction.

Around 1918, E.F. Benson moved to Rye, Sussex. He was inaugurated mayor of the town in 1934. There in his garden-room, the collie Taffy beside him, Benson wrote many of his comical novels, his sentimental fiction, ghost stories, informal biographies, and reminiscences like *As We Were* (1930) – over one hundred books in all. Ten days before his death on 29 February 1940, E.F. Benson delivered to his publisher this last autobiography, *Final Edition*.

The Hogarth Press also publishes *Mrs Ames, Paying Guests, Secret Lives, As We Were, As We Are, Dodo – An Omnibus, The Freaks of Mayfair, The Luck of the Vails, The Blotting Book* and *An Autumn Sowing*. *Queen Victoria* is published by Chatto & Windus.

FINAL
EDITION

Informal Autobiography

E. F. Benson

New Introduction by
Hugo Vickers

THE HOGARTH PRESS
LONDON

Published in 1988 by
The Hogarth Press
Chatto and Windus Ltd
30 Bedford Square, London WC1B 3RP

First published in Great Britain by Longmans Green and Co Ltd 1940
Hogarth edition offset from original British edition
Copyright © the Executors of the Estate of the Revd K.S.P. McDowall
Introduction copyright © Hugo Vickers 1988

British Library Cataloguing in Publication Data

Benson, E.F.
Final edition: informal autobiography.
1. Benson, E. F. – Biography 2. Authors, English – 20th century – Biography
I. Title
23'.8 PR6003.E66Z/

ISBN 0 7012 0589 X

Printed in Great Britain by
Cox & Wyman Ltd
Reading, Berkshire

NEW INTRODUCTION

The town of Rye stands like a pyramid on an isolated rock, crowned by its fine old church. With Winchelsea it is one of the Cinque Ports, having been added to the original five as far back as the twelfth century. At times of Anglo-French hostility, Rye was in the forefront of the fray. Both the town and the Norman church were twice badly burned by the French. Rye has been left with a quaint, continental appearance – sagging roofs of red tile, Georgian fronts concealing Jacobean and Tudor interiors, cobbled streets leading to sudden picturesque views, and the famous Mermaid Inn.

Rye was in earlier times a haven for smugglers. So many of the innocent-looking houses concealed vast intercommunicating cellars, the chimneys contained secret hiding places, stairways were hidden in cupboards. Distilleries were built on the coasts of Flanders and France, devoted exclusively to gin and brandy for export by smuggling. Pack horses laden with kegs could often be heard rattling along in the small hours of the night, as the illicit merchandise headed inland. This custom of evading the customs and "owling" (the smuggling of English wool to the Continent) died out in the nineteenth century when the lifting of trade restrictions took the profit out of the business.

Rye remained an undiscovered waterside port until the beginning of this century. Since then, it has become something of a draw for tourists. It was once said that there was scarcely a house in New England without a picture of Rye on its walls. The influx caused Rye's planners to preserve its quaint old world appearance and helped pay for its upkeep.

Lamb House has been described by Sir Brian Batsford, who leases it from the National Trust, as "a pretty, early Georgian house right in the centre of the town, with an unexpected acre of garden". It is, perhaps, most famous as the house of Henry James. One of his visitors in the summer of 1900 was E.F. Benson, who eventually succeeded him, living there from 1917 until his death in 1940. *Final Edition* was handed to the publishers ten days before E. F. Benson's death, therefore in the latter years of the 1930s he was busy writing it in the very heart of the town.

Rye, perched on its rock with its history of smuggling, presents a decorative, sleepy exterior hiding potentially dangerous undercurrents. In a sense, the same is true of E.F. Benson – custodian of Lamb House, 645th Mayor of Rye, Baron of the Cinque Ports, Freeman of the Borough, Hon. Fellow of Magdalene College, Cambridge, man of letters, biographer of Queen Victoria and Edward VII, planner of gardens and dog lover. At the time he was writing *Final Edition*, he was in almost constant pain from arthritis in both hips. He could be seen occasionally walking about Rye on two sticks. He is remembered as a kind old gentleman, yet with more than a hint of austerity, a forbidding character to some.

He abhorred the telephone which was housed in a room of its own and only used for an occasional business talk with his broker. He wrote either in his garden-room (alas, destroyed by a bomb in 1940) or in the summer-house of the secret garden he had inspired. We can picture him on sunny days wheeling his books into the garden on a hospital trolley with a plentiful supply of sixpenny notebooks to write in. He then sent his manuscript to be typed locally and at this point he revised it. He suffered from the depression to which his whole family had been prone, and his faithful manservant, Charlie Tomlin has said: "It was quite a lot to put up with the last two years, the last year especially." Here, at least on the surface, is a prolific and popular author in his twilight years, summoning with great difficulty the necessary energy to complete his hundredth book, and succeeding admirably. There is no evidence of any fatigue in his writing.

Yet the conservative image of E.F. Benson (or Fred as he was known) also concealed some interesting undercurrents. He was somewhat more than eccentric. A solicitor's clerk, William

Bryan, visited him at Lamb House in connexion with his will and was astonished to find him "in bed immaculately dressed (from the waist up, at least) in a tunic shirt with gold cufflinks and a tie, etc., rather than the expected night-wear". He adored mimicry, enjoyed memorising the dreadful poems Queen Alexandra penned on the deaths of friends and preserved a scrapbook in which the printed name of Lord Desborough was inserted into a number of highly unlikely press-cuttings. He was obsessed by the artificial behaviour of socially ambitious women, whom he studied with the same close attention with which he observed the birds in the sky. He disliked Edward VIII and used to mutter: "Pity my father didn't drown him."

Fred's father, Edward, had missed this opportunity when, as Archbishop of Canterbury, he christened the boy in 1894. Edward White Benson had been left an orphan and was brought up by the Bursar of Trinity College, Cambridge. He became a junior master at Rugby and then the cane-swinging headmaster of Wellington. He met his future wife, Minnie Sidgwick (whose father founded the Society of Psychical Research), when she was twelve, sat her on his knee and proposed to her. Their wedding came six years later and, although it was a difficult marriage, she bore him six children, none of whom ever showed any interest in the opposite sex. After the Archbishop's death (in church, sitting next to Gladstone) in 1896, his widow Minnie shared her life and bed with Lucy Tait, the daughter of the previous Archbishop. In her diary the primate's widow made the plaintive plea: "O Lord grant that all carnal affections may die in me . . ."

In *Final Edition* Fred writes more freely about his parents and brothers and sisters than hitherto. He did this in the knowledge that he was the last survivor of the family and there would be no revenge. Nor does he seem to have felt any particular affection towards his brothers. They were a complex family, most of whom wrote prolifically. The eldest brother, Martin, died young, but Arthur (A. C. Benson) became Master of Magdalene College, Cambridge, after a successful stint as a famous Eton housemaster. He is best remembered for the words of "Land of Hope and Glory" and left behind him a lengthy diary which has been described as "much more pungent than would be expected by all but the most intimate of his friends".

Hugh (R.H.Benson), the youngest son, was a zealous Catholic writer and apologist, who destroyed his nervous system by overwork: his best known work was *Come Rack! Come Rope!* He had the misfortune to become entangled emotionally and professionally with Frederick Rolfe (Baron Corvo), the author of *Hadrian VII*.

The elder sister, Nellie, formed an attachment with Dame Ethel Smyth, while Maggie acquired a lesbian friend in Luxor and another in England before succumbing to "violent homicidal mania" which caused her to be locked up.

Fred was rather looked down upon by his brothers and sisters who thought him a worldly trifler. He loved to be part of society and his mother chided him, "Fred playing with his Earls and Countesses". In consequence, he was very much the loner of the family. Unlike the others, he was a keen sportsman, very good at skating, winter sports, tennis and golf. He had an early success, which was somewhat damaging to a potentially serious writing career, when *Dodo* was published in 1893. It is accepted that the central character – "a pretentious donkey with the heart and brains of a linnet" – was based on Margot Asquith. Needless to say, she was upset by the novel and thought the portrayal somewhat exaggerated, but Asquith himself confessed that Lord Rosebery warned him not to marry her by saying: "If you want to know what Miss Tennant is like, read *Dodo*." The success of this novel caused Fred's pen to overflow, but many of his later books were very facile in content.

Fred's early life included working for the British School of Archaeology in Athens and the Society for the Promotion of Hellenic Studies in Egypt, and he enjoyed a phase in Capri, then a Sapphist haven. At one point he shared a villa with Somerset Maugham and John Ellingham Brooks, the homosexual husband of the lesbian painter Romaine. To what extent Fred was a disciple of the louche activities for which

Emperor Tiberius was noted when he was on Capri remains unclear. There are a few dark hints buried in *Final Edition*, much quoted by Benson fanatics. It is instructive to observe how Fred dealt with Lord Henry Somerset's plight in *As We Were*. We now know that Lord Henry was accused of homosexuality by his wife and fled to Italy, where as an old man he dwelt in Florence, a very tall Don Quixote in broad-brimmed hat and gold monogrammed carpet slippers, who took the air in the side-car of a motor-cycle to the delight of the crowds. In *As We Were* Fred was reluctant to spell out the truth: "Lady Henry became aware of things in her husband's life that made it impossible for her to go on living with him . . ."

He says little more that is concrete on the subject. Similarly, in *Final Edition* he introduces us to Count Fersen and describes taking opium with him. Of the Count, Fred writes:

His antecedents were reported to be sensational, for it was said that he had been officially ordered to leave French soil owing to some scandal in which he had been involved about the celebration of a Black Mass. Probably foundationless . . .

We now know from James Money's admirable book on Capri that the creepy Count (the original for Compton Mackenzie's Count Marsac in *Vestal Fire*) was sentenced to six months' imprisonment in France on a charge of inciting minors to debauchery. By the spring of 1905, this information was known on the island.

With his acute interest in people and scandals, Fred must have known this and therefore we must be prepared to read between the lines. He plants pointers to a scandal but is reticent of writing of matters best left unsaid. There is also a passionless quality in him. Sir Steven Runciman who knew him well from the 1920s until his death, detected a "fastidious distaste for physical contact" and a lack of emotional involvement with anyone. This quality is reflected in the famous Mapp and Lucia novels with their gentle mockery of middle-class social standards, where the characters score points not at the bridge-table itself but by who they can get to the bridge-table in the first place.

Fred wrote these novels in Rye, setting the action in Tilling, a fictional Rye named from the river Tillingham. The topography is accurate and Mallards is Lamb House. He claimed that the characters were drawn from figures in his past, that he himself was variously Miss Mapp or Lucia (though the latter seems to be based partly on the relentless hostess Lady Colefax). He was first inspired by an invitation to tea from an old friend of his father's. Because his friend's wife was late, no tea could be served, as local protocol forbade it. Instead, the two men sat gazing at the family budgerigar and discussing Henry James. Over the years Fred had developed a retentive memory which delighted in such tiny nuances of pretentious social life. His novels have been praised for giving a strong impression of "carefully distorted portraiture", and gradually his love of society found fulfilment in gently mocking its protagonists and those who aspired to join it. But, again, there is reticence. We are left in no doubt about the inclinations and proclivities of Lucia's friend, Georgie, though nowhere in those novels is there a hint of any misdemeanours.

Fred knew that *Final Edition* would be his last book. It is the nearest thing that he created to the scene at the end of a detective novel when the sleuth reveals the secrets to an astonished and believing audience. We have been warned by Fred's biographer in the *Dictionary of National Biography* that while this and *As We Were* contain "real value as sources for social history and personal anecdote" the student "may hesitate to take them literally". But the book evokes the nostalgic qualities of Rye at that time and its entertaining anecdotes are imbued with warm sympathy and gentle nostalgia. There is a portrait of his manservant Charlie Tomlin which ends: "Twenty-one years have passed since then, and presently he will come into the garden-room at Rye and tell me that it is time to change for dinner."

Final Edition contains much about Fred's hopes and fears. He defines ambition when writing of John Ellingham Brooks:

. . . a man who aims low and is eternally incompetent of hitting his mark does not arouse either pity or interest. But to aim high, though with whatever futility and indolence, is a different matter.

Fred was aware that he had often dissipated his talent, by being "uncontrollably prolific". Yet his energy and his wide knowledge will always command our interest and respect. He has recently acquired wider popularity in two television series of the Mapp and Lucia novels. In true Benson style, Rye on the small screen was not as straightforward as first observed. The cobbled streets belonged to Rye, but the Mallards scenes were filmed at Swan House, and those of the garden at Chilham, Kent. Nor was the church tower that of St. Mary's, Rye. The series was filmed in full and glorious summer-time with plenty of vintage cars and bright flapper costumes. There was period charm and metaphorical knives went into backs from time to time. Some loved it, and some loathed it. To me it seemed like Agatha Christie without the murders.

Hugo Vickers, London 1986

Sources: A. G. Bradley, The Mermaid Inn, Rye (London, The True Temperance Association, pamphlet); James Money, *Capri* (London, Hamish Hamilton, 1986); Cynthia and Tony Reavell, *E. F. Benson: Mr Benson Remembered in Rye, and the World of Tilling* (Rye, Martello Bookshop, 1984)

INTRODUCTION

I READ not long ago in some essay full of witty fireworks that by the time that most autobiographical writers address themselves to their task they seem to have forgotten, through the lapse of memory, everything in their lives which was worth recording. That discouraging verdict haunted me: I turned it over and over in my mind while I was meditating on the pages that follow, but came to the conclusion that, however just it might prove to be in the case that now concerned me, a court of appeal would not, in nine cases out of ten, uphold it. Indeed, as I thought over various very entertaining volumes of the sort which I had recently read, it appeared to me that not only had their writers retained their recollective powers in the most amazing manner, but that some of them had brought up, as an unnecessary reinforcement to memory, imaginations of the most magical kind.

Not only did they remember and record interesting experiences which had never happened to themselves, but experiences which had never happened to anybody. One distinguished writer, for instance, told us how, in the days of national anxiety preceding the death of King Edward VII, he had driven, evening after evening, to the gates of Buckingham Palace to read the bulletins posted there. Always round the gates there was so thick a crowd gathered on the same errand, that the police had to make way for his motor to approach them. But, as a matter of flat fact, the King was not seriously ill till the day before he died, and up to that evening there had not been issued any bulletin at all, nor could there have been a crowd pressing to read it. I am inclined to believe that our autobiographer did make that one expedition to read that one bulletin, and that it produced so poignant an impression on him, that, in the lapse of years, his imagination got to work on it, multiplying it subconsciously into a series of expeditions. It was not his memory that had failed but his imagination that had flowered. I think it would be pedantic to call such a result a falsification of fact: it was rather an enhancement of fact.

For a similar enhancement we are indebted to an even more distinguished writer who described how, at eleven o'clock on the morning when the Armistice was declared on November 11, 1918, he stood by his open window and listened to the solemn booming of the hour from Big Ben in the Clock Tower of Westminster. No one with a literary sense can read that passage without emotion, for the author described his reactions with consummate art: the strokes beat into his mind the blessed sense that the scream of the shells was silent at last, and the world had awakened from the long nightmare. But, again as a matter of fact, Big Ben did not strike at all at eleven o'clock on that morning. When first the German air-raids began, the mechanism was disconnected, lest the sound should supply the night-raiders above the darkened town with topographical guidance and it had not yet been linked up again. Only a pedant would quarrel with the imagination which evoked from silence the emotions which the striking of Big Ben would otherwise have inspired. Big

Ben, however, did strike at noon that day, and no doubt our author heard it then.

Another romantic memory, which cannot be accounted for at all, except on this theory that it is the privilege of some to remember with detail and distinctness what never happened to anybody, was given to the world when, on the death of Swinburne, Mr. Oscar Browning published in *The Times* some most vivid recollections of the poet when they were boys together at Eton. He described how on the day that Tennyson's *Maud* appeared, he and Swinburne raced to the bookseller's after early school to secure copies of it, and how he outran Swinburne and got there first. A vivid picture: one positively sees the two small boys, spurred by poetical passion, sprinting along to be the first to secure the Laureate's latest. But, alas, Mr. Oscar Browning had been, for a historian, careless about his dates. *Maud* was published in 1855, and Swinburne had left Eton two years before. There was no such race. Mr. Browning need not have run.

Photographs exposed to the light quickly fade, but these imaginative pictures of emotional moments (though they have never happened), when put away in the dark, certainly develop fresh details and decorations, and it is only natural that they should. Hardly ever does the mind grasp the full significance of any incident immediately. It broods over it, it considers its relation to the past and its bearing on the future, and this play of the imagination, without which it remains a frozen fragment, has a tendency to enlarge and embellish, for the imagination is essentially a picture-making faculty, and as such it arranges and groups and composes. It is, for instance, a legitimate and time-honoured device of biographers and autobiographers alike

—with the notable exception of Pepys—to give us verbatim reports of conversations between themselves and other important people long after these have taken place. For the dramatic construction of such it would be pedantic to deny the author the reasonable use of composition and imagination, provided he exercises them with discretion. But the late Mr. Frank Harris threw all moderation to the winds. He describes somewhere an intimate discussion he had held with Oscar Wilde on the subject of sex, as they sat together in their sleeping-car while the train roared through the night from Paris to the Riviera. It is a most picturesque piece of writing, admirably composed.

Wilde had lately been released from jail, and his friend was taking him away to some quiet hamlet where, it was hoped, he would regain his power to work. But the account always seemed to me suspect; the arguments were close and polished and eloquent, the conversational styles of the disputants were exactly the same; they must also have shouted their elaborate periods at each other to drown the din of the express. It has been now proved that they did not take that journey together at all, and a reader justly resents that so detailed and forcible a scene belongs to the realm of romance and not personal reminiscence. It arouses in him a distrust of the writer rather than admiration of his prodigious memory. As fiction, it would have been convincing. The same reader would have felt that (in spite of the roaring train) it must have happened just like that and he is chagrined to know that, presented under the guise of a personal experience, it had no existence. As for Mr. Harris's *Contemporary Portraits* in which he gives us his account of personal interviews he had with celebrities of the day, there is no reason to suppose that any of them took place. He read up, it has been abundantly proved, little-known sources of material about them, and enthroned himself as their intimate friend and confidant. Carlyle, Whistler, Meredith, Verlaine, and Wagner, Anatole France, and Matthew Arnold all opened their inmost hearts into his receptive ear. In all probability (they were dead and so could not give an authoritative denial) none of them did anything of the sort. Mr. Ernest Newman took him in hand over his account of his friendship with Wagner, and when Mr. Newman had finished with it there was nothing left. We can form our own conclusions about the rest. These conversations were admirably written, and if Mr. Harris had only called them *Imaginary Portraits* no one could have quarrelled with him. Walter Pater, it is true, had already used that title, but there is no copyright in titles.

Readers then may properly demand of autobiographical authors that they should depend on their memory or their documents, and that when memory fails as they struggle to push their way along the overgrown paths of the past they must make sure that an imprudent step on to an attractive patch of vivid green should not land them in a bog-hole. In setting their scene no one will grudge them a reasonable licence in decoration in order to adorn what would otherwise be a bald narrative. But caution is required. Among these volumes which I have enjoyed so much, I came across a description of the house which has long been my home and where now I write. The author speaks of it as "majestic": "just the sort of house," he says, "which Henry James had come to England, forty years before, to seek." No one would have been more surprised than Henry James to learn that. Lamb House has a modest dignity of its own, for it was built in the reigns of Queen Anne and King George I, when pretentious jerry-building for moderately sized houses was not so well understood as it is now, but its majesty is limited to three fair-sized bedrooms on the first floor, four fireless attics above, and three little parlours. Our author then speaks of its "immense" lawn surrounded by walls of grey stone. But, as the result of recent measuring, I find that it would be impossible to lay out a tennis court on that immense lawn, unless some player stood on a gravel path or the adjoining rose-bed to receive a moderately fast service, which another delivered from under a walnut-tree which stands round about the base-line opposite. The net would have to be attached to a red hawthorn on one side if the other post was to stand clear of a flower-bed. True, there would be left outside the court a few small triangles or trapeziums of grass, but I look in vain for further immensities. In vain, too, have I looked for the "walls of grey stone" which, we are told, surround this modest plot. They appear to be entirely constructed of red brick. . . .

Enough of these cautionary reflections. I go back to a day of early summer in the year 1900 when first the green front-door of the majestic house confronted me. It had no handle, no hole for the insertion of a latch-key, but only a large brass knocker. Henry James had met me at the station, we had walked up to Lamb House together, leaving my luggage in the care of the outside porter, and now by a dexterous twist of the knocker he lifted the latch within.

CHAPTER I

IT was a great honour and something of an adventure to be asked to stay with Henry James in this house at Rye which he had lately bought. He was an old friend of my family, and we were on terms of familiar adoration with the entrancing folk of his earlier novels, Roderick Hudson and Christina Light, Gilbert Osborne and Isabel and Daisy Miller and the rest, but we could not all follow him when he declared to my mother that his work of this period was "subaqueous," and that he had now got his head above water. Some of us—I refuse to damn myself directly—would have liked him to have continued amphibious, at any rate, for ever. Six or seven years before, he had consented to read through in manuscript my earliest effort in authorship, and it still appals me to remember that it was not even typed when submitted to him. He was certainly appalled also, for he wrote acknowledging the safe receipt of a sheaf of ill-written text, saying that he had not realized that it was so substantial a work. I wonder how far he penetrated into it: not far, I hope, for a comparatively small section, deciphered with difficulty, must have convinced him that *Dodo* was not a work about which it was possible for him to be encouraging. He wrote me two or three long and kindly and brilliantly evasive letters about it. He called it "lively," he called himself "corrosively critical" though he made no criticism, except that he did not find it as

I

"ferociously literary" as his taste demanded. "Hew out a style," he said, "it is by style we are saved," and I drew the obvious conclusion that, for the present, I was not.

He disappeared next morning after a preoccupied breakfast to a room built in the time of George II, which stood in the garden, close to the house and at right-angles to it up a flight of eight stone steps. The bow-window on the north looked straight down the cobbled West Street. On the left was the front of the house, and just below this window the street made a sharp turn to the right, and at the end of it was the disused churchyard above which rose the west front of the church. When Henry James had withdrawn himself here for his morning's work, none might disturb him, and as lunch time approached one sat in the garden by the steps waiting for him to emerge, and could hear his voice booming and pausing and booming again, as he moved up and down the book-lined room dictating the novel on which he was at work to his typist. The clacking of the keys of her machine formed a sort of castanet accompaniment. Such at this time was his mode of composition: he made elaborate notes of the course of his story and with these in his hand he spoke his pages. To use his own metaphor his book when thus fully planned was like a portmanteau which he had packed with such economy of space that, when he closed it, he heard it "beautifully creaking": now he had only to open it and, in this dictation, take out and unfold its contents.

This habit of *viva voce* composition impressed itself on his talk, giving it an incomparable richness. On it ran, as when he was dictating in the garden-room, in decorated periods with cursive corrections till he found the exact word and the perfect phrase. The effect was that of a

2

tapestry of speech being audibly designed and executed. He worked a panel of this for me one morning when he came out of his shrine an hour before the usual time, and, with splendid parentheses and side-lights explained to me that the book on which he was engaged (it must have been *The Wings of a Dove*) was finished. But I have already exhibited that piece somewhere, and I have a more sumptuous example which my brother Arthur entered in his diary. He wrote it down immediately after it was delivered, and it is certainly the best record of Henry James's unique utterance. The subject was the work of the novelist Mrs. Oliphant, then lately deceased:

"I had not read a *line* that the poor woman had written for *years*, not for years. When she died, Henley—do you know the rude, boisterous, windy, headstrong Henley?—Henley, as I say, said to me: 'Have you read *Kirsteen*?' I replied that, as a matter of fact—h'm—I had not read it. Henley said, 'That you should have any pretensions to interest in literature and should dare to say that you have not read *Kirsteen*!' I took my bludgeoning patiently and humbly, my dear Arthur, went back and read it, and was at once confirmed, after twenty pages, in my belief—I laboured through the book—that the poor soul had a simply *feminine* conception of literature, such slipshod, imperfect, halting, faltering, peeping, down-at-heel work—buffeting along like a ragged creature in a high wind, and just struggling to the goal and falling in a quivering mass of faintness and fatuity."

Surely to the trained ear there was never a finer passage of picturesque prose in the making, prose glowing in the melting-pot, ready to be poured out into the mould. He was soaked and saturated in the creation and criticism of literature: they permeated his being, an organic part of it. Friends and literature were his passions, and when he talked to a friend the most trivial incident must be dipped in style, as in Tyrian dye: he put what he wanted to say in a chiselled casket of words. One day he paid a call on a neighbour in Rye and he wished to tell us that when the door was opened to his ring a black dog appeared on the threshold. But he could not bring himself to say "black dog," for that would have been a scarcely decent *déshabillé* for his information. "And from the dusky entry," he said, "there emerged something black, something canine." And below that formal and entrancing talk stirred the spell of his geniality and benevolence, of his absorbed interest in all the qualities, rich and poor, of humanity. He disliked certain of these with singular intensity; anything approaching rudeness or inquisitiveness was abhorrent to him, rousing in him just such a sense of sickened pity as he felt for the work of poor Mrs. Oliphant. On the other hand he treasured and fondled all that responded to his fastidious instincts and to his affection. "I am singularly accessible," he wrote, "to all demonstrations of regard." An unfriendly deed or word on the part of one whom he had treated as a friend was final. He did not want even to see him again.

One afternoon I played golf at Camber. Beyond the links in those days extended the stretch of tussocked dunes bordered by shining sands, which now is covered with a confluent rash of small perky bungalows and bathing-suits hung up to dry, and is resonant with motor-cycles and loud speakers. He met us after our game at the club-house and gave us tea, in an ecstasy of genial nebulosity as to what we had been doing. "Some be-flagged jam pots,

4

I understand, my dear Fred, let into the soil at long but varying distances. A swoop, a swing, a flourish of steel, a dormy": and he wrote to Arthur saying that he thought I put golf too high among intellectual pursuits. On other afternoons we walked very slowly with frequent pauses for salutations to his friends, a child, a station-master, or a dog, for each of whom he had some special word, through the cobbled streets of the town and out on to the levels of the sheep-grazed marsh, with the sky above enormous as at sea.

I do not think he took much notice of the aspects of nature; he was scarcely more conscious of them than is a man, deep in thought, of the comfort of the arm-chair in which he sits. Nature, at any rate, only appealed to him fitfully, as the cool water and the plane-trees of the Ilyssus momentarily diverted the attention of Socrates from his philosophy and his Phaedrus, till at the end of their talk he invoked Pan and the deities who haunted the place to give him and his companion inward beauty of soul. Of all men that I have ever met he was the most Socratic—his mind was always occupied within on its own surmises and speculations. In the middle of light superficial talk it withdrew itself into depths of the element in which it functioned, like a diving sub-marine. Just so did Socrates stand meditating throughout a winter's night at Potidaea, unconscious of all but the philosophical problem that engaged him.

He laughed but little, but he was as full of humour as the packed portmanteau, "beautifully creaking." In these distant memories I recall his story of how on his way down to the High Street, he saw advancing towards him a woman whom he knew that he knew, but whom his racked memory failed to identify. As they drew fatally nearer each other, she made a bee-line for him across the roadway, and, still unidentified, opened conversation. "I've had the rest of it," she said, "made into rissoles." Recognition followed at once. "And then in fact," he said, "the cudgelling of my brain ceased, for I recognized my own cook and knew that she was speaking of the leg of lamb I had eaten hot and roast on Monday and cold on Tuesday."

Those few days at Rye scattered on the surface of my mind seeds of desire, barren at present, but so I take it, capable of sprouting should occasion give them a chance of growth. Rye has a spell, and I had come within circle of its enchantment. Lamb House and its walled garden, the cobbled streets with their Georgian houses, and, outside, the marsh, the golf, the empty sea-beaches beckoned, as by some secret gesture, with a promise of ideal content. But a young man of thirty, still very experimental in his tastes, and full of an energy for the due dispersion of which every day is too short, does not aim at content nor indeed desire it, and I did not contemplate living there. I thought of it as one thinks of some little town through which the express train passes, whistling and slowing down but not stopping, thus calling the attention of the observer from his window to glimpses of red roofs and fruit trees in flower and a stream wandering through meadows or broadening into a bathing-pool. He thinks for a moment, before he settles down to his book again, that existence here would be a divinely tranquil business, moving unjarred through springs and summers and fireside winters. He knows that he is only "making believe!" He does not inquire of any local agent whether he has on his books for lease or sale some pleasant little house with a walled garden. Rye remained exceedingly distinct and delectable in my mind like an image seen through a reversed telescope, but infinitely remote.

Indeed at that time, and for years to come, I had, like Homer's dawn, many dancing-places. I was much attached to London, where I had a small flat and numerous friends, I spent a winter month or so skating in Switzerland, perhaps another month in Scotland and yet another in Italy, and there was my mother's home, deep-buried in the country near Horsted-Keynes. Queen Victoria, after my father's death, had offered her Royal Lodge in Windsor Park: it had then been long unoccupied and had not been added to or modernized. Princess Christian, who lived close by at Cumberland Lodge urged her to accept it, but she did not think it would suit either her or her family and that such a tenancy would have implied a certain formidable dependence. She respectfully refused it, and experimentally, with many misgivings, she took a short lease of this house called Tremans where actually she lived for the remaining twenty years of her life.

It lay off a Sussex by-road, sunk deep between sandy banks, and indeed a more amiable house could not be imagined. From the gate a short avenue of tall Scotch firs formed the approach, turning past a low-walled lawn to the door. There was a small wing of grey stone, built by Thomas Wyatt, kinsman of the poet, the rest was of red-brick, completed in the seventeenth century.

Inside, a series of sitting-rooms, opening into each other, was panelled with oak and furnished with big open fireplaces, backed with old Sussex iron-work, where from the first chills of autumn till summer weather began, there burned a mixture of peat and logs, and the smell of wood-smoke, faint and aromatic, lingered there the year long. The house was spacious, but there had been poured into it vast quantities of furniture from Lambeth and Addington which my mother could not bear to part with, and it was full to overflowing. In a narrow lobby outside the dining-room was a piano, a two-manual organ from Addington, a tall glass-fronted Sheraton bookcase, a mahogany console table, and a life-size statue of Rameses which my sister Maggie had dug up in the Temple of Mut at Karnak. Squares of lawn and garden surrounded the house, there was an orchard of pink-flowering cherry, and the domain extended over a couple of hayfields to the stream at the bottom of the valley.

An immense yew-hedge separated the flower-fringed kitchen-garden from the road, and over the stone wing of the house sprawled a big vine, covered in the autumn with clusters of small tight grapes. They were no good for eating, so were evidently meant to drink, and out of them one year, I must irrelevantly mention, I made three bottles of white wine, following instructions given in the *Encyclopædia*. I crushed the bunches, skins, stones and stalks into a large bowl, and left them to ferment. Wine-making seemed a very simple process, for presently, exactly as the *Encyclopædia* had foretold, the mixture began to bubble and throw off alcoholic fumes. The Saccharomycetes, or microscopic fungi (*vide Encyclopædia*) were evidently at work. After the prescribed period I raked off the scum of skins and other debris, and bottled the wine.

The vintage of *Clos Tremans* (1900) remained in the cellar for a year or two, and was then examined by the manufacturer. A beautifully clear liquid with lumps of solid matter (probably tartaric acid) met his gratified eye, but in his capacity as wine-taster he was not so well pleased. The liquid was of incredible acidity, and having strained and rebottled it he put in a quantity of sifted sugar, since it seemed incapable of developing grape-sugar of its own, and corked it up again. The further history of that unique vintage is, alas, unknown, because I forgot about it. Perhaps, still lying in a cobwebbed corner of the cellar at Tremans, it may have matured (who can tell?) into a beverage for the gods. I would advise the Saintsbury Club, which dines twice a year in the Vintners' Hall in order to drink moderately and wisely of priceless vintages, to make inquiries. *Clos Tremans* is forty years old now, and may possibly be near its best. . . .

My mother herself had no touch of the true lover of the country who finds there both tranquillity and stimulus. Fields and flowers and the green-powdered woodlands of spring were always external to her, pleasant to look at, but not nutritious. They did not feed her: they left her the hungrier for varied and constant human intercourse, and the wholesome grist from the grinding of many minds. For close on forty years of her married life, beginning when she was a girl of just eighteen, she had been immersed in my father's eager businesses, at Wellington College, where he was the first Headmaster, at Truro where he was the first Bishop, and finally at Lambeth and Addington during the years of his Primacy. She missed also the management of two great houses with their streams of guests, she missed her pride in running them to perfection. Most of all and with a need of the spirit, she missed the sense that her time was *not* her own, that life was no longer a series of incessant calls and interruptions, while at any moment my father might want her. "I saw him first," she wrote to a friend, "when I was five, and I never had a time of conscious existence when he was not my larger self." Now she could order her day as she chose, but that brought with it no feeling of liberty, but rather of living in an uncharted vacancy. "No one," she wrote again, "can realize until they feel it, what the cessation of magnificent stimulus is *in itself*, apart from all the sorrow and loss that bring it in their train."

Personally she would much have preferred to live in London, but London was impossible, for my sister had for the last seven years been very fragile in physical health, and for her recovery country air and many daily hours out of doors were essential. My mother held that life was a piece of material given her to work on to the best advantage. The former piece, forty years of it, dating from the years of her girlhood, was now a finished tapestry, and this new length, as yet untouched—I quote the sense of her diary—was put into her hands. Something had to be made of it, but as yet she was at a loss for any design. All she knew was that somehow or other she must fashion it "into a garment of praise, not into a cowl of heaviness." Life, anyhow, was not meant to be negatively endured. But here was the root of the trouble: for forty years she had fashioned her life into a garment for another. She saw herself as not wanted any more. She was widowed, her three sons were grown up, they had their work to do, in which she could not help them, and it was not possible that they should need her with the same irreplaceable quality as my father had needed her. The emptiness of it! And the emptiness began to be peopled, dimly, as with shadows in the corners of a room when the light fades, with vague menaces.

In the new home Maggie's physical health rapidly improved, but there came with her restored strength a psychical change manifesting itself at first in runes and wayward eddies, as on the smooth surface of some deep-running tide. All through her long illness her intellectual and artistic interests had been very much alive: she sketched admirably, she (like the rest of the family) wrote stories, she had excavated with rich results the Temple of Mut in Karnak during her winters in Egypt, but the real bent of her mind was philosophical. As a girl she had gone up to Lady Margaret Hall, Oxford, and had taken a first in Moral Philosophy, and now she had been at work for several years on her book *A Venture of Rational Faith*. Just lately she had been editing an unpublished treatise by my father on *Revelation* and some addresses of his, delivered at Lambeth. She had soaked herself in these, they gripped her mind, with the effect that his very personality, dominating and masterful, and his sense of responsibility for the spiritual strenuousness of those round him began to take possession of her. Hitherto such traits had been non-existent in her, she had been indulgent and genial, leaving others to pursue their own paths, and never desirous of bending them to her own angle. For all the years of her ill-health, her mother had made life as easy as possible for her, adapting it to her invalidism, watchful and protective: but now in this strange psychical change Maggie began mentally to reverse their mutual relations. She saw herself in charge of her mother, not for her ease and comfort, but, as her father would have done, with this sense of responsibility for her bestowing herself in large aims and noble purposes. Words are almost too solid to express the fluid quality of this transformation, but definitely in her own mind she put herself in her father's place, and into her nature there passed as well something of his severity and of those moods of dark depression which sometimes obsessed him. Both she and my mother recognized this change in her and its origin. They talked of it, they admitted it, but the situation was not one that could be straightened out by discussion. There were agitating conversations between them, full of half-uttered hints and broken by uneasy silences; there were little frozen misunderstandings, tiny in themselves, but coalescing into slippery places. There was close, deep-seated friction. To my mother it must have seemed farcical, were it not for the tragic undertone that anyone should interpret my father to her; to Maggie it seemed that she was doing his will. Both felt that their relations to each other were changing, and that the change was undermining the confidence and comprehension which had hitherto existed between them.

There emerged a more definite cause for this estrangement, one that could be directly focused. For ten years now, in my father's lifetime and after, there had lived with us, as in her permanent and only home, the daughter of a former Archbishop, Lucy Tait, who in the matter of age came midway between Maggie and my mother. My mother's intimacies and emotional friendships had always been with women; no man, except my father, had ever counted in her life, and this long love between her and Lucy was the greatest of all these attachments; it was impossible to think of them apart. But Maggie, in the reinforcement of her health, resented this intimacy, and looked on Lucy as having an influence which helped to sever her mother from herself, and that she occupied a position in her mother's house which was properly hers. The feeling was intelligible enough, it was perhaps even inevitable, but where was the remedy? Lucy made a very solid contribution to the expenses of the house, for it was her own home, and therefore she must have a voice in its economy and management, but far transcending any such material consideration was the fact that my mother's life and hers were knit into each other. It was also extremely difficult for Lucy. The only alternative would have been for her to leave Tremans, and without her I am sure my mother could not have lived there. Maggie had her own companion and friend, Nettie Gourlay, who had spent winters with her in Egypt, and who now was at Tremans for weeks at a time. She was one of the most silent of human beings and quite imperturbable, but between her and Maggie there existed some deep affinity. Sometimes they went off together to Kampsholt Park, the home of Nettie's father. As an old man, he married a girl younger than his own daughter.

Very little of this profound disturbance appeared on the surface. Anyone staying at Tremans, even an intimate friend, would see only an ideal seemliness and tranquillity, a widowed mother and her daughter living each with the friend of her heart in a beautiful house in great comfort. Family prayers, as in most Victorian houses, began the day. The servants collected in a small dense crowd in the lobby of Rameses outside the dining-room, sang a hymn to the accompaniment of the organ, and my mother read a few prayers and some short passage from the New Testament with comments. Guests were not expected to attend. In fact, they were rather discouraged. Breakfast followed, and the post arrived with the late edition of the evening paper of the night before: morning papers did not come till mid-day. Maggie came down in the middle of the morning, and, if the weather served, established herself with her books and her writing and her Nettie in a revolving hut by the cherry orchard; one side was open to the air, so that the interior could be turned to face sun or shade as required. The ordering of the garden had become her job, and she strolled about with Taffy, her Welsh collie, at her heels and planned a new hedge of rambler rose or Penzance briar. My mother saw her cook, and let her green Brazilian parrot out of his cage. He adored her, but hated all others; so if anyone entered, he must be collected on the end of a stick and wiped back into his cage, for he pecked at the shoes of any intruder, uttering hoarse cries, and this hindered connected conversation. Lucy had a slip of a sitting-room adjoining my mother's, and helped her with her letters and read the morning paper to her. For a couple of hours a day at least my mother was occupied in Bible reading and religious meditation.

Maggie rested after lunch, and my mother and Lucy walked or drove through the country lanes. The peacock had discovered that he could see the reflection of his own gorgeousness in the black japanned panel at the back of the victoria, and, following it from the stables, strode after it, gazing thereon, as far as the end of the avenue of firs; and then refreshed, like Narcissus, by the contemplation of his beauty, rejoined his white spouse who was sitting on a clutch of eggs long addled. They came back from their drive: maybe they had seen a heron, or the horse had shied at one of those horrible motor-cars: they should not be allowed. Maggie's plan for a hedge of Penzance briar in front of the tiled sitting-out place in the garden was discussed, but Lucy thought it would cut off the view of the South Downs. Maggie was sure it would not, and Lucy, catching a glance from my mother said no more. She cordially agreed about starting some ducks, for the small weedy pond just beyond the stable-yard seemed predestined for ducks. The other parrot, Matilda, that accomplished linguist, had learned the parlour-maid's name, and this afternoon she had called out "Spicer, Spicer" in a voice so like the cook's that Spicer had hurried to the kitchen, and found nobody there but the scornful and silent Matilda. After tea Maggie lingered on, wanting to talk to my mother, but Lucy lingered, too, and so she left them together. It was a lovely June evening, and after dinner there was a nightingale singing in the wood below, and Nettie went to fetch a shawl for Maggie, so that she might sit out for a little and listen to it. But Lucy reported that there was a heavy dew, so it was wiser for her to sit indoors. Evening prayers followed. Beth, who had nursed all my grandmother's children and, in the next generation, my mother's, attended them to-night. It was her eighty-second birthday and she wore the silver brooch with "82" in enamel on it, which Arthur had sent her. Prayers ended as they had begun the day: Spicer brought four bedroom candles and placed them on the mahogany console-table opposite Rameses, and they all went to their rooms. Lucy slept with my mother in the vast Victorian bed where her six children had been born in Wellington days. . . . Since morning, tides of love had been flowing through the house, true and fervent religious perceptions permeated it. These might have turned the hours and their pleasant congenial trivialities (which, when all is said and done, make up a large part of existence, for its harmony or discord) into a day of happiness. Instead these trivialities stood dry and unrefreshed; little barren islands of grit and nothingness, and the bedroom candles brought the day to its dead end. There was no momentum left which would keep the pendulum swinging till next morning. Sometimes my mother's heart sank at the blankness of to-morrow and to-morrow. Yet somehow out of the material given her there must be wrought a garment of praise.

Winter came with boisterous winds roaring through the firs, and when they ceased, days of soaking rain. Maggie could no longer sit out in her revolving hut, but did her work in the long parlour above her bedroom. It was supposed to be haunted: some mediumistic friend keeping vigil there one night had seen little dwarfish figures dressed in brown running nimbly about among the legs of tables. When the winds blew, the open chimney belched stinging wood-smoke into the room, and when the rain fell large drops hissed on the logs, and those were more inconvenient than the little brown people.

At Christmas there was always a family gathering and a somewhat moral sense of gaiety. The servants, of their own pious propensities, sang carols outside my mother's bedroom window before day dawned, holly decorated picture-frames and door-lintels, crackers and the wearing of caps and the blowing of whistles accompanied dessert at dinner. When that was over the quartet at Tremans broke up for a while, Maggie and Nettie went to Falmouth for a month, and my mother and Lucy to Lambeth which had once been the home of them both. A monument of the Stone Age, Archbishop Temple, reigned there now: and as a young man when headmaster of Rugby was the author of one of the articles in *Essays and Reviews* which the Bishops in Convocation had condemned as unortho-dox. There had been violent clerical opposition to his first episcopal appointment as Bishop of Exeter, and he was much too old for taking up such a post as Canterbury and had no idea of the expansion of the Church of England in the Colonies. There was not an ounce of suavity or tact about him, and the Queen said to my mother shortly after his appointment, "The new Archbishop hasn't got any manners, and I'm afraid he's too old to learn now." He was an amazing mixture of savagery and almost senti-mental tenderness. Lord Halifax, father of the present Foreign Secretary and head of the English Church Union, told me of a frightful letter the Archbishop wrote him, saying that his Romish principles were abominable and that he was a traitor to the Church of his fathers. Deeply wounded, he sped to Lambeth, letter in hand, held it out to the Archbishop crying out, "That I should receive *this* from Your Grace!" and they both burst into tears. . . .

He scorned pain and physical ills as nonsense and rub-bish and was much harder on himself than on others. One day his doctor told him that he must have all his teeth out and off he went to the dentist but refused any sort of anæsthetic. After a number of difficult extractions had been made, the dentist said, "I think I'd better stop for to-day," and his patient, bloody but unbowed, replied, "I think you'd better go on." He grew very blind, and when my mother asked him whether he did not worry over it (a mild term surely) he answered, "Worry? Why should I worry? Not my fault. . . ." He had no compassion on people who bored him. A woman, sitting next him one night at dinner gave him a long and wearisome description of a railway accident. Her aunt, she said, had been in the train, and though there were several people killed in the compartment next hers, she was quite uninjured. "Wasn't that lucky?" she asked.

"Not knowing your aunt, can't say," replied the Primate.

As he lay dying he kept on drawing his hand from beneath the bedclothes, as if it contained something precious and showing it to his wife: "That's a beauty," he said, "and here's another." Soon, as she listened to his fragments of speech, she made out what he fancied himself to be doing: he was a boy again birds-nesting among the gulls on the cliffs of Lundy Island.

CHAPTER II

AT Tremans matters began to mend. Maggie finished editing my father's papers, and that strange psychical obsession faded. She took up her own philosophical book again, and deciding that it was becoming shapeless and obscure she scrapped the whole and remodelled it. There were no more of those frozen, agitating conversations with her mother about Lucy having come between them: it was as if her mind had emerged from some perilous dusk—was it dispersed altogether?—into the wholesome light, just as her body was overcoming her invalidism. Her broodings and depressions ceased; she recaptured her gaiety, and eagerly immersed herself in the affairs of the garden and the livestock. She had a family of blue Persian cats and no bolts or bars would keep the matron from hunting in the woods and bringing home a tender young rabbit for her kittens. She planned a system of education for Taffy, whose mind must not be allowed to lie fallow just because he was now middle-aged: he had his "lessons" every evening which demanded his utmost attentions. Her new hen-run grew populous, and her ducks throve on the stable pond. She insisted that my mother should keep pigs: they need not be murdered on the premises but sold when they were fattened: a small flock of cinnamon turkeys patrolled the cherry orchard. Lucy took a tiny house in Barton Street, Westminster, furnished it with obstructive furniture from

Tremans, and established an old servant as cook-house-keeper. It held two occupants comfortably, and the foursome could break up into two pairs. The day no longer came to a dead-end; it had stored up, by the hour of evening prayers and bedroom candles, sufficient momentum of interests and pursuits to set it going again in the morning.

A further factor in the restoration of the Tremans household was the frequent presence of my brother Arthur. He had been a hugely successful master at Eton for nearly twenty years, but he had long been in revolt against the fruitless drudgery involved in his work, and the barrenness, so he considered it, of the energy expended on classical education. Only a small percentage of boys, those who naturally had a scholarly bent, profited by it, and, as conducted, it was a prodigious waste of time for both them and their teachers. He also detested, as a mischievous idolatry, the worship of athleticism. He was longing to have done with a place which really he loved, and now he was asked to edit, with his friend Lord Esher, the first instalment, down to the death of the Prince Consort, of Queen Victoria's letters and diary. That was an admirable opportunity; the book was bound to be indispensable to historians of the future, it would be a full-time job for the next two years and he resigned, rejoicing in his freedom. Presently, to his dismay, he was in danger of losing it again, for the Headmaster of Eton, Dr. Warre, was about to retire, and, though he knew that Arthur's views on education and athletics were the exact opposite of his own, he told him that he was sure that he was the best man to succeed him. Arthur used his utmost ingenuity in dodging this crown of a scholastic career. He was convinced that Eton stood in need of radical reform, but he realized that the staff of masters did not agree with him, and formed the triumphant conclusion that he was not one of those dominating personalities who could carry through reforms in the teeth of opposition. The Governing Body wanted him, but he refused to send in his name as a candidate, or to pledge himself to accept if it was offered him. Though his evasion was successful, he was not satisfied, for when Dr. Edward Lyttelton, who meditated no such reforms and no such misgivings, was appointed, Arthur cherished some odd sense of grievance that the staff of masters did not put such pressure on him that he would have felt compelled to accept a post which he had done everything in his power to avoid. That was quite unreasonable, but he nursed this grievance, and for many years refused to set foot in Eton again. He established himself at Cambridge, when his work on the Queen's Letters which kept him at Windsor was done. Then he was elected a Fellow of Magdalene College, and, though gashed with periods of helpless misery, he entered on the most fruitful and happiest years of his life.

The key to the inconsistencies of his strangely self-contradictory character was that he had a double personality, sharply divided, with no connecting-point of contact between the two sides of his nature. In the first of these personalities, that which was in charge of his social and scholastic life and his relation with his friends, he was the most humorous and entertaining of companions, appreciative and incisively critical. He abounded in geniality, but the schedule of his day, its hours and occupations and companionships had to run exactly as he wished it: benevolent and genial though he was, he was also in that regard an absolute despot. In a small circle of company, or at *tête-à-tête*, he was the most stimulating but least dominating talker that I have ever met, never holding forth, but keeping the stickiest ball nimbly rolling, with the effect that the rest of the talkers got the encouraging impression that they were in peculiarly good form themselves.

He shunned all kinds of adventure, spiritual or mental, which were likely to stir him into disquieting emotion, and inwardly regretted it: somewhere in his diary he recorded "I want to be developed, but without discomfort." He had many intimate friends, but with the exception of his mother, they were all of his own sex, and he never wanted any other companionship. He distrusted women. "I *don't* like the sex," he wrote in his diary. "I don't like their superficial ways and their mixture of emotion with reason. Women, I think, when they get interested in one, have a deadly desire to improve one." Certainly he desired improvement, but it must be home-made improvement, easily evolved from within, and he resented anybody else taking a hand in it, just as he would have resented anybody washing his face for him. His men friends did not take such liberties, or, if they attempted them, he very promptly froze them up. Otherwise these friendships whether with young men or those of his own age were on terms of strict equality.

His powers of observation, of seizing hold of the crucial points in what he encountered, were extraordinary. Half an hour over a new book rendered him master of its merits and weaknesses, half an hour with a new person gave him material for a penetrating (and sometimes blasting) summary, and from a walk or bicycle ride he gleaned a dozen pictures, Japanese for clear-cut fidelity, of birds and riverside sedges, and sequestered hamlets and remote Georgian houses, and these he scribbled in his diary in that lucid and effortless English which flowed from his pen, unerased and uncorrected. That beautiful style was as natural to him as is the tortuous bungle of less fortunate writers. This diary, which grew into an immense document of four million words, was the outpouring of the first personality: its fate will be discussed later.

Then, returning from his long ramble, the second personality took charge during those three sacred daily hours to which no interruption was permitted, and whether at Cambridge or at Tremans, sitting in a large arm-chair, with a writing-board resting on its arms, he poured forth with the unerring swiftness of his diary-writing, page after page of those reflective volumes by which he was now getting so widely known, and in which his increasing circle of devout readers found guidance and uplift, but which were deplored by those friends who saw his humour, his critical incisiveness, his keen intellectual interests unused or unexercised in this stream of books, which they judged to be wholly unworthy of his gifts. *The Upton Letters*, *From a College Window*, *At Large*, *The Thread of Gold*, *Thy Rod and Thy Staff*, are among the titles. In these, through essay and homily and narrative, he depicted the second personality, patient, tender, tranquil, following the thread of gold through the involved labyrinth of life, withdrawn from the crazy tumult, and the lure of ambition and effectiveness. It was as if he was taking down the utterance of some inward dictation, which never paused for a word or a thought:

> "A thousand pages in his sight
> Were but an evening gone."

In those sequestered hours he was completely happy and what he wrote was completely sincere. He immersed himself in this Avilion world which was as real to him then as (when he came out of it) was the world in which he lived so critically and so genially. . . . When, at Cambridge, his servant came in to tell him that it was time for him to go to Hall for dinner, or, at Tremans, a gong boomed, he gathered up the drift of sheets scattered on the floor, to be sent unrevised to the typist next morning, and resumed, as by the process of opening a door into the next room and locking it behind him, his other life. The two were wholly dissociated, not a murmur, not an echo penetrated from the one to the other. He was perfectly aware of their severance and wrote in his diary: "In my books I am solemn, sweet, refined; in real life I am rather vehement, sharp, contemptuous and a busy mocker."

So, quit of his scholastic days at Eton, and having avoided the dangerous distinction which menaced him, Arthur began to spend much of his Cambridge vacation at Tremans, bringing with him his motor-car and his benevolent despotism. He loved the remoteness of the beautiful and perfectly ordered house, set in a network of country walks, where no intruder was liable to drop in for tea, where he was free to arrange the day in the mode that seemed to him to approach the ideal and where his despotism comprised so many agreeable plans for others. He never attended morning prayers, but came down towards the end of breakfast, with upheld hands of horror at the invariable pile of letters beside his plate, and spent the morning, under the control of the second personality, in writing long and sympathetic answers to the confidences of his admiring readers. Then the other took control again, and he hurried down to lunch, raging at the inconsiderate folk who wrote to him, because they had nothing else to do and destroyed his morning. Twenty-five letters, and he had not touched his new book: still, there might be a chapter to read, if my mother and Lucy and Maggie could bear it, after dinner. What a delicious leg of mutton. Tremans was the only house where food was perfect. And might Edmund Gosse come down for a couple of nights next week? And Spicer had told him that a large box had arrived for him: that was wine for the replenishment of the cellar. . . . About this afternoon. Let us all motor to Lewes, and then he and Lucy would walk along the ridge of the South Downs, and Maggie and my mother could continue their drive where they wished, and pick them up again on the road below the windmills by the Clayton Tunnel. They would get home by five for the sacred hours. He had to go up to London next day for a Fishmongers Court, an infernal nuisance, and he would bring Percy Lubbock back with him for a night. That piece of rough lawn outside the dining-room windows: it ought to be planted with daffodils. If Maggie approved he would order three hundred and everybody would dance with them next March. . . . After dinner if the promised chapter of the new book was not finished, he played bezique with his mother, and Lucy, tired with her long walk, dozed quietly unseen. Then came the first tiresome moment of the day. Spicer appeared at ten, while a thrilling game was in progress, and announced "prayers." This was an annoying interruption to the evening. Prayers killed bezique; or, if the chapter of the new book had been read, the discussion must be broken off to trail into the lobby where were the piano and the organ and Rameses II and the domestic staff assembled for prayers and a hymn. So prayers were abandoned when Arthur was at home. But my mother was firm about Compline at ten o'clock on Sunday evening. She intended to have Compline and did so. She begged Arthur to leave the family to their devotions and go away to the smoking-room, but he preferred to attend it, and resent it. "Compline," he wrote in his diary, "which I detest with every fibre of my being—the discomfort, the silly idiotic responses, the false sociability of it all." There was the sincere and vigorous voice of Personality I. But Personality II, if in charge of his pen, would no less sincerely have found a pensive seemliness in the household uniting their voices in hymn, prayer and psalm.

Arthur usually had a friend with him, a Fellow of Magdalene, or an undergraduate. George Mallory was one of these, who now lies beyond the range of eagles near the summit of Everest, or is embalmed in its gigantic glaciers. My mother had a discreet passion for so decorative a young man. She wanted to walk round and round him, admiring, and she wanted to call him by his Christian name, but she was afraid that Arthur would think her very daring. Or there was the picturesque Mr. H. E. Luxmore, an old Eton colleague, in a low collar and Liberty-fabric tie, knickerbockers and stockings that showed his small feet and, in the evening, a brown velvet dinner-jacket. He had a deep melodious voice, a clean-shaven handsome histrionic face, and there was a gratifying legend that at a crowded railway station some romantic girl had whispered "Wilson Barrett" as he passed. He was of a type to which Augustus Hare belonged, ready to read Jane Austen aloud to a deferential female audience, who thought him "such a dear"; and he made charming careful water-colour sketches in rich and sober colours. The high-minded tranquillity of Tremans was much to his mind, but he found my brother Hugh a jarring note. Hugh was too argumentative and perhaps not deferential enough, and Mr. Luxmore, like Valjean with his *mots cruels*, wrote to a friend in withering disdain of him and his official purple as a Monseignor, declaring that he was just the same "sharp insignificant little scug as he had been at Eton" which was a grotesque judgment. . . . The house, in these restored days, had a constant stream of most heterogeneous friends of the other members of the family coming and going; Mrs. Creighton, widow of the Bishop of London, who told my mother that she was too slack with her sons, letting them come down to breakfast at any hour they pleased; our old governess, Miss Mary Bramston, once held in much reverence by the family, for she wrote novels for which she received £20 down for the world rights (*Apples of Sodom* was one of them, and *Ellie's Choice* another); Adeline, Duchess of Bedford, and her sister Lady Henry Somerset; Duchess Adeline the younger was, even among intimates, liable to fits of consciousness of her rank and occasionally trailed clouds of glory from the abodes of light. She had brought with her on her husband's death James Woburn, the perfect ducal butler, who directed her diminished household with the same paralysing dignity as before. One night during the last war when she had just finished dining alone at her house in Berkeley Square and he had left her to her coffee he came back. He noiselessly shut the door and noiselessly approached to exactly the correct distance and said: "The Zeppelins have arrived, your Grace," as if they were guests at her evening party, come rather early.

Her sister had a flat in Gray's Inn, where not long before a Zeppelin raid had caused considerable damage, and in great agitation she told him to ring Lady Henry up at once and see that she was safe.

"Very good, your Grace," said he and went out, noiselessly closing the door behind him. He came back, again shut the door, and advanced to exactly the spot where he had stood before. "Her ladyship's flat has been blown to bits, your Grace," he said, "but her ladyship wasn't at home."

There were never two sisters less alike. Lady Henry had married the then heir-apparent of the Duke of Somerset and after tragic happenings had separated from him, her principle preventing her from forcing a divorce. She ran a home for inebriate women at Duxhurst and found humour in everything. When she laughed down the telephone her hearer had to laugh too. . . .

Then there was the new Archbishop, Randall Davidson and his wife who was Lucy's sister: there were friends of Maggie's who had been with her at Lady Margaret Hall, Oxford: tall effusive cousins of Lucy's who called her "Loo, darling" whenever they spoke to her and whenever they laughed showed their uvulas: my mother's widowed sister-in-law Mrs. Henry Sidgwick; the inimitable Mrs. Cornish of Eton: Miss Mary Cholmondeley, author of *Red Pottage*. All these were regular visitors, but for the most part, Arthur's periods were left free for his guests, for some of the others were not quite of his *genre*.

The reflective books flowed forth in these congenial surroundings. Sometimes Personality I had qualms about them and about the intellectual level of the multitudinous readers who valued and loved them, and so often told him so. "My desire is," he entered in his diary, "to write a great and beautiful book, and instead I have become the beloved author of a feminine tea-party kind of audience." Yet there might have been a remedy for that, if it had only been in his power to apply it, and by, fusing the critical humorous qualities of Personality I with the reflective quietism of Personality II to have made of them an amalgamated author. Perhaps it was impossible they should combine; perhaps he felt that he was too deeply committed to the feminine tea-party, many members of which would have found the collaboration very disconcerting. But it might have produced "the great and beautiful book."

My younger brother Hugh had been ordained priest in Anglican Orders by my father: in 1903 he had become a Catholic. As it has been stated that he kept his intention from my mother till he had quite made up his mind and that it half broke her heart that his father's son was submitting himself (in an official Anglican phrase) "to the Pope of Rome and all his detestable enormities," I may mention that from the very first he confided in her, and that so far from being broken-hearted, she fully recognized that this concerned only God and his conscience, and that, his convictions being what they were,

29

it was impossible for him to do otherwise. Directly after he had been received he was ordered to go to Rome, and she saw him off by the boat-train from Victoria. Before starting, the train moved backwards to couple up with a van or whatever, and she, standing on the platform by his open window, called out to him: "My dear, you're going in the wrong direction." It was like her at this emotional moment to say that, and they laughed the train out of the station. . . . He spent some months in Rome, and before he returned was ordained priest. He was bidden to a private audience with Pope Pius X, and had been instructed to take with him a white skull-cap, such as Holy Father wore and to present it to him: on which Holy Father would give him in exchange the skull-cap he was wearing that day as a keepsake. As Hugh took the new cap out of the tissue paper he dropped it, and he and the Pope both bent down to pick it up and nearly knocked their heads together. Holy Father grinned broadly and Hugh laughed. . . . Then Hugh had a request to make of him. It would be very difficult for him now to stay with his mother, for a priest had to say Mass every day, and the nearest Catholic church was a long way off. Would Holy Father therefore allow a room in her house to be licensed for this purpose? The Pope gave leave, but as Hugh was going, that domestic and most human old saint called him back. "You must get your mother's leave, too," he said.

So when Hugh returned to Tremans this Catholic shrine was established. There was a small timbered attic at the top of the house already licensed by the Bishop of Chichester as a chapel for the celebration of the Sacrament according to the Protestant rites: it had its altar

and its set of sacred vessels. This chapel and its properties, to which Hugh added a bell, was now devised for
its double use: it was common ground for the Churches,
though they never met there. Hugh brightened it up,
for at present it had a drab Protestant aspect. He hung
coloured Arundel prints on the walls, he procured a white
plaster image of the Virgin and painted it in bright
colours, and filled the windows, as in stained glass, with
painted figures of saints. These were strikingly visible to
tradesmen and others coming to the house and were known
in the village as "Mrs. Benson's Dolls," being regarded
with suspicion as signs of Popish tendencies fostered by
her son. When he stayed at Tremans he brought a boy
as server and daily said Mass at eight in the morning. My
mother's maid, bringing her early cup of tea, sometimes
reported with true Protestant detachment: "Mr. Hugh's
been ringing his bell very loud just now."

Hugh painted the dolls and furnished his chapel in a
spirit of deep reverence, but it was also great fun, for
there lay alongside his white-hot religious convictions,
knitted into them, indeed, a fabric of impishness. There
arrived for him one morning at breakfast time a parcel
from a biscuit manufactory, containing wafers for the
Mass, the supply of which was running low. "Hurrah,
they've come," he cried, and ate one or two, then passed
them across the table to me. "Aren't they good?" This
much shocked a Protestant cleric who was there (and was
probably designed to do so), but there was nothing to be
shocked at. At present these delicious wafers were no
more venerable than Albert biscuits—less so, in fact,
since Albert biscuits were named after the great and good
Prince—and were only remarkable for their pleasant

crispness. It was impish also when, playing croquet in those alternate moods of suppressed rage and blatant triumph proper to that savage game, he looked at his watch, dropped his mallet and said, "Oh, blow it, I must go and say my prayers." But he was not referring to his prayers when he blowed them but to the rule that enjoined his saying his office at mid-day whether he was playing croquet or not.

Like most converts, Hugh was more aggressively polemical than those who had been born into his adopted faith. He dragged in controversial topics: he extravagantly lauded the saintly monastic life of celibacy and contemplation, till Arthur who, in Personality II, had leanings towards such ideals himself, scribbled in his diary: "When Hugh talks about monks, I want to turn all monks adrift with a horse-whip laid on their backs and to burn down the monasteries." The family required little provocation to be argumentative, and it was impossible to sit silent under his pronouncements about the invalidity of English Orders (he was, after all, the son of an English Archbishop, and the fifth commandment is accepted by both Churches) or the Immaculate Conception. The latter, he informed us, had been predestined from everlasting, and Pope Pius IX had merely discovered it much as Columbus had discovered America or Isaac Newton the law of gravity: even the silent Nettie was moved to say "Rubbish!" below her breath. Then we were all heretics, and heretics would undoubtedly be eternally damned, though of course the mercy of God was infinite. . . . One night he turned on Aunt Norah Sidgwick, who with Balfourian calm had pointed out some fatal, logical flaw in his argument and said: "But I belong to a Church that happens to know," thus sounding the tocsin over the claims of the human intellect. His rules of war in these discussions were like Whistler's when engaged on the "Gentle Art." Whistler and he might pour irony and ridicule and insult on their opponents but no such reprisals were allowed to them. Hugh told us, for instance, *à propos* of the invalidity of English Orders, that the election of the Pope was always directly controlled by the Holy Ghost, but he bitterly resented an exasperated brother asking why the Holy Ghost always chose an Italian. "You hurt me when you say that," he complained.

He never set much store on human relationships: there he and my mother approached life from diametrically opposite starting-points. She once wrote: "I believe, and really I know from experience that there is a class of persons (of whom I am one) who *do* learn God through man. On the other hand I realize fully that there is another class of persons who learn man through God. The danger for the first class is that they should stop short at man and never get to God, for the second that they should stop short at God and never get to man." (She might have added that there was an even larger class of persons who begin with themselves and never get anywhere else.) Hugh belonged to the second class, and was not much concerned with human affections. His profession as a priest serving the glory of God was the first call on his emotional energies, and his books, entirely propagandist in purpose since he joined the Church of Rome, were devoted to the same service. Like Arthur, he had a deep affection to my mother, but otherwise the human race (except in so far that they had souls to be saved) were playmates and companions, pleasant and interesting, but not individually absorbing. In the whole course of his life he formed only one intimacy which had that quality, and disastrous was the end of it. The episode is so curious and it concerned so sinister and picturesque a personality that I give it in some detail.

Shortly after Hugh returned from Rome, a priest of the Catholic Church, he came across a book, just published, called *Hadrian VII*. The name of the author as set forth on the title page was: "Fr Rolfe (Frederick Baron Corvo)." Briefly it was in substance the story of a young Englishman who had been rejected for the priesthood by his spiritual superiors as having no vocation, and had been cheated, swindled and slandered by them. But he had never given up his conviction of his own Divine Vocation, and in the opening chapter of the book, a Cardinal and a Bishop wait on him in his sordid lodging, and, as accredited delegates of the Church, acknowledge that he has been villainously treated and misjudged. The Cardinal makes restitution for the monies of which various black-hearted priests have defrauded him, and admits him next day to Priest's Orders. He goes to Rome where the Conclave of Cardinals is being held for the election of a new Pope, and is himself elected. The rest is the history of his Papacy. . . . This book bowled Hugh over, and the personality of the author no less than his story fired his imagination, for, in spite of the fantastic plot, the book was blatantly autobiographical and inspired by the author's innermost self. He wrote to Fr Rolfe, of whom he had never heard, telling him that *Hadrian VII* was become his bedside book, and offered him any service he could render and his unstinted homage. Then his fervour was kindled afresh by Fr Rolfe's next publication: *In His Own Image*. Hugh exulted in these tales, told by Toto, a superbly handsome Italian lad, to his master Baron Corvo, about the ragamuffin young martyrs up in Heaven, who poked fun at St. Peter and were so friendly with the Padre Eterno, and *In His Own Image* joined *Hadrian VII* by his bedside. The naïve child-like faith exhibited in these stories was linked with just such an impishness as his own. A few critics hailed the mysterious Baron with his jewelled style as a curiosity rather than a new writer of distinction, but they did not rouse the interest of the public and only a few copies of each of these books were sold.

The two met, and before long they went on an ascetic walking tour together. Some people took an instinctive dislike to Rolfe at once, and further acquaintance con-firmed that impression. That was not Hugh's experience, and the walking tour, a sovereign test surely for a newly formed friendship, only deepened his fantastic admiration. His sympathy was also strongly stirred, for Rolfe told him how, as might have been inferred from *Hadrian VII*, he had been atrociously treated by perfidious priests of the Catholic Church and had been refused Orders. Hugh vowed that when he was a Bishop he would at once ordain him. At the end of the walking tour he asked my mother if he might bring him to stay at Tremans: she always made our friends welcome, and he came. This visit was not a great success: Arthur was at home and he did not take to Hugh's friend at all. He was quite nice to him, so ran her report, "but a mind that works in such a very different manner is not favourable to unfettered talk," a perfect periphrasis to express uncomfortable intercourse. But she was interested in him, and bade Hugh bring him again when Arthur was not there.

Rolfe was enchanted at having found someone who believed in his genius and in his vocation, but he wrote to his brother about this new friendship in very guarded terms saying that he had never met an honest Catholic priest yet. They were always up to some *porcheria* (dirty trick) and he meant to be wary. But they corresponded almost daily, and soon they agreed to collaborate in a Life of St. Thomas of Canterbury, as told by a contemporary monk, a form of narrative which appealed to both authors. They worked out the synopsis down to the contents of the chapters, and it was further agreed that Hugh was to do the actual writing of the book, Rolfe's business being to hunt up and supply picturesque medieval lore. For this he was to receive one-third of the royalties from the sales, and their names were to appear as joint authors. Hugh must have been a difficult collaborator, for after working furiously for weeks on something else, he turned with equal fury to St. Thomas and bellowed for more material. It must seem ludicrous to those who find in Rolfe's prose a fresh glory in English literature that in this collaboration he should only do the "devilling" for the writer, but it must be remembered that at the time Hugh's work had a very considerable sale and that Rolfe's had failed to find a public.

Then suddenly this friendship and collaboration were shattered. Hugh learned that for reasons concerning Rolfe's private life it was highly undesirable that Rolfe's name should be associated with his, and he proposed that he should effusively acknowledge in the preface to this book, the help Rolfe had given him, that the distribu-

tion of profits should stand as agreed, that he would
pay Rolfe £100 on the day of publication, but that his
name as joint author should be omitted. Many fair-
minded people will feel that, when once the terms of
partnership were agreed, Hugh should have stuck to
them, and that Rolfe's private life had nothing to do with
his researches into that of St. Thomas. But again it must
be remembered that Hugh was a Catholic priest, and that,
since this advice came from those to whom he owed
spiritual obedience, it was difficult for him to disregard
it. Simultaneously his literary agent told him that the
book would have a far better sale if it appeared over his
name alone. This was unfortunate, for it might be held
to have inclined him to make this new proposal.

Rolfe refused it, and Hugh then offered to efface himself altogether, and to hand over to Rolfe the entire rights
of the *Life of St. Thomas* which they had planned, together
with the chapters he had written. Such an offer, whether
Rolfe accepted it or not, acquitted him of any suspicion
that profit could have had any weight with him, for he
would thus receive nothing for it.

Rolfe refused that offer also. He had put his best work
into Hugh's two bedside books; the sales of these had
been negligible and he had no reason to think that a *Life
of St. Thomas* published under his own name would earn
him the fame and the affluence which he was convinced
were his due. He regarded this collaboration as more
likely to give him these than anything he could write
himself, for, whatever the comparative merits of their
literary gifts might be, Hugh was already a very market-
able author, and association with him promised to be
valuable. Rolfe may also have thought that it might tend

to rehabilitate him in the eyes of the Church which had refused to admit him to Holy Orders.

Now to make friends with Rolfe invariably implied that before long he would discover that you had a black heart (the first step led logically to the second) and he became what he called "a persequent enemy" who would cut off his own face to spite his friend's nose. He was in dire poverty at this time, but that he should find a priest guilty of such a *porcheria* was meat and drink to him. He had two lifelong obsessions, the one that the priesthood of the Catholic Church were bent on ruining him, the other, that all who professed friendship for him were scheming treachery. Hugh therefore was double-dyed in infamy; Rolfe denounced him to his Bishop, he wrote reams of calumny to his friends, and among them to Arthur. (Arthur sent one of these letters to Hugh, and he put it up on his chimney-piece for all his visitors to read.) Rolfe volleyed abusive and obscene postcards on him, he tried to damage and unnerve him by every means in his power, and he set to work on a new novel *The Weird of the Wanderer* in which he pilloried him as a dishonourable priest, describing his dress, his personal appearance, his stammering mode of talk, in savage caricature, and lest any should fail to mark his intention he called him the Reverend Bobugo Bonson. Hugh made several attempts at reconciliation with offers of aid, but Rolfe refused them all. There he was consistent. Exposure of a treacherous friend—to that warped mind all friends were treacherous at heart—was sweeter than any alleviation of his physical needs. Acceptance of help or, worse still, reconciliation, would have taken the honey out of life.

Throughout his life Rolfe was obsessed by this conviction that anybody who attempted to befriend him—it must have happened a dozen times in his life—was in reality weaving nefarious plots for his undoing. Broadly speaking, the reason was always the same, the false friend was jealous of him and feared that the world would recognize his transcendent abilities. For his own prestige therefore he had created himself Baron Corvo of Corvicastria (a town or a district of Italy unknown except as furnishing him with the title he conferred on himself), and being heraldically inclined, he designed his due armorial bearings. As Baron Corvo he wrote *In His Own Image* and *Hadrian VII*, and described in an English magazine called *The Wide World* how while staying at some ducal castle he was stricken with a paralytic trance, was prepared for burial and listened, perfectly conscious, to the requiems sung over him. But his barony failed to earn him respect or a sale for his books, and he dropped his rank and became a commoner again. A similar policy led him to adopt Kaiser Wilhelm II as his godfather, and that was a device not sufficiently thought out, for the Kaiser was only one year old when Rolfe was baptized into the Protestant Church, and it would have been stranger still if a Protestant Kaiser had stood sponsor for him when he was received into the Roman Church.

This paranoia inspired his writing, even as it inspired his life: he is the wealthy and beauty-loving patron of his magnificent Toto, or in *Hadrian VII* he is the persecuted youth who becomes the Vicar of Christ, or in *The Desire and Pursuit of the Whole* he is the adored and romantic lover of his young gondolier who turns out to be a girl. His bedecked and jewelled style fitly records those romantic and magnificent adventures. At its best it is extremely vivid and picturesque but it is at its best when it is at its simplest: at its worst it reminds us of the finer passages of Mrs. Amanda M. Ros, with whom be peace. The jewels are chiefly paste; he knew, for instance, practically nothing of Greek, but in order to convey the impression of recondite scholarship it was his delight to search the lexicon for sonorous words and anglicize them. This process does not enrich the English tongue in a literary sense, any more than does the coinage of terms for new chemical combinations or newly identified diseases of the spleen, and Rolfe's style often recalls the vocabulary of prescriptions and pathology. Sometimes "Latin served his end," and he wrote of "fumifi-cables" when he meant tobacco, and "gingilism" to signify loud laughter. It is twenty-seven years since he died, and some of his books have been reprinted, but they can never make any popular appeal such as he anticipated for them, if he could once get a hearing, and the interest he has aroused is mainly derived from the fact that it was this picturesque and depraved and devil-ridden person who wrote them. A series of indecent letters of his, for in-stance, describing his sexual orgies in Venice, and promising to procure for his correspondent similar delights was bought originally for £30, and next changed hands at £150. But never was there an author more convinced of the supreme quality of his genius, and of the plots of treacherous conspirators, whether publisher or priest or exposed friend, to rob him of due recognition. He worked with tireless energy: nothing but the sacred duty of stabbing the hearts of these traitors with epistolary Borgian stilettos would wean him from his pages and his polychromatic inks and exquisite medieval script which he had copied from some Italian manuscript. Essentially he belonged to the age of the Borgias which had so great a fascination for him, and for this reason it is as absurd to pass moral judgment on him as on Pope Alexander VI, whose infamies, no longer operative, do not morally concern us: they are merely amazing figures of horror and splendour.

Rolfe lived in a world of his own fantasies. He wore on his finger a ring, on the bezel of which was a sharp metal spur, so that when, as he explained, Catholic bravos tried to kidnap him, he could scar their faces from forehead to chin with this spurred ring, and thus they would be traced and brought to justice. His imagination, about which there are no two opinions, invested these fictions with just the same quality as a child's imagination gives to the stories he tells his nurse about the lion that roared at him from the shrubbery in the garden. The child does not really believe his tale; he knows he has invented it, but his invention gives him the spice of romantic adventure. It was so with Rolfe: he made up these stories of an Italian barony, of an Imperial godfather, of a conspiracy of Catholic priests fearfully weaving plots to kidnap him, in order to impress on himself no less than others the mystery and distinction of his own personality.

Throughout his troubled life Rolfe's imagination nourished both his megalomania and his conviction that those who offered him friendship were about to do him some bad turn. But never, having to his own satisfaction, detected their perfidy, did he pursue any of them with such fury as he pursued Hugh. Perhaps the bitterness of his disappointment at the collapse of the collaboration from which he expected so much accounted for this, and no doubt the fact that Hugh belonged to the detested and dishonest priesthood, for which Rolfe believed himself to have a Divine Vocation, added to his vindictiveness. But there may be something more. It is likely that he went to Hugh as a confessor, and that, under the seal, he disclosed some habitual vice which he was known to practise. Subsequently Hugh was advised by his spiritual superiors that there were reasons (presumably disclosed to him) why he should not associate himself with Rolfe over the book they had planned, and he suggested other arrangements. It would be like Rolfe's obsessed mind to convince itself that he did this in consequence of what he had told him under the seal of confession. There indeed would be just such a priestly *porcheria* as he was always on the look out for. The priest is bound by the most solemn vows to isolate all he is told in the confessional from what comes to him otherwise. He puts these secrets into a closed chamber of his mind and for the conduct and consciousness of life they have no existence. But if the same knowledge subsequently came to him from some other unsealed source he would be at liberty to act on it. This hypothesis may account for Rolfe's undying animosity.

Note. I am indebted for many of these facts about Rolfe to a book by my friend Mr. A. J. A. Symons called *The Quest for Corvo* (Cassell). In this brilliantly written monograph Mr. Symons has collected from those who knew and befriended Rolfe all that could be ascertained (or at any rate published) about him, and his record, written with complete detachment, is of absorbing and terrifying interest.

CHAPTER III

FOR a solid year of the early days at Tremans I had lived entirely with my mother, but this was not a successful experiment. It was, indeed, no place for a young man's permanent home, however much attached he was to the occupants. There were no neighbours, there was no physical activity in which I could find a companion, and the unmixed feminine point of view which underlay all intercourse stifled me. I believe that, feeling bored myself, and oppressed with the sense of being odd man out from morning till night, I made the worst of it, but even if I had made the best of it, there would still have been a misfit which could not be remedied.

Then my mother wrote me a very wise letter, suggesting that we should scrap the misfit: she wanted to know what I thought about it. I concurred and set up for myself in London, which no doubt would have been the wisest plan from the beginning. Elsewhere I have mentioned this situation, but I treated it with what now seems to me a fictitious sentimentality, and in this transaction there was really not a touch of it. My mother and I behaved like sensible people who were very fond of each other, and were sorry that this experiment had failed. It was a great relief to her that we scrapped it, and I remember awaking in my new flat, and being devoutly thankful that there was no one there but myself. Thereafter I constantly stayed at Tremans and found it and its inhabitants adorable. The mistake had been to make it a permanent home.

So, issuing from London, always with some unfinished novel in my luggage, for my trade which I pursued most industriously could be practised anywhere, I spent a month or two of the winter in the high Alps, and a summer month in Italy, for summer is most delectable in the South and winter among the snows. In the early autumn I sometimes went to Scotland, spending several weeks at Uppat on the Brora, fishing down that delightful river in the morning, and playing golf on the links there in the afternoon. Dunrobin Castle was a few miles off, where reigned Duchess Millicent of Sutherland, on whom the gods had bestowed a splendid position, natural magnificence and superb beauty. When she was at home for a ball or a party at Stafford House, she stood at the top of the double staircase looking of a beauty and gorgeousness altogether beyond the human. Then for the arrival of Royalty she went down into the hall, where the great doors, never opened except for them and the welcome of a new bride of the house, were thrown wide and she escorted them upstairs. They sat on a dais; the huge room was lit only by the soft light of sheaves of wax candles. The Duchess stood for a while on a low platform near the door so that later arrivals should easily see her and pay their respects. Not even the responsibility of these solemn functions quenched her sense of humour. One night when the room was absolutely crammed I observed her half-sister Lady Warwick pressed close to the bosom of a woman with whom for years she had not been on speaking terms. Neither could get away: they were sardines. I felt our hostess would enjoy that, and pointed

44

it out. She had hardly taken it in when with a quivering finger she pointed out two others in similar predicament, whose affairs had lately brought back to Venice contentions as bitter as those of the Montagues and Capulets. Prudent folk in their gondolas on the Canal kept a wary eye ahead, and if being Montagues they saw Capulets advancing up the water-way, they buried themselves in their books or were absorbed in the Salute. "Well, we are having a funny party," she cried.

One day, up in Scotland, she asked me to support her at a trying ceremony, for she had promised to open the newly laid-out links at Brora by driving off the first ball, and she was not a very steady golfer. She stood on the first tee between expectant lines of golfers, looking superb, and completely missed the ball. Disconcerted? Not in the least. She addressed it again, just grazed the top of it with the sole of her club, and it rolled into a sandy pocket not ten yards in front of the tee. She burst into a shout of laughter. "At last I've opened it!" she cried. . . . In turn she set me the trying task of writing in her visitors' book some verse or epigrammatic observation. Just above the place for my effusion was a very witty little poem by Lord Rosebery. She had asked him to write in her book the day before, but when, just as he was leaving, she presented it to him, he appeared to have forgotten the request.

"That horrible book of yours!" he said. "I can't turn out gems of wit at a moment's notice. . . . Well, where's a pen?" He thought for a few seconds and wrote eight lines, scarcely pausing. The poem, I remember, ended:

> "So, Duchess, though your servant staunch,
> I damn your album, root and branch."

It was read out, and there was great applause at this impromptu brilliance, when the voice of his younger son joined in:

"Why, that's what you were saying over and over to yourself all this morning," he said.

I usually spent some portion of August in the houses of a colony of friends on the north coast of Norfolk. The first point of call was "The Pleasance," at Overstrand, which I had known since the owner, Lord Battersea, then Mr. Cyril Flower, bought two small semi-detached villas that stood in a field by a narrow road running down to the sea, and there, like Kubla Khan, he decreed unique and astonishing pleasure domes. No one quite knew what happened to the villas; he himself was puzzled about it. They were not pulled down, but were ingeniously embedded, like flies in amber, in the structure which grew up round them. For years it was in a state of architectural flux, expanding and flowing in all directions, a dining-room here, there a loggia with red-brick pillars, new bedrooms and sitting-rooms upstairs, a hall and a library, a drawing-room across which ran a row of arches. Outside every year something astonishing was contrived, a courtyard of crazy pavement on which were placed marble Venetian well-heads without wells, beyond which was an angled monastic cloister of rough-cast with a tiled roof plenteously planted with stone-crops.

Lord Battersea bought land and yet more land, and for enclosure and defence against the sea-winds he planted grey poplars and thickets of buckthorn, below which were gay flower-beds, and there was a rose-garden with more well-heads. He levelled the ground for a tennis court, and built a thatched pavilion furnished with deep divans where the exhausted players could rest: two bronze Japanese storks straddled beside the door. Then he got tired of tennis and took to golf, and straightway the levelled tennis court was dug up and moulded into artificial undulations. Part was grassed, and part was planted with tussocks of heather and outcrops of rock, like a grouse moor. Below it, surrounded by more brown rocks on which stood more Japanese storks, he dug a water-garden in the pools of which lilies floated and goldfish expired. Beyond the lane that led from the village to the beach, he planted an enormous kitchen garden, where grass walks framed in espaliered pear-trees reflected the influence of Albert Dürer's wood-cuts, and since it was not sufficiently signorial to cross the public dividing roadway through doors in the palings, he tunnelled a passage underneath the road faced with white glazed tiles; unknowing guests sometimes hastily turned back from it, thinking it must lead to a lavatory. . . . Outside the garden he made a private cricket ground and beyond it built stables, where was a luxurious little flat which he lent to friends, or occupied himself when enlargements to the house rendered it uninhabitable.

Lord Battersea was of the type which Disraeli called "the magnifico," and he had a genial, careless consciousness of his own splendours that seldom left him. No one in the least like him exists now, this is why I speak of him at some length. As Cyril Flower he had sat in the House of Commons for many years as a Gladstonian Liberal, and had been a Whip. He married Miss Constance Rothschild, daughter and co-heiress with her sister, of Sir Anthony Rothschild of Aston Clinton, and he and his wife lived there with his widowed mother-in-law for the hunting season. He was a very fine rider and had more than once won the Parliamentary steeplechase. In London they had a mansion, Surrey House, at the corner of the Edgware Road, opposite the Marble Arch. After his retirement, with a peerage, from the House of Commons, he was offered the Governorship of Victoria. With his excellent brain, his very handsome presence and his instinct for splendour he was the very man for such a post. But Lady Rothschild, who had the same possessiveness with regard to her daughters as Queen Victoria, refused to part with her Constance for so prolonged a period, and the matriarchal will of an extremely firm old lady prevailed. It was a regrettable prohibition, for her son-in-law was still in vigorous, exuberant middle life. He was ambitious, and it closed his career for him, forcing him into idleness when he should have been hard-worked, and giving his native magnificence nothing to exercise itself on except palatial projections of himself. Surrey House was full of the unassorted opulence that he loved. There was a fine ballroom at the back with *boiseries*, possibly by Grinling Gibbons. Next it was a dining-room, lit entirely from above, since it had no outside walls, panelled to the top with yellow and rose-coloured marble from some Italian church or palace, which he had found stored in a stable at Brescia: high-backed brocaded Venetian chairs were set round a lapis-lazuli table. These treasures were rich and precious, and all of them, particularly the Italian marbles, looked as if they were not quite at home. But soon Surrey House was little used for he did not care to be much in London now that he had nothing to do there; social functions where he was only one of a crowd were not at all to his taste, and he concentrated his creative energies on the Norfolk coast.

He filled his house there with an extraordinary mixture of admirable and deplorable objects, but it was the possession of them rather than the beauty of them that he appreciated. "I've got such masses of things," he would say, "that I don't know where to put them. . . . Yes, that's a Whistler. He asked me such a price for it that I thought his cheek ought to be rewarded. . . . Duveen offered me anything I liked for those hawthorn jars. . . ." There was a fine Tintorretish portrait of a Pope, a Rossetti of the young Swinburne, a bronze by Gilbert and some rose-jade bowls. Then, with a slight descent from these high altitudes, there was an Etty of a brown man and a white woman dallying in a barque of mother-of-pearl, and life-size crayon portraits of himself and his wife by Mr. Sands, who had an immense Victorian vogue, he with his hunting-crop, and she wearing her famous pearls. Then, with a precipitous fall, there were doorway curtains of split cane and glass beads, and throne-like chairs and a table of parchment and ebony and mother-of-pearl with tassels of coloured silks depending from its edges. Each item of this amazing jumble faithfully reflected his ambiguous tastes.

As he said, he didn't know where to put everything, and sometimes he chose curious places for them. One day Queen Alexandra popped in on an unannounced afternoon visit from Sandringham, and found nobody at home but a young man of dishevelled appearance who had just returned from playing golf in a high wind. So they made a private tour of the house, a species of exploration which the Queen much enjoyed, for her appetite for looking into other people's bedrooms and dressing-rooms and bathrooms was insatiable. Before she could be stopped, she plunged into a small useful apartment near the front-door and found there a large photograph of the beautiful Lady Dudley: she thought this a very odd room in which to hang it. And in Lord Battersea's sitting-room was a photograph of his young valet in flannels with a cricket bat which instantly she pronounced to be a photograph of George Curzon. When she made up her mind on such points nothing would shake her. She determined, for instance, that Landon Ronald was the composer of *L'Enfant Prodigue*, and though he disowned that distinction, telling her that he had only played the piano accompaniment to it when it was produced in England, he never induced her to believe otherwise.

Lord Battersea was a very handsome man; he had fine features and silky grey hair brushed back from his fore-head and a Jovian beard. His wife was plain and stout and infinitely amiable. She had a boundless fund of vague goodwill for the world in general, and for her husband an unbridled admiration. This fondly expressed itself in long enraptured glances, in calling him "duckie" or "lovie," in laying a caressing hand on his head as she passed his chair, and these little tributes sometimes exasperated him. He was coming up across the garden one morning from his early bathe, dressed in the bright colours he affected, a green tam-o'-shanter, a blazer and a pink shirt, and as he approached the loggia where we were breakfasting, she could not curb her fervour. "Does not dearest Cyril look too beautiful this morning?" she cried. "Dearest Cyril I was saying how beautiful you looked!"

It was too much, as John Brown said when Queen Victoria gave him a plated biscuit-tin on the Prince Consort's birthday. "Oh, Connie," he called, "how *can* you be so silly? . . ." On his motor there was a horn which when the bulb was pressed, emitted gay bugling sounds. He loved to tear about the country at sixty miles an hour, and sitting beside the chauffeur, to press the bulb on coming to a corner or passing through a village. She inside, was divided between terror at this excessive pace and admiration of the music. "Are we not going too fast!" she said to her companion, "and does not Cyril use the horn beautifully? He makes it sound just like a bugle." When he was present, she had eyes and ears for no one else; and absently asked her neighbours at table ridiculous questions and did not listen to their answers. One night at dinner—he dined in a ruby-coloured velvet suit—he referred appositely but with Rabelaisian frankness to an unsavoury divorce case that was in process. "I call it 'Love's Labour Lost,' " he said. "Cyril, how can you?" exclaimed Lady Battersea in a shocked voice from the other end of the table, and put up her hand to hide her blushes. But she could not maintain a disapproving attitude and beamed at him. "Dearest Cyril, you are too brilliant!" she cried. " 'Love's Labour Lost!' Is that not clever? Did you hear what dearest Cyril said, Mr. Balfour?" And when her admiration ceased to boil over, she asked Mr. Balfour if he was not very fond of reading. . . . That night or another, Lady Dorothy Nevill, with her dainty aged face, smooth as a girl's, and her stories of early Victorian days when the world was just as gay as it was now but more discreet, was staying at the Pleasance, and Sir Edgar and Lady Speyer came in to dinner from their house "Sea Marge." She had been a professional violinist before this, her second marriage, and now played much better than she had ever done then. She had brought her Stradivarius with her, and after dinner played exquisitely for rather a long time. Lady Dorothy laid out her game of Patience as usual, but was distracted by the music. Under cover of vigorous bowing she whispered to me: "I 'ate that scratchin' sound."

There were always fresh embellishments and extensions planned ahead for this Xanadu; there were dozens of gardeners to do his bidding without, and within, his architect was confabulating about a baronial hall to join up the monastic cloister to the house. He saw himself, in the eyes of others, masterful and opulent. He talked broad Norfolk dialect to the gnarled fishermen sunning themselves on the benches overlooking the sea, and as he went to play his morning round of golf, he talked to children going down to the beach with their spades and buckets with genuine *bonhomie* and the consciousness that he was giving pleasure. He played foursomes only, partnered by the professional of Cromer links, against his valet and some friend, for he was no performer himself. The professional usually managed to pull him through, but there were difficult moments, for he did not at all like being beaten, and his opponents had to miss a very easy putt sometimes to avoid this. He went forward before his partner drove, and if he found the ball on the edge of the rough, he kicked it on to the fairway, and if caught in a bunker invisible from the tee it might be lifted out. Whether there were stymies or not, depended on who laid them. There was an atmosphere of incense abroad, and everybody chorused "Good shot, my lord" on the smallest excuse. One morning his caddie made a sad mistake. He had teed his lordship's ball and then turned away, and hearing the impact of the club made the usual salutation from mere habit. But his lordship had only topped his ball into the rough just in front of the tee. . . . Though his wife sometimes overdid it, he loved the sense that the gnarled fishermen and the caddie and the gardeners admired and adored him. But he was a shrewd man, and he must have known what stuff and nonsense it all was, and I am sure that below this breezy swagger there was fear and perpetual apprehension, and that this magnificence was a protection against that. He knew that it was a sham, and when he died it was found that he left nothing but a mountain of debts. His wife's devotion and loyalty were unshaken. "You can't judge dearest Cyril as you would judge anybody else," she said. "He was a genius."

When my visit to the Pleasance was over I was often a guest at a house which stood only a few hundred yards away from a gate in the palings of the garden, so that my portmanteau could be transferred from the one to the other on a wheelbarrow. This Danish Pavilion had been a most admired mansion in the *Rue des Nations* of the Paris Exhibition in 1900. Little did I think, seeing it there on the banks of the Seine, gabled and beamed and roughcast, that the interior would prove so hospitable. Sir George Lewis, the solicitor, had bought it, and now with fresh rooms and offices and garage added to it, it stood here in a delectable garden-plot, screened like the Pleasance from sea-winds by poplars and buckthorn. The family, Sir George and Lady Lewis and their unmarried daughter Katie, spent their summer holidays here, but it was not from Denmark nor yet from Paris that was derived that radium of mental alertness and friendliness which pervaded the house like a sea breeze. Lady Lewis, like her husband of Jewish blood, had the same gift as my mother of presiding as hostess over the hospitalities of her house, and simultaneously enjoying them as her own guest. Nobody ever doubled these parts as successfully as they. Spontaneous talk (did they direct or follow?) critical and appreciative talk, ranged over countless topics, particularly people. Both thirsted for anything characteristic and personal, but neither took any interest in gossipy tittle-tattle. Lady Lewis's very courteous: "Really! You don't say so!" with which she acknowledged such news was precisely like my mother's: "I must remember that," which meant that it already lay in fragments in the waste-paper basket of her mind. Animated discussion—and how good a test that is of real vitality of mind!—flourished over any question however trivial or nonsensical. It was argued, for instance, that when Phil Burne-Jones (of whom presently) wrote certain rhymes about smart patronesses of a charity bazaar and said of Lady Curzon:

"No one so fair is
In all Buenos Ayres"

he did not necessarily mean that she was very good-looking but that the ladies of Buenos Ayres were remarkably plain. Finally Sir George, who had listened intently, pronounced that this wouldn't hold in law: the implication was obvious. Just so, when at Hawarden there had been a vivid debate as to the proper method of drying a sponge before packing it. Mr. Gladstone waited till all had said their say, and then broke in: "You're all wrong," he proclaimed, "the only effective way to dry a sponge is to wrap it in your bath towel and stamp on it." One morning Lord Battersea looked in: some small trespass (or whatever) had been committed in his garden and with a sort of jovial patronage he said: "I shall have to come to you, Sir George, for six and eightpence worth of advice. . . ." "You won't get much advice for six and eightpence," was slightly discouraging.

In the Danish Pavilion at one time the telephone was in the passage outside the dining-room that led to the kitchen, and one night there came a trunk call for Sir George during dinner. He left the door open, so in those intermittences in conversation which fall on the least inquisitive when somebody is audibly telephoning, no one could help hearing his sympathetic voice: "Yes, yes, I'm Sir George Lewis. . . . Oh, is your husband going to divorce you? I *am* sorry. . . ." But most likely he averted that, for his shrewdness and kindness and amazing common sense composed innumerable domestic shindies which, but for him, would have exploded into scandals. His clients were his friends. "If anyone comes to me in trouble," he once said to me, "he doesn't often leave my office without feeling comforted." When he retired and his son took his place, he carried on the same tradition. A friend of mine, not very well-off, was in a very awkward place. She was being blackmailed over some disastrous letters, and I persuaded her to go to "young George" and tell him exactly all about it. In a very short time she got her silly letters back without any of the odious publicity which would have been inevitable had she prosecuted. But no account for services rendered accompanied them, and when she wanted to know what her indebtedness was she learned that there was none. "Very pleased to help her," he said. "The man was a dirty brute. . . ."

Golf, still rather high with me among intellectual pursuits, occupied most of the day; my opponent sometimes was Dr. Edward Lyttelton who was now Headmaster of Eton and had a house at Overstrand. He had a theory at one time (which he did not hesitate to put into practice) that if when putting you turned your back to the hole and, bending down and straddling the legs putted between them, famous results would follow. He ate no flesh foods, and sat outside the club house at lunch, while others were tearing at toxic chops with teeth that were never meant to be carnivorous, and nourished himself on raisins and nuts and other joyless anti-uric substances. He was economical about golf balls and went on playing with one till it was paintless and scarred with wounds. His brother Spencer one day, partnering him in a foursome, declared that the ball he put down had acquired a bias like a bowl from long battering, and in a moment of reckless generosity (for he also made friends of golf balls) gave him a new one which Edward at once sliced over the edge of the sand cliff into the sea. . . . Spencer was grim and blunt and bearded and rich: he lived alone in a house in Hill Street, into which no friend even penetrated. He was a bachelor, he sang in the Bach choir, and on being asked if he had ever in his life kissed a woman, he replied: "Once. On the brow." I think it must have been the same woman who when walking with him, was seized with a fit of sneezing. Her nose was streaming, and she found she had no handkerchief. A short dialogue followed.

She: "Lend me your handkerchief, Spencer, I haven't got one."

He: "Shan't."
She: "But what am I to do?"
He: "Sniff."

Golf over, one returned to the Danish Pavilion. Lady Speyer and Phil Burne-Jones, perhaps, had come across from "Sea Marge" for tea. Her masseuse or her manicurist had been summoned from London to-day, and Phil had made a marvellous sketch of her Pekinese dog being massé'd. There was a game of tennis going on, or Katie Lewis was finishing a game of golf-croquet with Sir John Hare. He used sometimes to toe a ball into a more favourable position for himself, when his opponent's eye was elsewhere, but never resented being asked to put it back. (He and Lord Battersea would not have enjoyed playing against each other: each might have suspected the other of cheating, but everyone else knew that it was only their fun.) Lady Hare was at tea: she had dined last night at the Pleasance, and described the high-born astonishment of dearest Connie on learning that when Sir John was acting, she dined with him at 6 p.m. or even at 5.30. She could hardly believe it: "Dearest Cyril," she cried, "Lady Hare often has dinner with Sir John at six o'clock. Is not that extraordinary? 'The Pair of Spectacles,' Lady Hare. How I enjoyed it! Are you fond of the theatre?" Or, on Sir Edgar Speyer's birthday, there was a party at "Sea Marge" and for this occasion his gifted little daughters made a surprise treat for him as Queen Victoria's children used to do on their father's birthday. They composed and recited poems in his praise and honour. One began

> "My father is a banker,
> As rich as rich can be."

(Is not that an unconscious echo of R. L. Stevenson?)
Another—why do I remember it?—spoke of London
Transport, in which as Chairman of the Tubes he was
interested:

> "Thomas Tilling, Tilling's Bus
> You're the only Bus for us:
> As you roll along the road
> With your great enormous load."

Perhaps they inherited their poetic gifts from their
mother who, later, when the whole family left for the
United States some few months after the outbreak of war
in 1914, became a distinguished writer of *vers libre*.
Never was there so silly and tragic a business as their flight.
Sir Edgar was a Baronet and a Privy Councillor, and as
soon as war broke out he severed his connection with the
Speyer banking house at Frankfort, and his brother James
Speyer's branch, frankly pro-German in New York. He
wrote to the Prime Minister, Asquith, offering to resign
his honours and Asquith replied expressing the fullest
confidence in him and refusing in the King's name to
accept these resignations. But there came the trouble.
For the last three months before the war Lady Speyer
had been at the very top of the wave in London: people
had intrigued to be asked to her concerts in Grosvenor
Street where Richard Strauss and Debussy were her
guests, and now many of these cut her dead. She was
asked to remove her girls from their school in London,
or other parents would withdraw their children; her aid
in war-work was declined. She had the highly-strung,
impetuous instincts of the artist and she could not manage
to restrain ill-advised retorts. Ludicrous scandals were

spread about them: she and her husband were supposed to signal to German submarines at night from their garden at Overstrand. It became intolerable and they went to New York where, it is hardly to be wondered at, Edgar Speyer joined up with his brother James. It is not often that our rather fair-minded people behave with malicious cruelty.

Lady Lewis and her family were entirely free from any touch of snobbishness. It would not have given her one particle of pleasure to entertain the entire Royal Family because they were royal, nor did she think a story the more interesting because it was about a Marquis, but distinguished folk, chiefly those eminent in the Arts, naturally gravitated to her house, for they loved its unique quality of humour, intelligence and warm-heartedness. Dame Ellen Terry, Sir James Barrie, Sir Edward Burne-Jones, Elizabeth Robins, Augustine Birrell, Max Beerbohm, Paderewski, Harold Samuel, John Sargent and Dame Ethel Smyth had all been intimate there, and at her incessant hospitalities in London very pleasant things occurred. Miss Muriel Foster, for instance, one of the very finest of English *lieder* singers, was dining there one night, Paderewski being also a guest. He had never heard Miss Foster sing, and suggested that if she would sing he would play, and so it was. Dame Ellen Terry recited at her annual New Year Party, Sir Edward Burne-Jones scribbled his inimitable pencil sketches for the daughters, Max Beerbohm bestowed the manuscript of his unpublishable poem "Ballade Tragique à double refrain": Dame Ethel Smyth swept into the house with her violinist, her flautist and bassoonist, and her bag of golf clubs, and held practices for the forthcoming performance of some composition of hers at the Queen's Hall. Their hostess (one of her own guests, I repeat) made native air for them all, and I do not suppose there was ever a house where so many gifted people in many lines were so much at home.

Sir Edward Burne-Jones's only son Philip was an intimate of the Lewis family, partly for his father's sake, partly because—though with rabid spasms of annoyance—they were very fond of him. I knew him intimately and the better I knew him the less did he seem to me to resemble any other human being. He had a huge sense of humour, the warmest of hearts, the savagest of tongues, and a unique power of exasperating his friends to boiling point, but of restoring relations again by something so apt and absurd that they could not be angry any more. One day he had a frightful row about nothing at all with Lady Frances Balfour who, seeing red, told him to leave her house and never come back. White and trembling with rage Phil obeyed. But next morning he found in an illustrated paper a picture of two seals at the Zoo having a violent quarrel. With heads close together and wide-open mouths they bellowed into each other's faces. Phil cut it out and sent it to Lady Frances with the caption "Don't let us behave like seals at the Zoo!" Who could resist that? He quarrelled like a child, he made it up like a child, and like a child he could sometimes behave like a demon.

By profession he was an amateur painter. He was brought up, of course, in pre-Raphaelite circles, and imbibed as a dogma the doctrine of infinite finish. But he lacked the artistic fervour that demands finish for its fulfilment, and perhaps he did not understand that unless there is inspiration in the picture, finish only accentuates the lack of it. He never really cared for his work, it was never anything approaching a passion with him (that was why he remained amateur), and while "le peintre Rubens s'amuse d'être ambassadeur" the extremely sociable Phil only amused himself by being a painter. But as a caricaturist, whose pen, bubbling with malicious laughter preserved for his victims their human identity, but rendered it ridiculous, rather than by a coarser art robbed them of any semblance of humanity, his work was worthy to be ranked with that of *Caran d'Ache*. It was a thousand pities that when he took up art as his profession, he promised, in answer to his father's request, to be a "serious" artist, and not professionally adopt the lighter vein at which he excelled. . . .

During the last war collections of eggs or vegetables were made on behalf of hospitals. In country parishes the vicar often assembled these in his church, and there appeared on a certain church door the notice "Ladies are requested to lay their eggs reverently in the font." Of course I sent this to Phil and was not surprised to receive from him a caricature of a friend who was not in high favour with him just then in dinner-gown and pearls sitting on a font with her skirts tucked up round her, and a strained expression on her face. Venom inspired these drawings as often as Phil's eye for the ridiculous, and I have a series of aspects of Sir Claude Phillips, the notable art-critic, whom he detested because he invariably slanged the exhibitions at the Royal Academy of which Sir Edward Poynter, who had married one of Phil's aunts, was President. He appears as a fat nude Cupid with a white moustache, a Boy Scout, or, during the war as a territorial officer making love to a German Frau. They are scarcely caricatures: they are portraits of Sir Claude in unlikely circumstances.

Phil took his colour from his surroundings instinctively, like a chameleon. Another of his mother's sisters was the mother of Mr. Stanley Baldwin, and the moment he became Prime Minister, Phil became a red-hot Conservative, ready to live in the last ditch for the cause. Up till then he had been in principle though never in practice a Socialist, but though he professed the greatest sympathy with the down-trodden masses he detested any contact with them.

Just so did Lady Carl Meyer, who, as she fingered her priceless pearls and ordered her Rolls Royce, tell us that we ought to have no private property at all. It belonged to the masses.

Another of his mother's sisters was the mother of Rudyard Kipling, but their contacts were few, for Kipling detested the gaieties of the social world for any unexpected call from which Phil would have laid down his palette and rung for a taxi. Phil furnished Kipling with the climax of one of his most notable stories, *At the End of the Passage*, in which a man had died from the terror of some haunting presence. Those who know the story will remember how a friend photographed the dead man's eyes, and obtained a negative of something so dreadful that he smashed the plate to bits, denying that there was any image on it. His moods changed colour as swiftly as his principles. One moment he was in the gayest spirits, cackling with laughter; the next, some infinitesimal offence caused him to resemble the fretful porcupine, which, according to ancient books on natural history discharges its quills at anyone who approaches it.

His health was very poor. There was nothing definitely wrong, but he hardly knew a day of the comfortable physical serenity which most people take for granted. "I've consulted every doctor up one side of Harley Street," he said, "and I'm half-way down the other." In addition to these visits, he sampled every kind of quack tonic he could hear of, and took anybody's advice. His housekeeper did not think he ate enough plain nourishing food, and prescribed a diet that might have been digested by a young navvy in full work. I dined with him when this new régime was introduced and we had a thick white soup, a thick white fish, a beefsteak, and treacle pudding, and Phil topped up with a dose of cod-liver oil and some port. That night I first heard the domestic wireless. Phil had just bought an expensive set. It required a good deal of coaxing before it ceased howling at anyone who touched it, but in the middle of this nourishing dinner it came through very clear and we listened to a hospital nurse lecturing on pyorrhea. "Perhaps I ought to have all my teeth out," said Phil. . . .

Another night the *venue* was with me. I had lately redecorated my house at staggering expense, and he was a little vexed that I had refrained from consulting him, for he would have recommended Morris wallpapers covered with sprigs of willow or groups of spring flowers, and "tapestry" curtains full of pomegranates. He looked in silence at my beautiful unpatterned walls of lapis-lazuli blue and apple-green, and then witheringly remarked "Very clean." In my sitting-room there was a newly acquired picture of Dieppe by Walter Sickert, of which I was terribly proud. But Phil with his ingrained pre-Raphaelite principles was bound to protest. "A smudge," he said. "I see nothing whatever in it, except that he has signed himself 'Sickert' as if he was a peer." Naturally I could not let that pass, so I told him he would soon be signing himself "Jones." Instantly the bleak wind ceased to blow and he drew a picture of himself with agonized face tripping up in his peer's robes. . . . I had a wireless set now, and before we settled down to our game of chess I switched it on, and something not wholly unknown, Beethoven's C Minor Symphony, came through; so, without consulting the programme, I mentioned what it was. Not long afterwards at his house he turned on his set, and instantly exclaimed "Beautiful, isn't it? Elgar." It was certainly the Love Duet in Lohengrin. "Elgar, I think," he corrected me, and turned to the programme for my undoing. He burst out into that delightful laughter. "I'd better confess," he said. "I wanted to show you that I knew music things, too. So I looked it up, but I mistook the time. It's Elgar next."

As Phil himself said, he had never learned to paint. He saw vividly, as his pencil drawings testify, but he never tried to solve the problems of painting. They bored him and he shirked them. He painted a quantity of small three-quarter length portraits, which he induced his friends to commission. There is one of Lord Rayleigh, the eminent scientist, which is quite admirable. The face is less than profile, and he is busy with retorts and bottles on the table of his laboratory. The tall bulky man with face turned away and stooping shoulders is not only a fine observation of Lord Rayleigh, but connotes also the scientist intent on his experiment, indicated by bottles with reflected light on their stoppers, and retorts with dark liquid within. But Phil never wrestled with such problems as how to paint the planes of a human face, with muscles underlying the skin and bones underlying muscles, nor above all of the individuality of eyes and mouths. He could make nothing of them. He painted a similar three-quarter length of Henry James, but that is no more than the profile of a gentleman with a beard. He painted a portrait of Rudyard Kipling, and that is a profile of a gentleman with a moustache. If in a hundred years' time that portrait of Lord Rayleigh appears in some exhibition of early twentieth-century art, critics will hail it as a little masterpiece and search in country houses for more examples of Burne Jones, junior.

Sometimes he disappointed those who had given him commissions. Sir Ernest Cassel, for instance, walking with him, and approaching, after dusk had fallen, the house where they were staying, saw two girls sitting in the brightly lit room within. A very charming subject, the garden beds outside growing cold and colourless and this warm welcoming interior behind, but certainly of appalling difficulty. Phil solved it by painting this cheerful interior with the dusky evening light coming through the windows, which was not the same thing. He painted also a full length life-size portrait of Lady Diana Manners as a girl in fancy dress of the Velasquez mode; the gold braid of it was of pre-Raphaelite finish. It was in full face, and the elaborate costume only called attention to the fact that nobody was wearing it. He asked her father to come and look at it, hoping for a purchaser, though the price £800, was perhaps high. The most courteous of men could find nothing to say about it but: "Yes, that's my little Diana."

This portrait formed the chief exhibit of a one-man show of his pictures at some Bond Street gallery. Several of his more intimate friends, who did not want his pictures, but felt that they were bound to give him a send-off, came very early on the morning of the private view. Lady Speyer got there first and bought a small water colour landscape for £10, which was the lowest price: the two others who closely followed her had to pay rather more. Phil was constantly there, waiting for an influx of visitors, but one day, tired of looking at his pictures all alone, he asked two or three friends to lunch with him at the Ritz and brought them back to the gallery, where he found that three Queens, Alexandra, Mary and Amelia of Portugal had come and gone in his absence. That was bad luck, but he made very funny pictures of three Queens in enormous crowns with their noses glued to the exhibits in an otherwise empty gallery. . . . He had the gift, which most of us lack, of laughing at himself and his own trials with wholehearted amusement.

He was a victim of that strange affliction, agoraphobia, and if he had to cross an open space alone with no wall or railing close by to steady him, he had distressing fits of staggering, painful and very humiliating. He used to describe with gusto how a woman called her two small children to keep close to her as he approached. "Don't go near that tipsy old man," she cried to them. He abhorred dogs. I have a nightmare memory of him and Miss Ethel Cadogan, who doted on them, gibbering at each other one Sunday morning in the road outside his house. She (it appears) had connived at, if not encouraged, her pack of Pekinese entering his front garden and using it as a public lavatory, while she stood outside, waiting till they had made themselves comfortable. Phil emerged, white with fury, and Miss Ethel Cadogan was red with fury, because—she averred—Phil had tried to kick one of her sweeties. So they slanged each other. Phil wrote to her afterwards to apologize for his share in the shindy, and Miss Cadogan, I am sorry to say, while accepting his apology, suggested that what had prompted it was the discovery that she had been a Maid of Honour to Queen Victoria. That was a pity: she need not have dragged that in, but it added to the Firbankish quality of the romance. Ridiculous things were always happening to him; he seemed to attract them. He was staying once at Lord Elcho's house at Stanway, Arthur Balfour being also of the party. Phil left early one morning, and found waiting for him in London an anxious telegram from Arthur Balfour's valet, asking him if by mistake he had packed the Prime Minister's false teeth. . . . Such random anecdotes reconstruct for me that elfin and beloved personality, sharp and savage and so easily appeased, so eager to give pleasure and to enjoy.

He and I once stayed together at the home of that astonishing and stimulating woman Miss Marie Corelli, at Stratford-on-Avon, of which she knew herself to be the social and intellectual queen, but sometimes had reason to regret republican tendencies among her subjects. I do not know whether she is widely read to-day, but throughout the 'nineties and well into this century she produced a series of dizzy best-sellers, which she sincerely believed were masterpieces of literature. This made her very happy not only for her own sake but for the sake of the world. It is not, however, as an author that I celebrate her, but because she lived, furiously and excitedly, in a bellicose romance of her own devising, which she was persuaded was real. She was the victim of persecution mania, but instead of cowering under that she made it into an orgy of triumphs. The critics, she was convinced, were in a conspiracy to ignore her, but instead of making up to them or asking them to dinner, or to stay with her at Stratford as a more worldly-wise author might do, she declared war on them by forbidding her publisher to send out any copies of her new novel for review, stating on a slip that if they wanted to read it they could buy it at the bookseller's like anybody else. It sold in the usual staggering numbers, which proved, to her ecstatic enjoyment, their uselessness and impotence.

Her books—those that I have read of them—dealt with cosmic and prodigious subjects: there was the *Romance of Two Worlds* which showed how occult spiritual forces could be brought to control the material world. The Prince of Wales, later King Edward VII, thought very highly of this work and recommended it to Queen Victoria. There was *The Sorrows of Satan* which showed how the powers of darkness could enable the owner of a horse never entered for the Derby, ridden by his valet, to win the Derby: there was *Barabbas* which had the Crucifixion for its subject and expounded a sensational theory about Judas Iscariot. She grappled with magnificent themes with all the reckless energy and *désinvolture* of her temperament, but I doubt if she could have written a work of fiction founded on the stream of consciousness, for her stream of consciousness was like a series of geysers continuously exploding.

These days were of hectic activity. She came down as we were breakfasting and upbraided us for our laziness in not being up earlier, declaring that she had done two hours' writing already. . . . Here there was a moment's awkwardness, for her devoted companion, Miss Vyver, who lived with her, imprudently began: "Oh Marie, you were fast asleep an hour ago, when——" but a glance silenced her. Then when we laggards had finished breakfast we went out into the garden. She had got a set of bowls, for bowls were an appropriate pastime in the garden of an Elizabethan house at Stratford, and Miss Corelli and I played bowls, while Phil and Miss Vyver, who had more modern tastes, shot at a target on a tree with an airgun. These sports accomplished, she took us up into a small tower, where was the sanctum in which she worked, and she showed us the pen with which she had written *The Sorrows of Satan*. There was some interesting furniture: a child's chair, a child's sofa, memorials of her early years. Then one of us remembered that summer time began that day, and she told us that there was no summer time in her house. "God's time," she observed, "is good enough for me," as if, at the creation of the world, He had also created a clock, wound it up for all eternity, and had said "This is the correct time." This principle made a slight dislocation in the day, for she had asked some friends in the neighbourhood to come over for lunch, and they arrived an hour too soon, when she was extemporizing to us on the piano. They ought to have known that Miss Corelli permitted no interference with God's time. She gave us some delicious hock to drink, and told us that King Edward had recommended it to her when she lunched with him at Marienbad. At her worst I confess that she was rather a snob and liked to bring in the names of the exalted ones of the earth whom she had known.

When the friends had gone she took Phil for a row on the Avon in her gondola, and held a rug in front of their faces when she saw a man with a camera on the bank, because she was sure he was one of those miscreants who were always lurking about in the attempt to photograph her. Occasionally she allowed an "authorized" photograph of herself to appear, as a counterblast against these libellous snapshots. "I hate publicity," she told me, "yet the papers are always coupling me and Hall Caine together, and he is always advertising himself. As for knowing him, we've never met, neither the one nor the other. . . ." She sent me out in her motor to see Anne Hathaway's cottage, and the garden of Old Place, and when I returned, she had cut a bouquet of Madonna lilies, and we went to the church where Shakespeare was buried, and she laid them with a curtsey on his tomb.

More bowls, more talks about the decadence of English fiction, its lack of ennobling purpose, the impotent jealousy of critics, and next day she motored us over to Warwick Castle. The castle had been let, and so her friend Daisy Warwick was not there, but she sent in her card to the American tenant Mr. Marsh, saying that she would like to show it to her party. Mr. Marsh most kindly welcomed us, apologizing for his wife's absence, for she had stomach-ache, and he confided to me that it tickled Mrs. Marsh to death to live in a castle. We followed Miss Corelli as she took us round the suite of rooms overlooking the river, and showed us the pictures. The finest of them all, she said, was yet to come: this was the marvellous Canaletto which hung in the last room of all. "There it is," she cried, as we entered, and pointed triumphantly to the portrait of a man by Franz Hals.

"That's the great Canaletto." As we drove away she called our attention to Caesar's tower, where, she explained, Julius Caesar lived when he came and conquered Britain. Phil was not feeling very well that day, and by the time we reached home he was completely exhausted. Miss Corelli made him lie down on a sofa in the drawing-room and administered warm brandy and water in a teaspoon, with words of encouragement in baby language: "Now ickle droppie more," she coaxed him, "and then a snooze till dinner-time, and as bright as a button again. . . ."

In a work of fiction a character like hers would appear preposterous; the least critical reader would reject it as fantastically unreal, but I am sure there was never a woman so primitively genuine. She was convinced of her supreme genius as a writer and of the monstrous but unavailing malice of the critics. She raged when she spoke of them and told me with what infinite amusement she regarded the poor things. She spoke with pity and disdain of the gossipy mischief-makers of Stratford who were always caballing against her, but assured me that they were as impotent as the critics to disturb her serenity, whereas she was really a very pugnacious woman, and loved a good scrap. Yet Miss Vyver, her companion, spoke with tears in her eyes of Marie's sweetness and simplicity, the lovingness and kindness of her child's heart. And that I am convinced was true of her also.

Every generation, if we may judge from the regretful moans of the previous generation about the hurry and bustle of modern life, lives too fast and too feverishly: these are a recurrent dirge. But there is another side to it: our grandmothers certainly, busy over their needlework and their carriage exercise, the making of lavender bags for their linen, and the management of their households, would have been aghast at the idleness of their descendants who have so much time on their hands that they play bridge or sunbathe for half a long summer's day and half the short summer night.

In earlier generations there existed, although always rare and remarkable, a type of woman who has now quite vanished. We may call her the Sibyl, and though hard to define she was unmistakable when met with. She was thoughtful, she was intellectual, but she must not be confused with the *bas bleu*, for mere learning had no part in her equipment. Often indeed she was literary, and often her attainments as an author were connected with her Sibylity, but the highest attainment did not qualify her. Jane Austen, for instance, was no Sibyl, and Emily Brontë may be taken as the precise opposite. The Sibyl's quality was primarily a condition of the soul. If she was an author it was involved with the moral responsibility which her gifts as such entailed on her. She never shone socially, she never entranced a company by her spontaneous brilliance, but during the evening—here was her hall mark—you would observe that members of the party were brought up to her singly for an audience, as she sat, a little aloof, middle-aged always, and grave and truly serious. Possibly she might not say anything Sibylline, just as a nightingale may not sing though you wait under the dark night, a little chilly, on the chance. . . .

I take George Eliot to have been the best example of English Sibyls: it was on her contemporary reputation as the greatest novelist England had ever produced that her Sibylity was based. She and Mr. G. H. Lewes, with

72

whom she lived, were "at home" to their friends once a week, and, as at a French salon, conversation was general, but she, though the crown of the gathering, took no part in it. She sat always in the same place with a vacant chair beside her and favoured guests were brought up to her in turn and she conversed with them in her low earnest voice, which was described as being like an organ, leaning a little forward, and giving each her full attention. As Sibyl, she, who in her books created some of the most humorous characters in fiction (the aunts, for instance, in *The Mill on the Floss*, and Mrs. Poyser in *Adam Bede*) cast aside all lightness. My uncle, Henry Sidgwick, who knew her well, was never quite certain whether he had ever heard her say anything humorous. He suspected her once, but did not think the evidence was convincing. The occasion was when a lady-caller told her that her son had an attack of jaundice. "Poor boy," said the mother. "He was very frank about it, and did not attempt to conceal it." After she had gone George Eliot said: "No amount of dissimulation, Mr. Sidgwick, would conceal the fact that your face was bright yellow. . . ." Was there a humorous intention there, or was she gravely considering the quality of the boy's apparent frankness? He thought it an open question.

The ever-present sense of her moral responsibility as a leader of thought was a religion to her. In *Daniel Deronda* she quoted a line or two from Walt Whitman as a heading to one of her chapters, but when the book had gone to press, she regretted her imprudence, and tried to get it cancelled, fearing that, since in these headings she quoted no poet except Walt Whitman, her readers might mistakenly think that he was her favourite bard.

Similarly, when *Theophrastus Such* was published seven months after G. H. Lewes's death, she required her publisher to insert a slip saying that it was written before her bereavement; the public must not think that she had spent the early months of her widowhood in writing. Mrs. Gaskell sent her a very enthusiastic letter about *Scenes from Clerical Life*, and she forwarded this to a friend "because it did honour to Mrs. Gaskell. . . . If there is any truth in me that the world wants, nothing will prevent the world from drinking what it is athirst for." Apart from her public responsibilities she regarded herself, almost from outside herself, with a similar reverence, and announcing after G. H. Lewes's death her marriage to Mr. Cross, she wrote: "Mr. Cross finds his happiness in dedicating his life to me."

Another Sibyl of later date, whom I faintly remember, was without literary distinction herself, though of literary environment. She was an extremely beautiful woman, of despairing pre-Raphaelite type, and in her presence laughter was never loud nor conversation frivolous. She was stamped with the hall mark of Sibility, for constantly at social gatherings people were taken up to her for the privilege of a few private words and came away refreshed and vaguely ennobled. . . . On one occasion she had been enshrined after dinner in a small sitting-room apart from the general company, and her hostess made a mistake, I think, in bringing the inimitable Mrs. Cornish, wife of the Vice-Provost of Eton, for an audience. Mrs. Cornish had a touch of the Sibyl herself and people were brought up to her; she made mystic utterances, she wanted no uplift of any sort, for she had got plenty of her own, and it might perhaps have been foreseen that two Sibyls would not hit it off. In any case, after a very short interview Mrs. Cornish returned to the general company, rather fussed, rather impatient and not refreshed. "Such a kill-joy!" was her comment.

These notes on the nature of Sibyls made in pious memory of a vanished type, serve to introduce the gifted and delightful Miss Mary Cholmondeley, who combined with the Sibyl's quality rich and humorous characteristics. In the heydey of her career before the incessant claims of her friends on her wisdom and her sight imposed too great a strain on her, she lived with her two sisters Victoria and Diana and her retired clerical father in a flat in Knightsbridge. Though the eldest, no material cares of housekeeping fell on her shoulders, all was managed for her. She had written two admirable books *The Danvers Jewels* and *Red Pottage*, and *Red Pottage* had the same sort of success as George Eliot's *Scenes from Clerical Life*. Not only was it a very popular book, but it had great distinction: it was an etching of delicate and acid workmanship, the characters were bitten into the plate. Thoughtful and highbrow people, literary and intellectual people sought her out, for she was wise and sympathetic and suggestive, and gradually she became a recognized Sibyl. The rôle suited her very well, for she took it seriously, conscious, though without the slightest priggishness, of her responsibilities.

When she was engaged on a novel she took little part in social functions, and went the same walk every day by the Serpentine, for she did not want fresh sights and sounds and new contacts to disturb her mental atmosphere: and during these periods of gestation she never read books by other authors for fear that her own style (a very good one) should be affected. If a friend wanted to come and have a talk, he must not drop in, even if she was quite at leisure, but he had to ask for an appointment and a time limit, twenty minutes or half an hour that day or another was assigned, or her sister Victoria, who devotedly guarded her, said that her next few days were overfull already and did not permit it. A few friends of the most intimate circle were allowed to call without an interview having been arranged for them, and if she felt she was up to it, she saw them. If for some reason a coolness occurred, they were liable to be told that the privilege was withdrawn.

All this was very Sibylline, but her sense of humour sometimes led her to laugh at herself, which Sibyls never did. She and I were once bidden to a week-end party at Lady Rothschild's but she decided not to risk it. She suffered from asthma, and described to me how it had suddenly attacked her the last time she paid a visit, and how she was carried out of the house in an invalid chair, wrapped in a cloak over her dressing-gown with closed eyes and grating breath. "It was not," she said, positively parodying the Sibylline quality, "the sort of impression I had intended to make." And no undiluted Sibyl would have written to a friend: "If I have not lost my temper during the day, or been sarcastic to my sister because my throat hurts me, or cross to my maid because I had got my feet wet, I lie down at night feeling that there are not many people as saint-like as myself." Nor was the Sibyl functioning when at the close of a long letter to a friend in a very grave responsible style about a further book *Prisoners* (about which there was trouble in her intimate circle) she added, "Just as an afterthought, to show I can

still take an interest in others, I ask after your health. . . ."
She was poking fun at the Sibyl there, much as Jane
Austen might have done.

She and her sisters were "At Home" sometimes to a few
friends in the evening. These were small exclusive entertainments, and the manner of them was Sibylline. Those
bidden received a card on which was inscribed "A cup
of tea" with a dainty little sketch touched with colour by
Victoria of a tea-pot and a steaming tea-cup beside it,
and the hour was half-past ten. Mary made out the list
of her guests: they must have a quality about them, they
must be those who, on their way home (as Henry James
said) "from their feverish, their reverberating dinner-
parties" would like to refresh and compose themselves
by an hour of quiet cultivated conversation before going
to bed. It was therefore an honour to be asked, and she
liked this honour to be appreciated, for after a couple of
refusals you were not asked again.

These gatherings consisted of twenty or twenty-five
guests, greeted by the sisters on their entrance. They
talked in pairs or in little groups after the manner of the
English, and Victoria and Diana moved about among them,
detaching one or adding another, ensuring circulation,
while Mary, like George Eliot, was a fixed point and, in
her low earnest voice, which she never raised, conversed
with her visitors in turn, and then Victoria took them
away to make room for others. But before long Mary
began to find these parties rather a strain. She felt herself responsible for their animation, and people who have
left their fireside or their dinner-parties are difficult to
animate at half-past ten over a cup of tea and conversation. Perhaps she did not carry quite the guns necessary

for a hostess who sat in a corner undiffused. They did not expand: they did not earn a reputation for brilliance, and she gave them up.

Red Pottage has fallen into most undeserved oblivion; it might easily, by this time, have been established as a minor classic. No novelist ever had a more diverting hand in dissecting and exposing a certain type of men, who are highly esteemed both by others and themselves as persons who lead a useful and high-minded life. But this pleasing skill caused trouble when she published *Prisoners*, and in spite of brief spasms of anguish, she thoroughly enjoyed it. Quite a high percentage of her middle-aged bachelor friends whose number she herself computed at about a hundred, claimed or complained that they were her models for one of these respectable gentry, whom with manifest glee she exhibited in this very popular book, as an exquisitely selfish and complacent prig. She protested that she had none of them in her mind when she invented, entirely from her inner consciousness, this peculiarly odious character, Wentworth, who was the making of her book. She ought to have left it at that. Instead, stimulated perhaps by the resentment of her victims, she retorted that, now her attention had been called to this undesigned resemblance, she saw it herself. In other words, now that they put on the cap, she admitted that it fitted them admirably. "They refused," she said, "to be comforted," though it was not comfort they wanted so much as blood. My brother Arthur became the test case, as it were, among the injured. He had been great friends with her, and was on the select list of those who might call without making an appointment. She had stayed at Tremans. They had had many Sibylline talks together, and now she had put, verbatim, into the mouth of Wentworth, many of his contributions to these conversations. She continued to plead the right of an artist to present a "type," and took it as a high compliment to her skill that her type so closely resembled individuals, which, in vulgar parlance, gave the whole show away, for when portraying her type she had put into his mouth the utterances of an individual with whom she was intimate. She shifted her grounds and pointed out that in *Red Pottage* she had been unjustly accused on the same grounds. She affirmed that parishioners from forty different parishes had written to her that in the figure of a peculiarly fatuous clergyman in that book, they had instantly recognized their own pastor, whereas she had never set eyes on any of those gentlemen. Did not that prove how true was her presentation of a type, when so many total strangers were instantly recognized as being examples of it? But that was not to the point, for in the present instance, it was not total strangers but intimate friends who were the complainants. My mother, who thought that Arthur had been grossly and intentionally caricatured, did not believe a word of these justifications, and called it "a piece of savagery on Mary's part: she wanted to scratch." But she remained on perfectly friendly terms with her, ignoring the savagery and, I think, slightly amused at the hullabaloo. Arthur, however, was not at all amused; he was hurt and angry, and Mary Cholmondeley solemnly withdrew from him the privilege of visiting her without an appointment. As he had no further intention of visiting her at all, he bore the privation well. The whole affair was a storm in a tea-cup, but the gale was violent and a great deal of hot tea was spilt.

Nowadays Sibyls have disappeared. Unlike poets they were made, not born, and nowadays nobody makes them. It is many years since, at any social gathering of thoughtful people, I have seen, sitting quietly in a corner, a woman of middle age, to whom a series of guests, male and female, were conducted for private audience. I do not think that the Sibylline type is extinct; there are probably many women who have the due qualifications; it is the audience rather, the revering circle of those who made such into Sibyls that has failed. And there seems to be little chance of recovering the manner of the uplift which they certainly communicated to the devout. Oscar Browning, for instance, was a constant worshipper, so he told me, at the shrine of George Eliot, but his recollection of these audiences never went beyond what he said to her. He remembered, it is true, her "tenderness," but that might mean anything. Mrs. Cornish thought her Sibyl was a kill-joy, and Arthur only recalled, with fury, what he had said to Mary Cholmondeley. I am inclined to think that there was something Freudian about the Sibyls. They evoked, not by calculated catechisms but by some subtle and silent penetration, bubbles from the consultant's subconscious self, and he was so much interested in these when they came to the surface, that he forgot about Freud.

The Blessed St. Theresa, so runs a legend, set off one winter morning before it was light to attend Mass. The church was a long way off and her conveyance was a farm cart. The cart upset on the rough road, and St. Theresa was thrown out into a wet ditch. She was very much annoyed, and cried out: "O Lord, no wonder you have so few friends, when you treat them like this! . . ." The story, so characteristic of St. Theresa, might with the same fitness be told of the late Lord Halifax, who at the age of over ninety retained the exuberance of his youth. To him the two worlds, visible and invisible, were absolutely one, and he was as much at home in the spiritual and eternal Kingdoms as he was in the material and transient world in which he took such enjoyment. In person he was slight and thin. There was something of the woodland, as of a deer, in that alertness of movement, something perennially boyish in the eagerness of his mind. As a young man he had been equerry to King Edward VII, then Prince of Wales, but, being a militant Anglo-Catholic, he thought his convictions might become a source of embarrassment and resigned, giving him a prayer-book for remembrance' sake. The chief aim of his life was the re-union of the Church of England and Rome, and though a great friend of my father's, he regarded him, as well as his successors at Canterbury as sadly lacking in the zeal and boldness by which alone this could be accomplished. The burning of a few Bishops on Tower Hill, he said, might help, and for the cause he would certainly have gone to the stake himself.

He used often to spend a month of late spring in Italy. One year, he and his friend and contemporary, the late Lord Stanmore, took the Castello at Paraggi close to Portofino, and Father Waggett was among their guests. It stood walled off from the road on a small fir-clad sea-girt promontory and there was a levelled platform on the rocks from which one could take a header into deep water. One morning I returned from a long swim and found the three others had finished their bathe, and, without a stitch of clothing between them were arguing violently about the Holy Trinity. "My dear Stanmore," said Lord Halifax impatiently, "such nonsense! There are Three that bear witness in Heaven, of course the Holy Ghost came down at Pentecost, but he's there just the same! . . ." At tea one day there came in a gossiping tongue from a house near, which dropped some vague scandalous hints about the character of a rather queer Englishman who lived near by on the coast, and said it was better to avoid him. If there was one thing that Lord Halifax hated without reserve, it was this kind of mischievous stuff. He jumped up. "I shall go and call on him at once," he said.

In the autumn he invited me to a tour—it amounted to that—of the family houses in Yorkshire. We went first to that noble place, Temple Newsam, just outside Leeds, which had been left by his sister, Mrs. Meynell-Ingram, to Lord Halifax's son, subsequently Viceroy of India and now Foreign Secretary, with a life interest to his father. There was a big house-party, among whom were Princess Louise, Duchess of Argyll, and her husband. She was an extremely handsome woman, far the handsomest of Queen Victoria's daughters. Like her eldest sister, the Empress Frederick, she had high artistic gifts and there was no trace of the amateur about her sculpture. She had charm and bubbling gaiety and the same exuberant vitality as our host. We drove over to Fountains Abbey one day, where after extensive sight-seeing Lord Ripon was to meet us and give us lunch at his agent's house. But he was late and the Princess was hungry. She had seen quite enough of cloisters and ancient refectories and wanted a modern refectory properly equipped. As we padded about, rather like the lions in the zoo waiting for their keeper to bring them their dinner, she spied a smallish man in a bowler hat walking away from us. The wish was father to the thought. "Ah, there is Lord Ripon," she said, "he has gone to the ruins to look for us. Let us go after him, and we shall get our lunch." We gained on him fast, and when we were close to him: "Lord Ripon," she called out, and he turned round. It wasn't Lord Ripon at all, but an astonished stranger. "How dreadful!" she said, and there were peals of laughter.

Another day we went to Bramham. It had been built by some remote collateral of my family, Robert Benson, Lord Bingley, Chancellor of the Exchequer in the reign of Queen Anne. His only child, a daughter, had married a Lane-Fox of that period, and Lord Halifax's daughter had married Mr. George Lane-Fox of this period, and so Bramham was Halifaxian too. The house had been much damaged by a fire and was not yet rebuilt, but the garden had been kept in condition. Le Notre, who had laid out the gardens at Versailles, and, in England, at Wrest, had planned it, and water, as in all his garden-architecture, was a feature here with small lakes, one above another on the hillside. The Duke of Argyll had not come out on this expedition, and I seem to remember the Princess murmuring something on our return that she expected to find him reposing in bed, writing poetry.

From Temple Newsam we went on to Hoar Cross. It, too, had been a Meynell-Ingram property, and Mrs. Meynell-Ingram had left it to her younger brother Fred Wood, who had taken the name of Meynell. There was a fine church there, built, I think, by her husband, and the Kensitites, those militant Protestants, had their eye on it, suspecting Popish practices. I could see nothing there to arouse their Crusading fervour, but after church on Sunday morning, Lord Halifax showed me how, by turning a concealed switch or touching a button, panels in the walls painted to resemble solid stone rolled up like blinds, disclosing the Stations of the Cross. This gleeful device, for the thwarting of Kensitites, somehow reminded me of Hugh.

And so to Hickleton, Lord Halifax's own home near York. The church adjoined the house, and there every morning at eight o'clock he attended Mass, accompanied by his dog who lay reverently beside him. There was a day of driving rain, and he had a raging cold and cough. One of the party, tiring of a day in the house, announced at lunch that he was going out for a walk whatever the weather. Lord Halifax instantly said that he would go too. Remonstrances were useless. "Nonsense," he said. "When you've got such a bad cold as I have, nothing matters. It may get better, so why fuss over it? Or if it gets worse, you develop pneumonia and die, and then there's no more bother!" Out he went, and of course the wetting did him no harm. But he viewed the two alternatives with the sincerest unconcern. In his latter years his chaplain always accompanied him when he went out walking, for if he fell down he would not be able to get up unaided. Lord Halifax turned this into a game. He delighted in leaving the house by some unlikely door and giving his chaplain the slip. One day when he had succeeded in doing so, he observed that his companion was on the road behind him, probably in pursuit. So he jumped down into a ditch and hid behind a bush till he had gone by.

There was yet another home, Garrowby, on the hills

beyond the plain of York. What I best remember of a day's excursion there is being shut into some big dark chest or cupboard at one end of the house and being told to open a door or push a panel in the side of it and walk along the passage which would be disclosed. The passage turned sharply, and immediately round the corner was an awesome figure against the wall with a mask for a face. After recovering from this shock one had to continue the solitary pilgrimage; it was dark and as one shuffled along in the gloom there were strange tappings and chucklings from which it was easy to imagine the most sinister causes. This passage was Lord Halifax's gleeful contrivance for producing a pleasing terror in those who, like himself, appreciate the childlike luxury of being frightened and uneasy. He was intensely interested, as his collections of genuine ghost stories show, in apparitions and supernatural phenomena, but he also loved the ghost stories of fiction, whose only object is to terrify. I wrote several, as desired, for his special discomfort, and read them aloud to him. He was getting rather deaf, and sat close, with his hand up to his ear; and, if the story was fulfilling its aim, he got more and more uncomfortable and entranced. "It's too frightful," he said. "Go on, go on. I can't bear it!" This passage at Garrowby was his own original ghost story in brick and mortar.

CHAPTER IV

HUGH having returned from Rome, a priest of the Catholic Church, though less than a year ago priest in the Orders of the Anglican Church, was living in the Catholic Rectory at Cambridge. He soon became known as a very fine preacher. Whenever he was in the pulpit the church was crammed, and, once there, his stammer, which in talk was often very troublesome, ceased to exist. (I observed him at dinner one day drinking champagne which he disliked, and asked him afterwards why he had done so. "B-b-because I couldn't say c-c-claret," he replied.) In addition to his parochial duties he was pouring out propagandist novels. Writing with him, as with Arthur, was a passion, and was also the source of his income, and his spiritual superiors allowed him to drop parochial work, for which he had neither gift nor liking, and serve his Church more congenially to himself and more effectively to others by writing and preaching. Personally I cannot read propagandist fiction with pleasure, for I detect and resent the gritty powder in the jam. But among his novels is a book of the highest spiritual beauty, *Richard Raynal, Solitary.*

There were drawbacks to Cambridge. The University authorities looked upon him with suspicion as dangerously attractive to undergraduates as a preacher, and as a direct proselytizer. Conscientious Alma Mater was fussed about the Protestant staunchness of her young people, to whom she herself gave no religious instruction whatever, and Arthur was asked to induce Hugh to leave Cambridge. He very properly replied that the right thing for the University to do was to get some Anglican preacher of equal force and eloquence as a counterblast. As for Hugh's attempting to proselytize, there was not the faintest truth in it.

It was disagreeable. Also he hated living in a town, and he wanted to be completely independent, solitary when he chose, under his own roof. He suggested to my mother that he should build a bungalow in the cherry orchard at Tremans, where he would live with a Catholic manservant who would look after the bungalow and serve him at Mass every morning in the joint Anglican and Roman chapel with the dolls in the windows. There he would be an intermittent hermit, buried in his novels, or going forth to preach, and sending word across to the house whenever he felt disposed to lunch or dine there or seek society. This scheme was quite impracticable (my mother, for instance, did not want a bungalow in her cherry orchard) and it was soon abandoned, for he happed upon Hare Street House, a most dignified little manor, Tudor in parts, and, later, Georgian, near the village of Buntingford in Hertfordshire. It was for sale and after agonies of indecision as to whether he could possibly afford it, he bought it. And there he lived for the remaining seven years of his life, as happy, or so I judge, as it is possible for a human being to be. The core and purpose and illumination of his life was the service of God, and his writing, which he enjoyed above every other occupation not only furnished his income, but, being directly propagandist was in the same service.

When he lectured or preached in London, in the big cities of the north or in America, these engagements had to be booked up months beforehand, and never in hall or church was there an empty place. His eloquence was certainly remarkable, but it was the sheer spiritual power of his personality which had such a hold on all who heard him. Very occasionally he took a holiday: he used to stay with Lord and Lady Kenmare in Killarney in the forest and shot or went deer-stalking. One day he killed three stags and proceeding on his butcherous way came across an old, old Irish woman dying by the wayside. He gave her the last rites of the Church, Absolution and the Viaticum, and waited with her till she went forth on her journey. A perfect day. Then from holiday or mission he hurried back to his beloved Hare Street. There were always one or two Catholic friends of artistic tastes living with him and sharing the expenses of the house who gave him exactly the society that he liked best. He made strict rules for himself. He said Mass, of course, every morning, he had hours set apart for prayer and meditation and hours for exercise. A Trappist silence must be observed at breakfast time, but that perhaps was indulgence rather than discipline, for Hugh felt morose at that hour and did not want to talk. Their recreations were those of monastic establishments. There was a Tudor brew-house adjoining the house, and this Hugh at once turned into a chapel, building a cloister of communication. He and his friend Doctor Sessions made themselves wood carvers, and carpentered a rood-screen before the Sanctuary, with figures of saints and angels. They made a statue of Our Lady, set on a bracket where demons writhed beneath her feet, and on feast days she was decked in a fine satin robe, and she wore an ever-lengthening necklace set with small gems given by his friends. For exercise they cleared the long-neglected garden, relaying the lawn, repairing a flagged terrace, painting a greenhouse, and converting a potato patch into a rose-garden—Hugh in flannels of inconceivable shabbiness and such shoes as a tramp discards by the way-side.

Inside the house were decorative employments for the dark hours. Mr. Gabriel Pippet designed a frieze representing the Quest and the Attainment of the Grail to hang round the parlour where Hugh worked: the figures cut out in coloured cloth were stitched on to a brown background of canvas. The guest-chamber, also, had a frieze of home manufacture: this depicted a procession of highly disquieting robed skeletons, stepping the Dance of Death. He merrily consecrated this room to the use of heretic Anglicans who stayed with him, in the pious hope that waking in the night and finding themselves encompassed with these gruesome reminders of mortality they might be moved to fly to the only true fountain of salvation. The brethren stitched and snipped very gaily after dinner at this proselytizing piece till the bell for Compline summoned them to the chapel.

The house was largely furnished from the overcrowded rooms at Tremans: chairs and tables and linen and many folio volumes of Christian Fathers which my mother had brought away from Lambeth, and (naturally) had never been opened since, and which Hugh now was allowed to bring to Hare Street, and never thereafter opened them either; and there was a large uninspired three-quarter length portrait of my father in robes behind the head of the table in the dining-room. In the drawing-room was a Bechstein grand piano, on which Hugh occasionally played a plain-song chant or two very loud in odd moments. A scurrilous postcard from Rolfe might be found on the chimney-piece, and chained to a perch was a young sparrow hawk. Hugh intended to train it and ride out with it on his wrist a-hawking, but I think it escaped and went a-hawking on its own account. From morning till night the hours were filled with manual tasks and religious offices. Hare Street House was to revive the traditions of Little Gidding, and be a humming dynamo of prayer and physical labour in house and garden.

Personally he lived with the utmost economy, his only luxury was a prodigious consumption of the cheapest cigarettes that he could find. His catering was of the plainest, he never drank wine except when a guest was with him, he never took a taxi if he could possibly avoid it, his clothes were of the most venerable. Such economies, which concerned himself alone, had a purpose, for there was always the fear in his mind that his power of writing would fail, or his vogue pass, and he intended to relax none of them till he had an invested income, say £300 a year, which (in those days) would enable him to continue to live at Hare Street, when his earning days were done. Economy in personal expenses is a habit. It grows on the addict like some laudable drug, and I fancy that he continued to take it after his very modest estimate of future contingencies was reached. On the estate itself he spent a good deal, for he knew to whom he meant to bequeath it, and it must be a desirable and complete inheritance with endowment for upkeep. He bought a fresh strip of land to ensure a more permanent privacy for house and garden, he built a pleasant house in the paddock beyond the garden, which he at once leased to a devout Catholic lady. He installed electric light with an engine to generate the power, and a system of central heating. Great was the triumph when the latter was complete, and on a rather muggy evening he had the furnace piled with coke, and visited all the rooms to satisfy himself that the heat was intolerable everywhere. "Isn't it s-p-plendid?" he cried, profusely perspiring.

While he was in the first ecstasy of possession of this home of his own and its expansion, a gale of trouble, after these tranquil years, swept over Tremans. There were warnings of its approach. Maggie, who for the last three years had been living in a sunshine of serenity, occupied and happy, was shadowed from time to time with clouds of a dark depression which got between her and the normal pleasures of life and roused in her what she called "a thin, harsh, critical attitude." Once again, as when she was editing my father's treatises, she became censorious and disapproving, but now, instead of wanting to manage and direct, she went back to the early days of her invalidism and longed for my mother to take care of her again and protect her from the fears, vague and unformulated at first, with which these depressions filled her. She felt herself menaced. There was something threatening her which she could not deal with alone, but with that yearning for protection returned the conviction that Lucy had stepped in between her mother and herself. The fears of evil presences pressing in upon her began to express themselves under more definite aspects, and, as in the baffling uncertainty of gathering dusk she caught glimpses in the faces of passers-by, of brutish instincts and lusts lurking below a smile or a casual glance. She knew these were disordered imaginings having no reality; she knew that the world was still wholesome and sweet, but they made a veil of haunted darkness through which, when it encompassed her, she only caught remote gleams of the interests and pleasures that lay outside.

With a courage that would not admit the possibility of defeat she set herself to fight this menace. She clung to all the friendliness and normality of the world, writing to a friend with eager intentness of the yells of welcome her dog gave her when she returned to Tremans, of the big brood of turkeys and the ducks in the stable pond, and the "powdery" look of the woods in spring, and of spring's "starry" flowers, forget-me-not and small white clematis. . . . Or in Cornwall again for the winter she wrote of Mr. Fox's sub-tropical garden at Falmouth, with the palms and fruiting bananas, and the birds that scolded if you had brought no tit-bits for them; and of watching from the cliff the yellow-legged herring-gulls paddling in the rock pools of the shore and the edges of the sea. "I long for new eyes and ears," she wrote, "and a new heart to appreciate more poignantly what I take for granted. . . ." Of one thing, whatever happened, she was resolved: "not to transgress in the smallest way any of the things which are due in tenderness and faithfulness to other people."

She went back to Tremans and passing through London she came to my house. The fear of what was approaching had deepened in her mind to a certainty, and "I wanted to see you first," she said. Then came sleepless nights and days of profound misery. One morning my mother telegraphed for her doctor to come at once, and Maggie implored him to defend her and others from what she might do. An hour later she was in the grip of violent homicidal mania.

Next morning I had an express letter from my mother, telling me about it. "We are in very deep waters," she wrote. When I got down to Tremans the violence of the attack was over and Maggie was natural and affectionate. But she must have known what had happened, for she asked me if she would have to be sent away somewhere. Arrangements had been made for her to be taken in at a home where she would be under restraint till certain formalities had been put through, and she left quite quietly, kissing my mother and patting her dog. Some near relative had to see her again before he signed the petition that she should be certified, and a few days afterwards I went over there. She was frightened and agitated. She said there was no world outside the room in which she was sitting. And I remember how the printed lines of the form which I had to sign jigged up and down as I read them. It was difficult to force the pen on to the blank space.

I recall these days once more in order to realize with what courage, a courage so steadfast that it seemed effortless, my mother faced them. She accepted them as the Will of God and in His Will was peace. At first she used to visit Maggie in the private asylum near London where she was now moved, but before long she refused to see her any more, for she was convinced that she was perfectly well, and that her mother had contrived this plot to get rid of her burdensome presence at Tremans where she and Lucy would now live peacefully and happily together. "But it isn't *Maggie* who believes that," my mother said. "It's this disorder, this cloud." Her realization of that and of her inward essential peace was never shaken. "No, I can't be unhappy," she wrote. "Deep down I am conscious of nothing but gratitude and joy and love." Through long years she waited undismayed, and just before the end there came a day. . . .

There was more trouble yet. Arthur was now settled at Cambridge, as a Fellow of Magdalene College, leading the life for which, like Hugh, he felt himself most fitted, and which like Hugh, he so thoroughly enjoyed. His physical health was excellent, he was interested and successful in his College work, and now that the task of editing the first series of Queen Victoria's letters was done, he swung back to the reflective volumes and essays which had found both here and in America a very large public. The diary was as pungent as ever, he described "the shady and dicky-looking peers" smoking in the library of the House of Lords with the reflection that "these are the brightest jewels in Britannia's crown." His activities mental and bodily appeared all to be functioning with the precision and smoothness of steel piston-rods.

He began to suffer from fits of depression. At first they were intermittent, and for days together he was free from them. But they spread a film of misgiving, like rising skeins of mist, between him and his normal enjoyments and interests, and they worried him. Just then came Maggie's collapse, and this affected him in the most terrifying fashion. She had had these preliminary symptoms, this eclipse of enjoyment, this feeling of some veil sundering her from the normal pleasures of life. These symptoms resembled his own, and, always minutely observing himself, he fancied that the same road down which she had passed was opening in front of him. The fear took root. It was in vain that doctors assured him that his trouble was a neurasthenic affection which had nothing to do with his mind, and his misgivings thickened into a fog of apprehension and misery. He had certainly been overworking, but he was incapable of administering to himself the obvious remedy. He could not loaf, for leisure was not a relaxation to him, but a load of heavy time dumped down on him. He stuck to his jobs and particularly to his writing as a means of diverting his thoughts from himself, but he could not have adopted a more disastrous régime, for his books, built up of introspection, only focused his attention on himself. He had a house near Ely, and tried idleness there, but he could make no hand of that. He came back to Cambridge and found the cheerful contacts and relationships of college life as intolerable.

He left Cambridge, and was put in a nursing home for a rest-cure, but that only gave rest to a body that was in no need of it, and gave his mind full leisure to torment itself. He wrote in his diary a despairing summing-up: "I would not live one moment of my life again, and I would like the memory of it all to perish, and the very spirit within me to be blotted out." Yet to a visitor he might appear to be in very cheerful case. I went to see him one morning, and, broadly smiling, he hailed me with the mystic remark: "I've joined the best stationmasters." He explained (an explanation seemed called for) that in recognition of his work on Queen Victoria's letters, the King had made him a Commander of the Victorian Order. "When the King is going by train," he said, "he confers the C.V.O. on the station-masters of the places where his train stops, and the M.V.O. on the others. . . ." And then he went on to say that he was getting worse every day. . . . He spent a month in Italy, which he detested, he went for motoring-tours in England with friends whose company he liked best, and still this intangible, inexplicable load of misery refused to be lightened. He spent months with my mother at Tremans and to her—he could no more help it than can a patient in fever help having a high temperature—he poured out his long daily lamentations, as they strolled about the garden paths, he, huge and robust and helpless, and she so small and so steadfast. Never was her wisdom more manifest. She told me that she refused to listen to these woes with her heart, and, letting herself be distressed by them, lose herself in barren sympathy. She listened to them with her head only, for the devising of anything that would encourage him. Sympathy, so ran this admirable gospel, was useless unless it quickened your wits to be of use. But it was difficult. He disliked being told that he was on the mend, for this neurasthenia dug its claws deep and resented, as if it was a sentient independent creature, a bird of prey, any hint that its grip was relaxing. . . . Then out of nowhere there came remissions, chinks of brightness, as between drawn curtains in a dark room. He almost averted his eyes from them, as if they were a false dawn. But they were real, and, with a sweep of curtains and a rattle of rings, it was full daylight again.

On the instant he became precisely the same person as he was before those two years of eclipse. They had left no scar on his mind, they were no more than a sneeze. He did not regard them as a danger signal, and if it was the overwork of incessant writing that had caused his breakdown, he hastened to put the same strain on himself as before. To him it was not a strain: it was his manner of enjoying life to the full, and he set to work on a new book, *Thy Rod and Thy Staff* to record the mental anguish he had been through. Books, diary, college work started off again, full steam ahead. Unabated was the vigour with which his two personalities resumed their expression of themselves.

Like Henry James he prized above all achievements of his own, signs of affection spontaneously offered him. He never sallied out of his own fortress to seek friendly invaders, but, so to speak, he left its walls ostentatiously unguarded, for them to enter and find welcome. As well as contemporaries and old friends there were among these many young men up at Magdalene and other colleges. He contrived—or rather it was natural to him—to associate with them, on equal terms. The quality of youth called to him, and though sometimes he moaned to himself that they looked on him as an amiable old buffer, that quality and its attraction for him bridged the gulf of years. If they came to consult him, he never pronounced, he never spoke as the experienced to the inexperienced, but made himself inexperienced and considered the question from their standpoint. But there was always a barrier, beyond which they must not trespass, a keep in the centre of his fortress into which he could retreat, barring the door behind him. It was no use knocking at it, for no answer came, or, at the most, an upper window was opened and a few frozen words sent the would-be intruder about his business.

In comparison with these younger companions his contemporaries sometimes seemed stale and dreary comrades, and he described with peculiar virulence the dinner of some social club to which he belonged: "It seemed to me a vile thing to see the kind of mess people make of their lives—the inevitable mess—and then become pursy and short-winded and red-nosed and stupid beyond words." Even the decorum with which they (and he) performed their University duties raised a snort of impatience. "We saw the D.D.'s and B.D.'s in black gowns and cassocks floating out of the Senate House after listening to the Lady Margaret Professorial practitioners. They looked like rooks in a rookery: I think I hated these meek cautious respectable men, so comfortable and fortunate, so down on all unorthodoxy or independence. I should have liked to give them a little real religion to suffer for." He did not spare himself, when, in such moods, he surveyed his own part in social functions, but told his diary what a sorry figure he had cut at some such dinner: "I was full of stories," he wrote, "and witticisms of a hard kind. I felt how I should have hated myself if I had met myself."

But these were only little whiffs of hot steam arising from momentary exasperations, written down, perhaps, chiefly because it was so easy to him to coin apt and corrosive phrases. There were brief panics that the fierce depressions were coming back again, but these were quickly dispelled. A heat-wave in the summer made him sleepless and apprehensive, but one night he and one of the younger friends set off on a bicycle ride instead of going to bed. They listened to the hooting owls, and lingered on a railway bridge hoping to see a North-Eastern express yell through the station, and soon the sky was tinged with the green of dawn, and at Grantchester "the mill with lighted windows was rumbling, and the water ran oily-smooth into the inky pool among the trees." When they got back to Cambridge it was day, and never had there been a night of such restorative magic. Sometimes he figured himself leading a withdrawn life among orchards in the deep country, but with the same dip of ink he acknowledged that the terrors would close in again and that he was only happy "in stir and fuss." Friendships and his academical work and good health and the expanding success of his books made him a very happy man though not content. No one to whom such incompatible schemes of life appealed could be that, for the two tugged against each other. The evangelist of a placid reflective life told him that his University work was a very second-rate affair, while the busy effective don looked with scorn on the cheap facility of the writing which so large a circle of readers found inspirational. Below his ceaseless in-dustry he recognized that his mind was essentially lazy, he did not take the trouble to think out these problems for which he prescribed faith and tranquillity, as if these could be procured at a chemist's, like a bottle of opodeldoc to be well rubbed in and for external application only. He almost despised the want of perception in those who found comfort and uplift in his medicine and took it to be the wisdom of one who through suffering had attained this enviable serenity. For two years he had indeed suffered intensely, but the wisdom which he had gained from them was to rejoice in his restored happiness.

Meantime at Tremans my mother was growing old in years. She had ceased now to wish to move in the mid-stream of London, and this life in the remote country to which she had settled down ten years ago for Maggie's sake had rooted itself in her. Moreover she never gave up hope that Maggie would one day be rid of her delusions and hostilities, and would come back here. It did not seem impossible, for there had been marked improvement in her condition; she had left the asylum and was under a doctor's care living in his house. . . . So my mother waited, and no one ever grew old with such grace and distinction. Her essential youth remained undimmed, and when fears and anxieties beset her, she stood outside them, and, writing to one of her sons, pleasingly poured scorn on them with capital letters: "The Rest of Life," she remarked, "stretches before me, a Desert Track, from which Death will be a thankful Emergence," and proceeded to discuss the Sackville case with singular acerbity. She had friends constantly with her, and sometimes she and Lucy spent a few weeks at Lambeth or she paid a visit or two in Scotland, but change tired rather than refreshed her, and she was glad to be at home again.

She took the gradually growing disabilities of age with glorious inconsistency. It vexed her that she had to spare her eyes, and not read or write for more than an hour at a time, but next moment she positively embraced that as an opportunity of becoming finer. "There is surely some splendid way," she wrote, "of making this limitation into a *PLUS* quantity. I am endeavouring to turn disabilities into powers. That must be the task of advancing years, and ought to be true right up to the gate of death." On the other hand, she felt it to be "so stupid" of her to be growing ever so slightly deaf, and be unable to follow some rapid discussion that was going on round the table, nor keep up with the flight of the shuttlecock and be obliged to ask what had made the others laugh. And it was stupid of her to be a little lame—somehow her fault—so that she could not go for "good" walks any longer. "But, oh, my dear," she said, "if you can bear a totter with a tortoise, do come out with me for half an hour before lunch." And there were moments of suppressed triumph, for when I brought Phil Burne-Jones to stay with her, and she asked him to go out for a totter, she found that in spite of her twenty years' handicap, her locomotive powers far exceeded his, and the tortoise had to wait while the hare rested by the side of the road. . . . Sometimes these disabilities were to be transformed into powers, sometimes they were her own stupidities, sometimes she made a game out of them and adopted strange quack dietings for digestion's sake, in which fried substances and sugar were taboo. A box of black, repulsive, digestive charcoal biscuits stood beside her at lunch, and, refusing the delicious dishes of her admirable cook, she munched these instead, till there appeared curled slices of fried plum pudding covered with a cracking caramel of sugar. So she ate two of them, and in her diet sheet, as in the confessional, recorded this transgression.

Her three sons, one from Cambridge, one from London or winter resorts in Switzerland, and one from Hare Street or preaching tours in America, were often with her in the years preceding the Great War. On a ludicrous occasion they were there together, each madly writing, one a reflective volume of essays, another a story of modern life, the third a propagandist romance. Somebody suggested that they should suspend their important literary labours for a day, and that each should devote himself to parodying the work of a brother. This was a congenial job, for though they all took their own work very seriously, there was not a vestige of mutual admiration between them, and they thought it would be very pleasant to give frank expression to the lack of it. So, like three Cains each preparing to murder an Abel, they borrowed copies of each other's books from my mother's collection of them, studied them closely, and sharpened their dagger-pens. After dinner all was ready, and my mother much looked forward to this feast of fraternal candour.

Arthur began. He had been studying *The Light Invisible* by Hugh, and he laughed so much himself as he read the impression it had made on him, that his eyes streamed and he had to wipe his spectacles. There was an aged and saintly Roman Catholic priest, who, after saying Mass, spent the morning alone in his parlour, sitting in his purple cassock, communing with the Unseen, and refreshing himself with nips of port from a decanter which he hastily concealed behind his breviary if anyone came in. For the rest of the day he doddered about his garden recounting his clairvoyant spiritual experiences, how, for instance, he had seen a woman dressed in a blue robe with stars in her hair standing by a bush of rosemary. She smiled and vanished, so it was not difficult to guess who *she* was. . . . My mother, by this time was laughing helplessly and hopelessly, with her face all screwed up, but Hugh sat, leaning forward, so as not to miss a word, puzzled and inquiring, and politely smiling.

Then it was my turn to read. I had skimmed through several of Arthur's books and presented the musings of a wise patient wistful middle-aged gentleman called Geoffrey, who sate by his mullioned window and looked out on the gracious flowing meadow below, where a stream ran between banks of feathery grass and willow-herb and loosestrife. His gardener had been rude to him to-day, and Geoffrey wondered how people could bring themselves to be harsh and discourteous in a world that teemed with loveliness lavishly scattered there by the Divine Hand, and he was afraid he would be obliged to dismiss this impercipient gardener. But as he mused on the gentle, peaceful, tranquil scene, memories of his boyhood came back to him, and he remembered walking to church with his hand in his father's on a mellow Sunday evening, after he had been reading the *Pilgrim's Progress*, and he asked him if the church bells were ringing from the towers of Beulah. . . . Just then the gardener came round the corner whistling "A few more years shall roll," and Geoffrey thought how beautiful and true that was, and how before many more of these seemly years had passed, he and the gardener alike would have to face the great mystery of death, trusting, he hoped, in the Divine Power which had hitherto so wisely and lovingly sustained them. So he beckoned him to come to the open casement where he sate, drinking in the fragrant odours of the wallflowers that so graciously blossomed below, and instead of dismissing him, he thanked him for the lesson his melodious whistling had taught him, and they sang the rest of the verse together. Then as it was growing chilly he closed the mullioned window, and, sitting in front of the fragrant wood-fire that sparkled on the hearth, he wrote a short article for *Christian Endeavour* about the opportunities the humblest of us are given every day to make the rough places plain, and took it to his resident typist as she sate in her little panelled parlour.

How much, he reflected, our typists do for us, and how little we do for our typists!

Once again my mother was helplessly giggling, but, as I read, I became aware of a draught or a frost or something inclement in the room, and looking up, I saw a pained expression on Arthur's face. . . .

"Now for Fred," said Hugh, and then it was my turn to know what a brother thought of me. Hugh's composition seemed to me to miss its mark. Those babbling puppets with their inane inconsequent talk had no individuality; there was nothing in them. Really this composition made no impression on me: I could not see the point of it. . . . But here was my mother for the third time wiping tears of joy from her eyes, and Arthur and, of course, the author were much amused.

"Oh, you clever people!" said my mother. "Why don't you all for the future write each other's books instead of your own? You do them much better. Give me all those stories. I shall read them when I feel depressed."

Such memories recall, perhaps through their very insignificance her eternal delight in the ridiculous, whether exhibited by herself or others, which was as integral a part of her character as her faith and her courage. Indeed, I must add an example or two more. A Roman Catholic priest in the neighbourhood brought a French Bishop who was staying with him to call on her. He had omitted to tell him anything about her beyond that Monsignor Hugh Benson, whose sermons he considered most effective instruments for the conversion of Protestants, was her son: he assumed, it was supposed, that she was a Catholic herself. They walked in the garden together, and he casually spoke to her of the deep joy she must feel in her son's denunciation of the heretical English Church, which kept so many souls from salvation. As they drove away the Bishop told his companion what a pleasant talk he had had with this charming and interesting woman, and learned that she was the widow of the late Archbishop of Canterbury. There was no need for the apologies that followed: she revelled in the absurdity. . . . Once she had invited a local branch of the Guild of St. Mark, which arranged outings for children, to have tea and revels in the cropped hay-field. She had meant to say a few words of welcome when they arrived, but her eye fell on their banner, the lion of St. Mark, very militant, all claws and teeth with the text "Suffer the little children to come unto me" inscribed below. The words of welcome had to be postponed till she composed herself again.

During these years before the war I saw very little of either of my brothers, who had formed a very close friendship. Their manner of life and mine (except that we all wrote furiously) were as different as they well could be. Arthur at Cambridge, where he was one of the most notable figures, found the academic *milieu* which suited him best; Hugh at Hare Street, now one of the most popular Catholic preachers, led a semi-monastic life, surrounded by a few like-minded men, which was of the same *genre*. Both of them had their professions which they strenuously and successfully pursued, while I had no career apart from writing. My works and days seemed to them both dilettante and frivolous. They regarded London and the social gatherings which I so much frequented with an amazed horror, and when obliged to go there fled back at the earliest possible moment to Cambridge or Hare Street. I spent a good many days in the year in the houses of friends, and they avoided such visits like the devil. They were ungregarious, and the gregarious and the ungregarious can never understand each other. Another point of difference, which is less superficial than it sounds, was that I devoted immense energy of mind and body to athletic sports: they were a pursuit to me and to them they meant nothing at all. Our tastes and aims and the environments occasioned by them were incompatible to the point of antagonism. They together and I apart drifted into benevolent indifference. We were all very prosperous and wished each other well.

Two or three summer months in Capri had now become for me part of the schedule of the year. I shared a house there with an old friend John Ellingham Brooks who, partly from laziness, partly from a flawless mental fastidiousness, made less of fine abilities and highly educated tastes than anyone I have ever known. He was short in stature and clumsy in movement, but his face was very handsome. His mouth had a thin fine upper lip priestlike and ascetic in character, but below was a full loose lower lip, as if the calls of the flesh had not yet been subdued. Handsome though he was I found him sinister in appearance. In the process of making a complete failure of his life as far as achievement of any sort went, he made himself for many years very happy: so perhaps from a certain point of view he may be held to have arrived at a success which is denied to most of us. Since he has died without leaving the faintest mark of his passage, and since the style and the charm of Capri in those years, its unusual and gifted foreign colony, has vanished as irrecoverably as he, I attempt an intermittent reconstruction of them both.

Some fifty years ago now, after leaving the University

and travelling in Italy, Brooks came over to Capri for a couple of nights, and then he travelled no more for the present, but sent to Naples for his luggage, and remained in the island for the rest of the summer. Capri cast its spell over him, he returned again and yet again, his absences grew shorter and then ceased. He had no ties that he valued in England; he had sufficient private means to enable him to exist quite comfortably without the need of earning money by work, and that I regard as the tragedy of his life. If he had been forced to work at however uncongenial a task, the fibre of application might not have atrophied, as it assuredly did in the absence of having anything definite to do, leaving him practically incapable of any sustained mental exertion. A brief interlude occurred in the unvarying progress of the years when he married, in a fit of aberration on the part of bride and bridegroom alike, an American girl who lived on the island, and was the heiress to considerable wealth. Why either of them should have married at all is quite inexplicable: I only record that they did. They soon found out that they had made a ghastly mistake and loosed themselves from their bonds.

His passion—it was not a pose—was for what he considered the masterpieces of literature. In English his idols were Meredith and Walter Pater, a strange combination. In Italian he read Leopardi before going to sleep at night, and d'Annunzio when he was waking. He studied Dante, he was familiar with the second part of *Faust* and Hérédia's sonnets. He never concerned himself with second-rate or third-rate vintages. He might sip them, tasting a pleasant flavour, but they were not of the *premier cru*, so why falsify the palate by accustoming oneself to inferior beverages? He read solely for the pleasure that reading gave him, and I do not think that he had the smallest touch of the creative gift. If he had, this fastidiousness, apart from his inability really to apply himself to anything, would have probably rendered it barren. But he intended to leave one work behind him: this was a translation into English of Hérédia's sonnets. He pictured it to himself as his *Omar Khayyam*, slender but immortal, of which every word and syllable must be a tessera in a polished and perfect mosaic. By 1910 he was, in his own manner, at work on this.

A subsidiary passion was music. He enjoyed it immensely, and here, his personal ambition was to be able to play a piano-sonata or two of Beethoven's, but as regards execution he was as incapable as of literary creation. If on a summer morning he determined to be industrious instead of bathing and basking till lunchtime, and if Hérédia did not respond to his wooings, he was content to think that it was no use trying to force inspiration, and in his shirt-sleeves, with a pipe in his mouth, he practised diligently, and genuinely felt that he had passed an industrious and busy morning. But in spite of this diligence he never applied himself. He never had any lessons, he could not memorize a dozen bars of what he so constantly played, nor practised scales or exercises, and the technique he evolved for himself was a complete obstacle to any progress. One of his conjuring tricks, for instance, was, in playing a descending passage with the right hand, to pass his second finger over his first (incredible but true, for how often have I made vain suggestions!) instead of using his thumb and passing a finger over it.

Lunch implied a quiescence for two hours afterwards, and Brooks mused over the recalcitrant passage of Hérédia till he fell asleep. He woke and watered the garden, or we went for a walk with his fox terriers, and after dinner came the social event of the day, when the foreign world flocked to Morgano's café, where the Juno-like Donna Lucia presided at the bar, serving syrups and liqueurs, till overcome with fatigue, she fell asleep in her chair, still smiling and statuesque. Maxim Gorki, then an exile from Russia was often there with a small band of disciples. They played games of cards with a purring mutter o conversation, until it was observed that the Master had ceased to attend and was leaning his head on his hand in meditation, and the mutter was stilled. Norman Douglas looked in after his day's work on *South Wind*, or Mr. Jerome, American vice-consul at Naples, resident in Capri, had a cup of coffee before his night's work, which often lasted till morning. He was a Roman historian of high erudition, living alone in a house encompassed by a walled garden in the centre of the town, and presently he strolled back to his book-lined library to renew his labours. Just now they concerned the Emperor Tiberius; he was convinced that his supposed infamies and perverted orgies were a malignant scandal invented by the historian Tacitus. Sometimes I went back with Jerome to his house, and he explained to me how the monstrous legend had arisen that when the Emperor had glutted his passion with these young folk he threw them off the precipitous rock where the ruins of one of his seven palaces still stands, and experienced the final sadistic thrill. All reliable sources, said Jerome, represented the Emperor as a gentle, kindly man, devoted to children to whom he used to give delightful treats at this palace on the edge of the easternmost cliff of Capri: the conjunction of a huge precipice just outside the palace gates was sufficient to account for the rest. There were many other legends which owed their origin to such conjunctions. A cleft in the rock on the Acropolis, for instance, was the sole source of the Athenian legend that Poseidon, god of the sea, had claimed Attica for his own, and in token thereof had struck the rock with his trident, and in the cleft salt water had welled up. . . . Jerome's table by this time was piled high with the books of reference he had torn from his shelves to prove his point.

Then up at Ana Capri lived Dr. Axel Munthe, though not yet of that world-wide renown which was afterwards so justly his, when he published his *San Michele*. But on the island he was a legend already, a doctor who, as he had revealed in *Letters from a Plague-stricken City* had passed through the epidemic of cholera at Naples, ministering to the sick through sleepless days and nights, without fatigue or fear. He had the healing touch, it was said; he had hypnotic powers which none could withstand, but was himself nearly blind. He could not face the brightness of the day, but at dusk he walked out, and the peasant folk looked on him with awe and affection as he passed, stilling a crying child, or laying a hand on an aching head. Sometimes he lived at his villa San Michele, or if the Queen of Sweden was his tenant there, in a fortress, Materita, beyond the village. . . . At Ana Capri also lived Mr. Compton Mackenzie, one of the group of younger English novelists of whom Henry James wrote an appreciation in the *Literary Supplement* which ranks among the most enigmatical pieces of English prose. (Mr.

George Prothero told me that he read half of it, and then suddenly found that he did not know what it was about. He began it again and read it all through, and thought that he understood it. So, to make sure that he had grasped it, he began reading it through for the third time but the gleam had vanished, and he was completely in the dark again where he forever remained.) Mr. Mackenzie had bought or leased the southern slopes of Monte Solaro down to the sea. They were a fine piece of perpendicular property, far too steep for cultivation of any sort, a scramble of boulders covered in places with treacherous vegetation, but he longed for them as for Naboth's vineyard, and put up a gate on the hillside leading to them, to show that his estate began here. The gate was purely symbolical for the property was quite unfenced. He was writing hard, and by a curious idiosyncrasy found he could concentrate most completely if somebody was playing the piano: so, if his delightful wife was not at leisure to make music, Brooks was sometimes called in to supply the necessary noise.

These great lights shone on a remarkable social circle. Down at the Grande Marina, where the excursion steamer from Naples anchored while the horde of tourists swept over the island for a few hours daily, lived the two Misses Perry, wealthy American spinsters of advanced and adventurous age. Miss Kate was close on eighty, and her sister Miss Sadie, though ten years younger, was not less vivacious. The house which they had just built for themselves overlooking the harbour quite outshone Lord Battersea's Pleasance and was comparable only to "Soyer's Symposium" which Mr. Benjamin Disraeli pronounced to be the most wonderful thing in the world:

"It is impossible," he wrote to his adored Lady Londonderry, "to conceive anything more various and fantastical." It was dazzling white, mainly of Arab architecture, with floors of Moorish tiles, and above rose a Gothic cupola, sheltering a bronze bell. There were loggias from whose roofs, screened by Italian trellis, dangled great bunches of yellow grapes, which, when dusk fell shone with the electric light concealed within. There were Oriental rugs and Chinese porcelain and refectory tables and weird modern pictures on the walls and saddle-bag divans and chairs set with mother-of-pearl, and in the garden stood a white marble circular Temple of Vesta. The two Vestals seldom left their precinct, but on Sunday afternoon they invited their friends there, and regaled them on ices and sugar cakes and caviare sandwiches and cigars, and a bewildering variety of alcoholic drinks, whisky and brandy and absinthe, and cup of white Capri wine, innocent-looking, with strawberries and herbs floating on it, but of staggering potency. Capri was not hide-bound by teetotal fads. Brooks was a great favourite there: he talked to Miss Kate about the Hérédia sonnets, and the difficulties of the Waldstein Sonata. The sympathetic old lady loved being confided in: she felt she was admitted into high artistic circles, and told him he mustn't work too hard.

The king of the Vestals' hearts was certainly young Count Fersen whom they both regarded with protective adoration. They had lately taken him on a tour in the Orient, and he had built himself a remote house near the ruins of the maligned Tiberius's palace and precipice. His antecedents were reported to be sensational, for it was said that he had been officially ordered to leave

French soil owing to some scandal in which he had been involved about the celebration of the Black Mass. Probably foundationless (for Capri was rather a gossipy place) but he led a fantastic life, as anyone was at liberty to do on the island without arousing more than a faint but kindly interest. I called on him one day, and after tea he proposed that we should go to his smoking-room for a pipe of opium. I was not an addict, but I went with him to the scene of the earthly Paradise. It was an undistracting room, dim and bare, with several couches against the walls, and he stripped off most of his clothes and put on an embroidered Chinese robe. His Italian servant vested himself similarly, prepared his master's pipe and his own, and they lay down on their couches. Fersen chattered away, and did not seem to be entering any kind of Nirvana, but Nino after a couple of pipes lay relaxed and quiet with large black eyes staring at nothing. It was all rather like a charade. . . . An end came to this close friendship between the Vestals and Fersen on the outbreak of the war in 1914. They expected him to fly to the succour of his native country now invaded by the barbarous Huns and never forgave him for his want of patriotism.

Then there was an American artist, Mr. Coleman, who occasionally was at home to his friends in his studio but in less Bacchanalian fashion than the Vestals. His pictures —picturesque corners and rugged old fishermen—had (for me) the curious quality of looking like bad copies of first-rate work, and he himself, white-bearded and rather majestic in manner, looked like a bad copy of Lord Leighton, once President of the Royal Academy. There was the English vice-consul, endeared to readers of *South Wind* as Mr. Freddie Parker. There was a Scotch lady,

Mrs. Frazer, who spent the mornings in the sea, well wrapped up in a thick serge suit. The annual ambition of her life was to bathe a hundred times during the summer; when she had reached her century the serious work of the year was done, and she had a holiday. She spoke in the Highland tongue, and on major festive occasions wore a great cairngorm, an heirloom, as big as a hen's egg, on her bosom, and the tartan skirt of her clan. After dinner she was easily persuaded to propose the toast of Bonnie Scotland, for which purpose she stood on her chair and in the correct ancestral mode put one foot on the table. She waved her glass, she led the cheers and started "Auld Lang Syne." . . . Among all the colony I cannot recall one who could be called "ordinary." There must have been some occult ingredient in the air of Capri which developed individualism. It contained also, like the water of Nepenthe, an oblivion-making quality, for, from the moment of landing in the island till the moment of leaving it, the seas and continents, the ties and the obligations of the rest of the world were deleted from the mind: nobody cared what happened anywhere else. Even the lights of Naples, strung nightly on the shore of the mainland like a necklace of gems, and the red glow of Vesuvius were no more than a painted drop-scene, in front of which was enacted the life of the island.

In 1914 I went out to Capri in the middle of May. Brooks was incessantly ruminating among the Hérédia sonnets and he read me one or two with the original before me for guidance. I had not the requisite knowledge or perception of French poetry to appreciate the subtlety of their perfection, but from what I knew of English, his translation seemed to me frigid and laboured.

It had not the primary call of beauty, nor any echo of it. He called my attention to some ambiguous phrase in the French of which he had rendered the ambiguity most successfully, and he seemed to regard the preservation of this obscurity as a triumph of translation. But, of course, so he explained, there was endless polishing to be done yet: there was endless roughness to be ground away before the clear fire shone out, and it would be a long while before his fastidiousness was satisfied. But patience and industry would achieve that, and he had no misgivings himself as to the ultimate quality of his work. For my part, I had nothing else, for I could not see how polishing could ever reveal a beauty that was not there. I admired, I envied (and I could have wept over) the sincerity of his conviction that he was at work on a gem of literary art, but dimly I began to foresee—just because of his sincerity—one of those tragedies whose insignificance constitutes their poignancy.

We had moved the year before into a most delightful house, which I had long coveted, taking a seven years' lease of it with option to purchase. It faced southwards; a terrace ran along its front and a plumbago ramped up the whitewashed rough-cast of the house wall. From the terrace ran out a short vine-covered pergola over the cistern for rain water, and in the garden, lying rather steeply down the hillside, grew a great stone-pine which whispered to the slightest breeze and roared when sirocco blew. Over the wall separating it from the footpath outside that led up from the town to Tiberius's palace and precipice hung a tangle of passion-flower and Morning Glory. The house was much larger than our previous quarters: there was a big studio built out at the back, and I intended to bring out more furniture from my overcrowded house in London. Two months was the limit of my stay here for the present, but I meant to come back half-way through August after a visit to Bayreuth.

Unclouded days succeeded each other: there was never so resplendent a June. Light winds blew from the north across the bay, with never an hour of sirocco. We breakfasted early before the sun grew hot below the pergola in the garden, then came the morning in the sea at the Bagno Timberino, with alternate swimmings and baskings, and on the way home a call at the post office for letters and papers brought by the mid-day steamer from Naples. I had an unfinished novel on hand, and after siesta worked at it till dinner, and resumed again afterwards instead of going down to Morgano's café, thus getting three or four undisturbed hours. I was anxious to prove to my beaver-instincts, now that I meant for the future to spend at least four months every year in Capri, that it was quite easy to be solidly industrious there. Brooks's return from Morgano's was announced by Beethovenish sounds from the piano in the studio, a-strolling in there when my own labours were done, I found him dreamily engaged on the Sonnets. As usual all that might be going on in the world outside the island seemed quite suburban, and when one Sunday towards the end of June I called at the post office on the way up from my bathe and read in the Italian papers that the Archduke Franz Ferdinand and his wife' had been murdered at Serajevo, I attached no significance to it. It was a horrid senseless outrage committed by a half-witted boy, and having ascertained from *The Times* atlas that Serajevo was in Bosnia I thought no more about it. A fortnight afterwards, with my finished story in my suit-case, I looked from the deck of a Channel steamer at the cold grey water streaming past, amazed that it and the clear crystal round the coasts of Capri could both be called the sea. On the fourth of August the flame of war had enveloped Europe.

CHAPTER V

HUGH and I were together at Tremans for three days before the end of August that year, by which time I had hoped to be back in Capri with fresh furnishings for the Villa Cercola. He was waiting to know whether his offer to serve as Chaplain to Catholics on the West Front would be accepted, and meantime he was sure that this was the battle of Armageddon, the last stand and overthrow of the hosts of Satan, after which the millennium would dawn on the warring world. And why look further than the Kaiser to find Anti-Christ? . . . On one of these days there was a total or nearly total eclipse of the sun, and though, on reference to the Bible we found that the darkening of the sun was not a phenomenon allocated to Armageddon, but to the Day of Judgment, something final and apocalyptic was clearly at hand. But whatever that might prove to be, the eclipse in itself was most interesting and must be carefully observed (for the whole heavens would soon be rolled up altogether and therefore this would be the last eclipse) and presently we were gazing at the reflection of the diminishing orb on the surface of a bucket of water, where it could be regarded without bedazzlement. The heat of the summer morning was chilled, the circular spots of light filtering through the foliage of the Penzance Briar became crescent-shaped as the eclipse increased: the birds chirruped as in the growing dusk of evening and went to roost. Then through the darkness and the silence there sounded the crackle of gravel under the bicycle of a boy from the post office with a telegram for Hugh. It was to tell him that Pope Pius X was dead. This added to the sense of doom and finality. But before long the black circle of the moon slid off the sun's face, the light and heat of the morning were restored, the birds went about their businesses again, and Hugh and I went to bathe in the hammer-pond in the woods.

He said Mass next morning for the repose of the soul of the Pope in the joint chapel of the Churches, and we went our ways, he to his beloved Hare Street, and I to London for my job of war-work. Air-raids were already expected, and, incredible though it sounds, rows of small lights to suggest streets were prettily laid down in Hyde Park, in the hopes that raiders from a height which must render them quite invisible, might rain their bombs on the Serpentine and the ducks and the Achilles statue. This pleasing device was soon abandoned, just as in September 1938 trenches dug there as shelters from enemy aircraft soon filled with water.

I never saw Hugh again. His offer to go out to France as a Catholic Chaplain was not accepted, and he was told to carry on with his own work. But there was something wrong; he had bouts of very severe pain, which was diagnosed as "false angina," on which his comment was that, though false, it was extremely plausible. It came abruptly and abruptly ceased, and in the intervals he was as active as usual. Early in October he was conducting a mission at Alverstone, and preaching at Salford, when it grew much more acute. Pneumonia developed, and completely conscious to the last, he died without reluctance or struggle, just ceasing to breathe.

I went down to Hare Street to find his will, which he had said was there, and to see if he had left any directions about the place and the manner of his burial. I hunted through drawers and boxes of papers in the parlour hung with the Quest and Attainment of the Grail, and at the end of long search discovered it among a few casual bills and letters lying on his writing-table, as if he had been looking at it just before he left. It was dated two years before, and in it I read wholly unexpected and elaborate instructions. He wished to be buried in his garden in a brick vault sunk beneath the ground and accessible by a small flight of steps. This vault was to be closed with an iron door which could be unlocked from within, "and the coffin," he directed, "should be lightly made, so that in the event of my being buried alive, I could escape, and that a key (of the vault) should be placed in the coffin." After a month it was to be presumed that he was dead, and the vault was to be sealed and closed. If these directions could not be carried out, he entreated his executors to make sure that he was dead by having an artery in his arm opened "in such a way that death would not be caused if I were alive (since this would be suicide) but that if life were still in me, the fact would be unmistakable." As he lay dying he had asked the nurse to make sure that he was dead before his burial: otherwise, as far as I know, he kept this fear of being buried alive completely to himself. But these directions, made two years before, show how real it was to him. . . . I have wondered whether a story of Rolfe's published in that remarkable magazine *The Wide World* had induced this obsession. In it, writing under the name of Baron Corvo, Rolfe vividly described how, in a state of suspended animation, he, pulseless and immobile, had been prepared for burial and placed in a strong coffin, which he had great difficulty in breaking through. . . .

It was quite impossible to build this vault under several weeks, but the alternative precaution was taken, and, in order to follow out his wishes as far as possible, the necessary permission was obtained that he should be buried in his garden. Cardinal Bourne, Archbishop of Westminster, came down to Hare Street, consecrated a piece of ground below the Calvary that Hugh had erected, and boys from the Westminster Cathedral sang the Requiem. Then there arose a difficulty about carrying out the other provisions of his will. He had bequeathed Hare Street House and the estate, with a fund for their upkeep, to the head of the Catholic Church in England at the time of his death, and thereafter to his successors. But his will had not been properly witnessed and was therefore invalid, so the whole estate legally passed to his next of kin. But we were all agreed that the intention of his will must be carried out, and the only legal way of effecting that was that Cardinal Bourne should bring a lawsuit against us claiming the estate under the provisions of the will, and that we should not defend it. When notice of this action appeared, a certain newspaper of strong Protestant principles, not quite understanding what the purpose of the suit was, highly commended the family's resistance to the encroachments of Rome, whereas the whole point of it was to give effect to these encroachments.

Cardinal Bourne much enjoyed being a small English Squire and often used the place as a holiday home. According to Hugh's wishes, the furnishing of the house was to be kept as it had been in his life-time, and thus it happened that a Cardinal of the Church of Rome ate his dinner under a portrait of the Archbishop of Canterbury. In all the history of the high prelates of the two Churches such a conjunction can hardly have occurred before. Over Hugh's tomb in the garden there was subsequently built a memorial chapel.

Arthur was now Vice-Master of Magdalene, and lived in a strange but most attractive house which he had contrived for himself in the College by adapting some cottages that stood there and building on to them. The ends of this long line of low roofs were two-storied. At one end up a narrow precipitous staircase were two bedrooms and a bathroom for guests, and below a room which was never used or even furnished, and his secretary's room. At the other end on the ground floor was a kitchen and a sitting-room for himself, and above, his servants' rooms. He built the one-storeyed connecting link between these two portions, a polygonal lobby and a passage flanked by a dining-hall forty feet long with a gallery at one end, panelled and hung with portraits, and his bedroom. Somewhere (I cannot place it) was a minute courtyard, impenetrable because of the grove of perennial giant hemlocks, six feet high, that grew out of the flagged pavement. Arthur hated heat, he hated what is called "a cheerful sunny room," and sun and brightness and any glimpse of a view, to his great content, were quite banished from his quarters, for his bedroom, sitting-room and lobby all faced due north, and a dense strip of shrubbery grew close up to the windows. In the dining-hall the windows also faced north, and were placed so high in the wall that nobody could see out of them.

The walls of his sitting-room were lined with tall book-cases, on the top of which were invisible electric lamps, and a series of copper urns: the floor, except for a passage between door and door, was a mosaic of tables, piled high with papers and japanned boxes, and the large arm-chair where he sat with a board across the arms, and wrote. The house was full of heterogeneous furniture: there were fine Chippendale chairs in his bedroom, a seventeenth-century refectory table in the dining-hall, masses of china, including a fine Wedgwood dessert service and quantities of rubbish stowed away in cup-boards, two great French ecclesiastical candlesticks six feet high, Queen Anne bureaux, a faked Elizabethan corner cupboard, Turkey carpets, early Victorian sofas, an elaborate American organ. But apart from a few family pieces, these were all his own acquisitions. He had seen them in sale-rooms or through the windows of curiosity shops and they had struck his fancy: he wanted them. He never made a speciality of any branch of collecting, pictures or furniture or books or silver, but merely acquired what he thought attractive and never gave it another thought. The whole house in bulk and detail was as much an expression of himself as is the shell of an oyster. He grew it, and I have dwelt on it, because at his death it vanished.

With the outbreak of war Cambridge became a vast deserted house with many of its dons and most of its eternally youthful family serving their country, but the house had to be kept in working order for the resumption of its traditional life when the war was over. For the present it was suspended: Arthur's tutorial work ceased, but that gave him more time for writing, and that was his passion. "I live," he recorded in his diary, "first to shape thought into word," and headlong was the shaping of it: within ten weeks after Hugh's death he had finished writing a life of him. Next year on the death of Stuart Donaldson he was appointed Master of Magdalene, and simultaneously there befell him the strangest of financial romances.

For years his "fan-mail" had been very large, for his quietist books and essays appealed to a vast multitude of readers. He knew himself that these books were not of any high intellectual or philosophical value, but through the medium of his lucid and beautiful style they awoke in many thousands of simple and thoughtful readers the perception of the beauty of a withdrawn and untroubled and unambitious life, as seen through the eyes of Personality II. He spent endless hours in writing sympathetic answers to these correspondents, who, he sometimes complained, seemed to have nothing else to do except to bother him. These admirers, his feminine tea-party audience, whom he had never seen, assured him that he had marvellously expressed for them what they had always thought but had never been able to formulate, and had given them the key to many problems of life which had always baffled them. More mundanely, a daring spinster told him in strict confidence that he would make a lovely husband and enclosed her photograph, to show, I suppose, that she would make a lovely wife. . . .

Between him and one of these correspondents there had been establishing itself, though they had never met, a real friendship. They wrote constantly to each other: Arthur told her of all that both intimately and super-ficially made up his life, of his rides in the Fens, of the affairs of his friends and family, of the joyless days of the long melancholy from which he had emerged, of his renewed happiness, and of his schemes for the expansion of Magdalene. She was American by birth, a woman of great wealth and culture, who had married a rich man of European nationality, and now, in advanced middle age, lived with her husband and family in Switzerland. She was one of those who had found inspiration in his books, and these letters, through which they had come to know each other had kindled a warm personal affection between them. Then one day there came a letter from her telling him what a joy it would be to her to be allowed to contribute to his schemes for the College, so that he could carry them out more fully. She had consulted her husband and her family and they thoroughly approved. At first it seemed to Arthur a proposal that it was impossible to accept. But again she urged it on him with a tact and a sincerity that made herself appear the benefited rather than the benefactor: she asked a favour rather than conferred it. He consulted a friend or two: their view was that he would be only the trustee or administrator of a fund, and that he would put himself under no personal obligation. He accepted, having as yet no idea of the scale of her bounty. During the next few months she made over to him securities and cash amounting to £45,000 and more was to follow. Of this he had entire control to spend as he pleased. He disclosed to the Fellows of the College the existence of this anonymous benefactor, he established a second account, and his magnificent vicarious gifts to Magdalene began.

Already he had been spending considerable sums on the College, and in the eleven years since he had been made a Fellow, he and the late Master had greatly raised its status in the University. Now the scope of his personal services was prodigiously enlarged by the administration of this endowment. He built, he adorned, he financed and he reigned. He had a genius for remunerative expenditure and these large funds gave it ample opportunity. He founded fresh exhibitions. He privately helped boys whom he believed would be a credit to the College, but who otherwise could not have afforded to come to Cambridge. Magdalene, hitherto hampered by poverty, went ahead in an amazing manner, and it acquired before his reign was over a position that gave it rank among the leading colleges. It might be said that his influence and personality backed by this affluence founded it anew. He was always looking ahead to find fresh expansions inherent in those already attained, and at the time of his death he was building another court to house the young men whom existing sets of rooms could not accommodate.

This fairy tale in the fortunes of Magdalene continued to preserve the strange feature already mentioned. As Browning said, "It all came out of the books I write," and never did Arthur and the veiled princess know each other's voices, except through the written word, nor ever did they set eyes on each other. Possibly one of them hung back from the idea of a meeting, more probably neither of them desired it, or surely it must have taken place. After this constant and intimate correspondence either or both may have felt that personal contact might involve anti-climax; in any case, this bodiless relationship entirely satisfied each, so why run the risk of the minutest disenchantment? The story might have furnished Henry James with a theme on which he could have constructed a masterpiece, tightly packed and "beautifully creaking." I can see myself reading it, enthralled and intrigued, up to the stage that it had now reached, but feeling uneasy that he would not be able to resist in the pages that remained a cruel, apt and ironical development. He might have permitted two middle-aged strangers, an American woman and an Englishman to encounter each other in the dismal opulence of Newport, and, thrown together at some social gathering to have talked to each other, still unintroduced, and have become conscious of some faint essential antipathy. He would have spared us, I fancy, the ultimate brutality of a disclosure (just as he would have spared us the banality of the obvious commonplace climax) but there would have been turns of phrase in their conversation, which reminded each of the prized and perfect letters, moments of uneasy suspicion loyally banished, questions that would have disclosed their identities stifled on the lips, and have left them thus. Or would he have permitted the romance of the two who never saw each other to come to its close as it did?

Eight years had now passed since Maggie's breakdown. Her mental condition had very much improved, and, as mentioned before, she was living now under the care of a doctor at Wimbledon. I used often to spend the afternoon there, or, in charge of her nurse she came up to see me in London. Before Hugh's death, she had even spent a night at Hare Street, and had gone down to Cornwall again. She still had many delusions, but it seemed now as if she did not believe in them herself: one only was tragically real to her, that my mother and Lucy had contrived this plot to get her banished from Tremans, so that they might live there together undisturbed. . . . Her memory was amazing: she liked talking of old days at Truro or Addington, and always after these visits she wrote me a long letter in a minute hand recalling other incidents which our talk had suggested. If Arthur was in London she went out with him to a museum or a picture-gallery, but soon there came a disastrous afternoon, for when it was time for her to go back to Wimbledon, she refused. There was no scene, she was quite quiet, and it was not long before her devoted nurse had her in hand again. But for him it was an unnerving moment, and her expeditions with him ceased. Then she had a sudden and serious heart attack, and she herself asked that her mother should be sent for. Just for a few hours she was completely herself again, tender and affectionate to her, but again the clouds gathered. Still, for a few hours there had been a complete break in them, and who knew that they might not pass altogether. Hitherto she had been in good physical health, but after this attack, her strength began to decline, and there were no more visits to London. She sat out in the garden of the doctor's house, making dim little unfinished water-colour sketches, or writing stories about her dogs and her Persian cats, and now she hardly ever spoke of her delusions. But always when I went away she asked if I could not take her back to Tremans.

Throughout the spring of 1916 she lost ground physically for her heart was seriously affected. One day, unusually, she began to speak in a hushed frightened voice of some creatures "not quite people" who lurked in a corner of her room, but she was not very sure about them, and smiled when I laughed at her. Next day I came to see her again, and now she laughed herself at the notion of the creatures that had been half real to her the day before. Not one shadow remained of the darkness in which she had dwelt. She had awakened that morning, very weak in body but with her mind unclouded and serene. Once more she asked that her mother should be telegraphed for, and when she came, we sat by her bedside, and there was no mention made of all that those two had been through. There was nothing left of the bewildered years which were lifted clean out of the lives of them both, nor did they speak of Lucy. But soon she got tired, and she said she wanted to have a good night and be ready for my mother when she returned in the morning.

She went to sleep. Once in the night she woke and her nurse heard her say to herself, "As pants the hart for cooling streams." Then, sleeping again, she died.

My mother had gone through these troubles with a faith which had never wavered nor questioned. Arthur, on the other hand, had to fight personal and intimate apprehension of which she had no experience. He attributed his first attack of neurasthenia to the shock it gave him to see Maggie after her collapse, and he had been haunted by the fear that his own wretchedness and want of power to enjoy were symptoms of a kindred malady. That fear, even in his renewed activities, had perhaps never quite left him. It was dormant, but not dispersed, and it had shown its lurking presence by his shrinking from seeing her again, after the unfortunate incident I have mentioned. He felt himself to be vulnerable. But that was all past now, and perhaps it was with the resolve to drag this fear out of its hiding-place and demonstrate to himself that it no longer had any force, that, during the year after her death, he busied himself in collecting her letters and writing a memoir of her. If this was so, it was a very unwise valiance, for this constant dwelling on her was almost bound to revive the associations which he hoped to prove to himself had no longer the power to affect him. Soon after his book was finished he found himself threatened again. He watched the approaching menace with a fascinated dismay, noting its symptoms in his diary, the swift nightly pageant of meaningless dreams incessantly renewed as if his brain was out of control, and the waking from them into an abyss of hopelessness. During the day the onslaughts were intermittent: he could take pleasure in reading for a while, but then "an agonized stupor came on, a nausea of the mind." His power of enjoyment was paralysed: the beauty of the external world and the sense of friendship withdrew themselves into some region with which he could no longer get into touch. "What it means to sit here," he wrote in his diary, "the soft wind rustling, butterflies poising on the buddleia, apples dangling, the garden I love beyond, the life I love all about, and have this horror over me, can't be even faintly guessed. It separates me from everything and everybody."

The assault this time was far more deadly than before, bringing him nearer to the dangerous verge, and he was sent to a nursing home which took in borderland cases, where every care would be taken but without restraint or loss of liberty. There was a certain risk, but alienists saw him and thought that such risk was justifiable, for to do more might have caused a final unbalancement. His imagination, that deadly and divine faculty, which always weaving for us fears and joys and projects and disappointments, had got out of hand. All of us know its freaks, how out of some small anxiety it augurs a ruin of disaster, or out of some small piece of good fortune a gold mine of prosperity, but we can keep it in reasonable control and refuse to give reality to its fabrications. But he had lost control of it, and yet he knew the unreality of the agonies it caused him. He wrote to me, for instance, to go up to Cambridge to look after some small businesses there, and said that he could no longer pay his servants their wages, and feared they might be starving. Then enlarging on this, he added that they might already be dead of starvation; perhaps the doors of his house would be locked, in which case I must break in. Yet he knew that he had made arrangements for his household to carry on there, and when a day or two afterwards I went to see him, he referred to this letter himself. "I can't think why I wrote it," he said.

Perhaps such miseries were better forgotten or unrecorded, but I write of them for the reason I wrote of other such, because their very darkness illuminates the same unfading memory. Within three years my mother had lost a son and a daughter, and now another son was again beset by this malady of the mind which made him daily long for death. None of these sorrows affected her inward happiness. It welled out clear and pellucid, for the spring that fed it was the faith which nothing could cloud. She wrote to a friend, "Faith is not a bundle of mere spiritual truths, but a *condition of soul* which I should describe as eternal life." That to her was the power which not only consoled but was the cause of her happiness, and that condition of soul was hers. She feared life as little as she feared death. Her interest in it and her joy of living never suffered abatement, though thinking of the great company of those she loved who had passed on, and who, she knew, were as truly alive as ever, again she wrote: "The dream that life is. And how one feels one must be waking soon or coming home soon to talk it all over!" A year more passed, and on Maggie's birthday she woke, and went home.

For a year after her death I kept Tremans just as it had been in her lifetime. There was not yet any sign that Arthur was making progress towards recovery, but once before he had completely thrown off a similar though not so severe an attack, and one clung to that hope. If he recovered and resumed normal life, he might wish to make his home here in vacations, or, if he never took up active work again, he might wish to live here. As yet, buried in wretchedness and in this new and profound grief, he was quite indifferent about the future.

As that year went by I became more and more aware that my mother had been the whole spirit and inspiration of the place and without her it was meaningless. Most of all it was meaningless to Lucy Tait; for the last thirty years her life and my mother's had been one, and for her there was only this aching emptiness. She bought herself a smaller house in the neighbourhood and lived there and at Lambeth with her sister and brother-in-law. At the end of this year Arthur was still in the same state of apathetic misery, and since I could not live alone in this big house buried in the country we agreed that we must part with the remainder of the lease. Sweetly and incessantly my mother's presence haunted it, but how false and unreal she would have pronounced any sentimentalizing over that!

Almost everything in the over-furnished house was knit into domestic associations, but it was evident that much of it must go to auction. Most of it had been familiar from the time when my father was appointed Archbishop of Canterbury thirty-five years ago, and much went back into the dim days of Wellington and my parents' early married life, and wedding presents of sixty years ago, and there were a few family pieces of one side or the other going back to the seventeenth and eighteenth centuries. But all family tradition would be broken in the next generation, for there were only Arthur and I left, and to anybody else these stacks of familiar things would have no significance. I marked a quantity of furniture and pictures and plate, to be sent to Magdalene in case of his recovery, for he had the associative sense, and loved material objects with memories attached to them, but I never have cared for such. I wanted to keep a few beautiful things, some miniatures; an Elizabethan corner-cupboard; a hexagonal Jacobean pulpit with carved and painted panels, now serving as a sideboard—my father had bought this as a young man on a walking tour near Bideford, as it was on its way from a church that was being restored according to the taste of 1850, to an old furniture shop—Egyptian antiquities from the excavation of the Temple of Mut in Karnak, but I wanted these because they were beautiful. The very bulk of familiar things that were mine for the taking (for Arthur had told me that the more I took, the better he would be pleased) surfeited me: it was like a piled-up plate of food, high and pyramidal, which kills the appetite. I did not want the antique (and partly modern) oak sideboard which had been familiar to me since the Wellington days, when,

as a small creature of five years old, I stood by it at breakfast time and had to repeat to my father the new verse of
a Psalm I had learned that morning, with all the previous
verses. That was a pleasant memory and immediately
preceded sausage. Nor did I want the set of steel en-
gravings of Raphael's cartoons, which hung in the dining-
room there, of which the enumeration was reserved for
Sunday morning. There was his big mahogany knee-hole
table, with drawers on each side, and a roll-top, and I
did not want to recall what that suggested. He sent
for me one morning in the Christmas holidays, went on
writing for a few minutes while I stood waiting, and I
saw beside him the report from the headmaster of my
private school, which I knew would contain some awful
revelations about my conduct during the last term. Or
what place or use could I find for the organ from the
chapel at Addington? It chiefly suggested the Sunday
evening Compline, which Arthur so detested. A copy of
the service, a thin volume bound in purple leather would
be just as efficacious as an evoking spell. Many other
things had delightful and beloved associations attached to
them, but I wanted none of them because of their associations. Why should one need material reminders of what
one already possessed the essence of?

Together with this work of selection went on the
vaster business of destruction. There were cupboards
full of papers, there were large wooden boxes, dating
from the exodus from Lambeth and Addington labelled
"Archbishop's Correspondence," and within, dossiers
about such businesses as the "Deceased Wife's Sister Bill"
and the "Lincoln Judgment," which had long been obsolete,
and which no one would ever read again. Then there

were boxes of my mother's correspondence, packets of letters from her mother to her, still in their envelopes brown at the edges, with crests on their flaps and early Victorian stamps. They described the excitement of travelling in a "steam-train"; they were full of advice to her when as a bride of just eighteen she left home; they inquired whether the new baby (now reading them) had been "weaned," and whether Edward's neuralgia was better. About these sentimentality prevailed, and I inconsistently kept some of these, though aware that no one would ever look at them again. There were her early diaries, too: the crisis over her extravagant household books, the full total of which she had been put off disclosing to him: her fear that in consequence he would not buy the riding-horse he wanted so much (riding was so good for him): the subsequent reconciliation, and, to mark his forgiveness, his generous increase of her allowance, which she thought so supreme a magnanimity.

She seldom destroyed a letter from her family, and there were hundreds from Arthur from the time he first went to school, and these I put among the pieces to go to Cambridge. She had kept also Maggie's bitter letters to her during the clouded years, and that was very puzzling, for she knew that they were no more than symptoms of Maggie's disorder, and not herself. And there was dangerous stuff that had better perish: a correspondence, for instance, in which three very well-known women had written to my mother some years before about a divorce case to the prospect of which some of the most exalted ghouls in the land were much looking forward as a tasty dish, but the wisdom of these four ladies deprived them of their banquet. And there were fragments and finds which seemed to date from an extinct era. Miss Victoria Grosvenor, whom I remembered many years before as a genial elephantine woman of middle age and a strong upholder of her sex's right to independence, had written to my mother saying that she had "crossed the Rubicon" and gone to a popular concert at St. James's Hall alone and unprotected! . . . She was jealous of her great size, and when she heard that Arthur was sixteen stone, her geniality faded for a moment, and she said to him, "Indeed, you're not!" I lingered over Miss Grosvenor: she was a very ardent churchwoman, and had asked my father's advice about going out to Japan as a missionary. The Japanese, she told him, had a deep reverence for ancient and distinguished lineage, and would listen with respect to a cousin of the Duke of Westminster when she recommended them to embrace Christianity. Her father, Lord Ebury, who lived to the age of ninety, had, as a small boy, gone out with the guns snipe-shooting over the Five Fields meadow land which stretched from near Hyde Park Corner down to the Thames, and separated the village of Chelsea from London. They had come into the ownership of the Grosvenor family by the marriage of the then Lord Westminster with Miss Davies, the heiress of this fortunately situated farm, and where Belgravia now stands had been these pasturages and marshes of the riverside, much of which was submerged by high tides.

I pulled out of a spider-webbed cupboard yet one more box: it was labelled "Family Miscellaneous," and miscellaneous indeed it was. There was a packet of unused invitation cards to a Speech Day at Wellington College, somewhere in the 'sixties of the last century, and tucked into it a note from Lord Derby, Chairman of the Governing Body, in the third person, saying that he would do himself the honour to attend my mother's garden party. There was a correspondence about a boy whom my father had expelled. The Governors asked him to reconsider his decision, and a copy of his reply informed them that if they had any intention of over-riding it he would instantly resign the Headmastership. There were some pen and ink drawings which he made for us children on half sheets of paper, when, with brushed hair and washed hands, we came down to his study for half an hour before bed-time, and he made pictures of castles and churches and biblical scenes, the youngest sitting on his knee and the elder ones standing round watching with bated breath the magic of his skill. There were antique photograph albums: these had cardboard pages with small oblong apertures for the "cartes de visite" of young men with whiskers and young women with garlands on their ringletted heads, and large apertures for "cabinet" photographs. I had no notion who these blades and beauties were, but near the end there was a "cabinet" of my mother, aged perhaps twenty, having tea in a summer-house with a croquet mallet leaning against a rustic table.

Next from this bran pie of relics I drew a portfolio with mysterious contents, a series of sheets of thick cartridge paper yellow with age on which were spread specimens of seaweed. Some were like the brown network of bare branches on a tree-top in winter, others had green fronds as of tropical plants in a jungle, others were like combed strands of red hair, and at the corner of each sheet was the scientific name of the specimen. There hung about them in addition to a peppery odour, the atmosphere of the leisurely diligence which had so charmingly displayed them. But what were they?

Then, with the suddenness of a train emerging from a tunnel, memory flashed into daylight, and I had to linger over Great-aunt Henrietta. I was staying at the age of five with my Grandmother Sidgwick, when her spinster sister Henrietta Crofts, came back from a visit to the seaside with a case full of lumps of seaweeds which she had collected. She invited me to come to her bedroom and see the beautiful destiny that awaited them. She popped each of them into her sponging-tin bath and gently led it about, this way and that till the fibres expanded in the water, and then floated it with infinite dexterity on to a sheet of cartridge paper. She spread the fibres out with a pin, as if she was playing spillikins, and they adhered to it by some glutinous quality of their own. She had collected sea-shells also on her holiday, and encrusted photograph-frames and the lids of wooden boxes with them, so that they became objects of celestial beauty.

As I consigned such relics to the clothes-basket for destruction—for what else could be done with a collection of ancient seaweeds?—I meditated on Aunt Henrietta. She was grim and formidable in aspect, but benevolent to my sisters and me, and she had a remarkable memory for birthdays and was lavish with half-crowns and five-shilling pieces. She treated us as if we were still infants, and on the morning of my sixth birthday (that manly age) which occurred soon after this seaweed business, she told me she had heard fairies singing in the garden, and thought that they might have come to offer their congratulations. So she went out into the garden to look for them, closing the front door and bidding me wait in the hall. In a minute or two I also heard singing in the garden, and knew quite well that the voice was Aunt Henrietta's. Presently something rattled into the post-box, and she tapped at the door calling to me to let her in. She entered in great excitement saying that she had seen a fairy hovering by the door and then flying away again. We opened the post-box, and there was an old seal-skin purse of hers, containing five shillings. . . . I did not like her to think that I still believed in fairies, but it would be tactless to tell her that, or even to thank her for her munificence, since she had nothing to do with it, so I feigned credulity and we went to tell my grandmother of this astonishing occurrence.

Aunt Henrietta seldom relaxed from her grimness into laughter, but when once she began to laugh, she, like Queen Victoria, could not stop. One day when she and grandmamma went to church together, she found she had forgotten her prayer-book, and she had to share her sister's which was old and weak. The print was very small and they both pulled at it so hard in order to be able to read the Psalms and make their due responses that the prayer-book came in half. Aunt Henrietta began to laugh, and, not being able to stop, she left the church with half a prayer-book in her hand and her face buried in her handkerchief.

For days, in the hot June weather, a bonfire flared or smouldered in the cherry orchard, and into it I cast everything which might make mischief if it fell into wrong hands—"when in doubt burn" was the safer course—and all such papers (and seaweeds) as nobody would have regretted if they had been destroyed years before. The smoke rose in spirals in the still air, and the heap of ashes grew. At last all cupboards and drawers were empty, the selected van-loads of what was to be kept were dispatched, and then came in the advance guard of the auctioneer to make the catalogue of what remained. Numbered tickets were affixed to furniture, books were gathered together in lots, strange miscellaneous bundles were gathered together in lots, strange miscellaneous bundles were formed of fire-irons and stair-rods. On the last evening that I spent there I found the gardener smoking a disconsolate pipe by his new asparagus bed that had yielded a marvellous crop that year. In all his life, he told me, he had never made such a good asparagus bed. . . . But all ties were not severed. Spicer, who had been my mother's parlour-maid for close on twenty years, was to rejoin me in a month or two, and with her came the house-boy Charlie Tomlin. Twenty-one years have passed since then, and presently he will come into the garden-room at Rye and tell me that it is time to change for dinner.

CHAPTER VI

HENRY JAMES died in 1916. I had been to Rye once or twice since the first visit I paid him there, staying with an old friend Lady Maud Warrender, in her house at Leasam. It was perched on a hill a mile outside the town, overlooking it and the broad lands of the marsh that melted into the riband of sea beyond. Music was her passion, and she had the most superb contralto voice. Her brother, Lord Shaftesbury, was a tenor, and so curiously alike were their voices in timbre that when they sang duets together and the parts crossed they were almost indistinguishable. It was there that I first met Edward Elgar, then beginning to be recognized as one of the greatest living composers, and perhaps of the musicians of all time. One morning he begged me not to go and play golf, as had been my intention, but come over to Winchelsea and "help him." He explained this mysterious errand, for I would not go without. Some forebear, his great-grandfather, I think, had been hanged there for sheep-stealing and Elgar's piety prompted him to search the churchyard to see if he could find his grave, thus establishing that he had received Christian burial: two searchers would make quite a short job of it. He asked me also to write four songs for him on the subject of flying, air-raids, and travel by air, and these he set for solo voice, chorus and orchestra. They were to have been a turn at the Coliseum, but he had some disagreement about terms with the management, and bundled them into a drawer, refusing to take any further steps about them. It was a pity, for he never wrote anything more characteristic. Search was made for them after his death, but it was as vain as the search for his great-grandfather's tomb at Winchelsea.

With Henry James's death I supposed that Lamb House itself would concern me no more, but in the preordained decrees of fate, or, alternatively, in the fantastic hazards of a fortuitous world, it began at once to concern me more closely. The house was let to an American lady, and she, being obliged to winter in the South, left her housekeeper there, and asked a very intimate friend of mine to occupy it if he wished for a month or so, and he in turn asked me to share his tenancy. I had war work to do in London, but a morning train there on Monday and an afternoon train back to Rye on Friday gave me week-ends in the house which I had imagined I should never enter again. Lamb House began faintly to assume a home-like aspect, for coming back on Friday afternoon I knew I should find my friend there. He was of neutral nationality, an artist of whimsical and imaginative work, and he established himself in the garden-room, once resonant with the booming voice of Henry James and the clack of the responsive typist, and plied his brush by the north light of the bow-window. Then Fate began to act with that capricious consistency that shows she means business. The remainder of the lease was offered to me: I could not take it, for I was already co-lessee of the Villa Cercola at Capri and hoped to resume possession at the end of the war, but this offer seemed a sort of nudge, an aside, on the part of Fate, to indicate that she was attending, and meant that Lamb House was coming nearer. I passed the offer on to a friend of mine, who accepted it. For the moment that seemed to put it further away again, but now the landlord of the Villa Cercola told me that he would not renew my lease after 1919, and that if I wanted to stay on I must purchase, and I had no intention of doing that. Simultaneously, Tremans was given up and my friend, to whom I had passed on Lamb House wanted for the future to spend his winters on the Riviera. Would I therefore consider taking a sub-lease from October till the end of March? I did not require much time for consideration.

And so it came about that lying in bed one morning, more asleep than awake, I found myself wondering where I was and what was that luminous patch on the floor near by. I did not really want to know, for, much more, I wanted to prolong my floating over those ambiguous shallows which lie between the deep waters of sleep and the shores of full consciousness. That is a precariously transient condition: too keen an interest in external concerns will cause the drifting craft to ground on the beach, while too complete an apathy of mind will take it out on to the deep seas again. It was admirable just to be conscious of existence, but not of its circumstances. I felt at home, but did not know where that home was. Then a noise, half-flap, half-crack upset the balance, and I was aware that the luminous patch on the floor was sunlight coming in through one window, that the noise was the flap of the blind drawn down over the other, and that I was in the King's room at Lamb House. I drowsily inferred that the wind must have shifted from the east to the south and that the sun had graciously appeared again.

Coming down to the small square dining-room I opened the french windows that give on to the garden and a very mild air streamed in. For the last three days a virago of an east wind had shrieked and scolded (there is no place outside the Arctic Circle so cold as the east end of the High Street in Rye when the winter wind blows from that quarter) and except for the starlings there had been no bird-business going on. Starlings take less notice of the weather than any other fowl: they strop their beaks on the chimney-tops and straddle about the lawn with their toes turned out in the bleakest of gales. They even continue their imitations of the notes of other birds (which must show a jaunty merriment within) under the most depressing conditions, for yesterday I felt compelled to steal out into the garden in volleys of rain to get a sight of the red-shank who was whistling just outside. Why a red-shank should leave the sheltered ooze of the river-bed for this garden perched on a hill in the middle of a town I did not pause to consider: that note was certainly a red-shank's. I tiptoed round the corner of the garden-room, and there on the trellis was a starling amusing itself with talking red-shank language. But he is a Mark Tapley among birds and, whatever the weather, maintains a bank-holiday demeanour. Now I make the birds' breakfast, chopping up the skin and bones of a kipper and the rind of bacon with pieces of toast. Starlings are good clowns at table: they gobble up some fragments and toss others into the air, and make scuffling runs at sparrows, who come too near the feast. They will not suffer other birds to partake: it is as if at a dinner-party those guests who, in the evolution of species, had a touch of true-blue starling

144

blood in their veins scurried round the table, fork in hand, and speared pieces of fish and flesh from the plates of the plebeian and drank their wine. They remind me, too, of a music-hall turn in which two conjurors sat down to a meal. There were some biscuits and sandwiches and a tea-pot and plates and saucers, and, instead of eating their food they threw the crockery at each other deftly catching it. Then they began to throw the biscuits and sandwiches and caught them in their mouths till they had eaten them all. So it was with the starlings: their stunt was to throw the kippers and bacon about, and under cover of the stunt to eat them. I must write a monograph on starlings. The garden, I have noticed, has too many prowling cats about. There shall be a bird-table, a flat wooden board on a support so high that cats cannot leap on to it, and pounce on my guests, and on the edge of the board I will carve the text: "Thou shalt prepare a table for me against them that trouble me. . . ."

This garden and the bird-haunted lawn are surrounded by walls of old red brick. To the south the gable-windows of houses in Watchbell Street can just blink into it: to the east are the roofs of houses in Church Square; to the west the ground falls sharply down to the level of the marsh, and over the wall appears the high ridge, eight miles away, of Fairlight: a row of Lombardy poplars, planted by Henry James, partially protects it from south-westerly gales. On the north stands Lamb House, and at right angles to it the garden-room already mentioned. A short flight of steps leads up to its door, and over the railings and the wire frame above an antique wistaria has twined itself, gripping these supports with tight coils in the manner of a boa-constrictor. Surrounded by these walls and buildings the garden has the same quality of urban privacy as certain college gardens at Oxford encircled by houses yet not overlooked. The trellis where the starling impersonated a red-shank screens the kitchen-garden: the rest is an irregular slightly-sloping lawn bordered by flower-beds set behind low green fenders of box-edging. In one corner is a flat rectangle of rock-garden, only lately laid down. When I first stayed with Henry James an ancient mulberry-tree stood on the lawn, but a gale split and rent it beyond repair, and now apart from the screen of poplars there are only four trees, three delectable, a walnut and two fine red hawthorns, and one detestable, a weeping ash. This consists of a straight thick trunk some ten feet high, from the top of which radiates a drooping circle of innumerable canes, tapering as they descend to the ground. In late spring they put forth their leaves, and the tree becomes more odious yet, for these form a stuffy tent or cave of thick foliage which from outside looks like the green crinoline of some goblin giantess. One's imagination pondered this sinister suggestion: the ash-tree perhaps was a Victorian witch of the woods, cut off at the waist and rooted there by some spell. Could I only discover and render the spell (Rye is full of spells) she might leave my garden and seek the woods again, which I should much appreciate. In any case the ash, as George Macdonald has told us in *Phantastes*, is not a kindly tree; a witch's blood indeed stirs in her sap, and a wise man, after dusk, will always keep clear of the range of her clutching fingers.

The house was built in the reigns of Queen Anne and George I. You enter (with a twist of the brass knocker), into a white panelled hall from which a panelled staircase leads to the first floor. A small oak-panelled parlour opens through french windows into the garden, and side by side with that is the dining-room. There are two similar rooms over these, one of which, also panelled in oak, is the King's bedroom, and it has a right to its royal title. For in the year 1725 his Most Gracious Majesty George I, returning from his beloved Hanover to the realm where he so cordially reciprocated the dislike of his English subjects, encountered a very violent gale and was driven for shelter into Rye Bay, where he was put ashore. News of the august landing was swiftly carried to the town, and Mr. James Lamb, Mayor of Rye, set out with horses and brought the King up to Lamb House to pass the night. Mr. and Mrs. Martha Lamb very civilly turned out of their own bedroom to accommodate him, and before morning, Mrs. Lamb, perhaps in consequence of this unusual excitement, gave birth to a son. The King was graciously pleased to be the boy's godfather, and since a violent snowstorm was raging which blocked the roads, he stayed on in the house for three days till the weather abated. The chance of getting His Majesty to attend the christening in person was too good to miss, and Master Lamb, in spite of the weather and his unusually tender age, was conveyed to the church, and the King stood sponsor beside the font. Intercourse during those three days must have been difficult, for Mr. Lamb could not speak a word of German, and the King of England not a word of English. Perhaps he brought with him for his solace, as Henry James fondly hoped was the case, one of his fat Hanoverian mistresses, but there is no record of her presence. . . . The King was mindful of his duties as a godfather, for presently he sent to Lamb

House a silver bowl weighing seventy ounces with the hallmark and date-letter of the year (K) and the inscription "King George to his godson George Lamb." The bowl is a beautiful piece of the period very solid and plain and of admirable design. Unfortunately it has long left the family, and only two years ago, still in mint condition and in its original leather case, it came into the market once more, and now belongs to the Marchioness Cholmondeley.

A grimmer incident connected with the family who built Lamb House and were so much concerned with the history of the town befell in the next reign. It is so strange and so full of improbabilities that it might well be rejected by the editor of some sensational magazine, if submitted to him as a piece of fiction, but it is true, and happened thus. In the year 1742 this same James Lamb was again Mayor of Rye. As such he presided on the Borough Bench, and he had lately inflicted a heavy fine on John Breads, the principal butcher of the town, for selling meat at short weight, and Breads was obsessed with the desire for revenge. On the night of March 16, young George Lamb, godson of the late King, being now a boy of seventeen, was to sail for France by the boat that started from the quay below the town, dropping down the River Rother as the full tide began to ebb. His father was to see the boy off and he promised to sup on the boat before it sailed. The Captain had ordered from Breads some extra viand to do honour to his guest, a joint perhaps of the *pré-salé* lamb for which the pasturage in the marsh, swept with the salt winds from the sea, is famous.

It was a raw night with driving sleet, and Mayor Lamb was suffering from an influenza cold, but when it was time to start, he put on the cloak in which he was so familiar a figure in Rye and set out. Just on the other side of the narrow cobbled street outside Lamb House lived his brother-in-law Mr. Alan Grebell, whose sister Martha, now deceased, had been the Mayor's wife. So foul was the weather and himself so poorly that James Lamb stepped in to Mr. Grebell's house, and asked him to take his place and see his nephew off. By all means, said Alan, and as it was already time to start, he got up and put on his coat. But James told him that this was not sufficient protection in such bitter weather, and gave him his own cloak instead. So the Mayor returned to the warmth and shelter of his own fireside, and Alan, now well wrapped up, went off across the churchyard and down the steps by Ypres Tower to the quay. Alan explained to the Captain how it was that he had taken the Mayor's place, but he himself was a very honourable guest. He had been ten times Mayor of Rye, he was highly respected in the town, and there was none except Breads who did not wish him well. The supper passed off very pleasantly with plenty of fine French brandy.

When it was time for the boat to sail, Alan said good-bye to his nephew, and, full of cheer, walked up the steps by Ypres Tower and so back across the churchyard to his house. The worst of the storm was past and between the scudding clouds the moon rode high and clear. Breads, meantime, had closed his shop in Market Street and went out, having put underneath his coat the stabbing knife which he used in his trade, wooden-handled with his initials cut on it. He hid himself behind a gravestone in the churchyard close to the path along which Alan Grebell would return. There was no one abroad on this wild night, and there he waited till he heard steps, perhaps not very steady, coming along the path from Ypres Tower. He lay close till they had passed him, and then, peering out, he saw the figure of the man he was waiting for, unmistakable in the Mayor's cloak, going homewards. Breads tiptoed up behind him, and stabbed him heavy and deep in the back below the ribs.

Then what would be purely incredible in fiction enters into this attested story. Breads, exulting in the thought that he had struck the Mayor his death-blow, casually chucked away his knife into the grass among the grave-stones, went back to his house, and drank himself tipsy. Grebell, unaware that he had received a mortal injury, or, indeed, any injury at all, walked on to his house, some eighty or a hundred yards away, and his manservant opened the door to him. He told him that some rude fellow had jostled against him as he crossed the church-yard, and bade him lock the door and go to bed. With the Mayor's cloak still round him he himself went into the parlour adjoining, and sat down by the fire. That a man who had been fatally stabbed should have been unconscious of it and that in this condition he should have walked home sounds as incredible as that his assail-ant should have thrown his initialled and blood-stained knife into the grass close to where he had just used it. But the Empress Elizabeth of Austria, wife of Franz Josef, was also fatally stabbed as she was walking to a steamer on the Lake of Geneva. She was unaware of her injury, went on board the boat and then collapsed and died.

James Lamb, who had gone back to his fireside, when his brother-in-law, wearing his cloak, went off to sup on the boat, passed a disturbed night. Twice before day he dreamed that his dead wife appeared to him in great distress, and told him that her brother Alan Grebell had been murdered. It was a very vivid impression, but, waking, he thought to himself that he was disordered with a touch of fever, and, in any case, no man of sense takes any count of dreams. But a third time he dreamed the same thing, and now when he woke day was dawning. He got up and put on some clothes, and still wearing his night-cap stepped across to Alan Grebell's house to re-assure himself that all was well, for he was uneasy that for the third time this dream should have troubled him. The servant who had let his master in last night was just coming downstairs. He opened the door to the Mayor and told him that Mr. Grebell had come in about mid-night after his supper, safe and sound. He had locked the door and gone to bed leaving him in the parlour. With the memory of that twice repeated dream in his mind, the Mayor was still not quite satisfied, and he went upstairs to peep into Grebell's bedroom and see him for himself. The room was empty and the bed un-slept in. This was strange, and he came downstairs again and looked into the parlour. Alan Grebell was there, still sitting in his chair by the dead fire with the Mayor's cloak round him, crumpled up and bowed together, not like a man who slept. A doctor was sent for, but the body was already cold, and when he examined it, he found the wound in the back below the ribs. The Mayor instantly had the servant arrested, for it was he who had last seen his master alive. He was questioned and he repeated exactly what he had said before, but the fact that he had locked the door after letting Grebell in, looked black, for there was no sign that the house had been entered during the night, and no one slept there but the master and the man. His detention did not last long. An hour later Breads the butcher came out of his shop, still tipsy from his night's debauch, and was staggering about Market Street crying out: "Butchers kill Lambs! Butchers kill Lambs!" for he still believed that the man in the Mayor's cloak whom he had stabbed last night in the churchyard was the Mayor himself. He was arrested, and during the morning the blood-stained knife with his initials cut on the handle was picked up in the church-yard where he had flung it away.

Three days later the body of Alan Grebell was buried in the family vault below the Clare Chapel in Rye church. The chapel was not in use at that time: it was walled off from the main body of the church and the town fire engine and other municipal properties were kept there. A slab in the floor over the vault records Grebell's numerous virtues and his distinguished services as Mayor, and how he met his death "by the cruel stab of a sanguinary butcher."

James Lamb, as Mayor of Rye, presided over the bench of magistrates before whom Breads was tried for murder. A verdict of guilty was returned, and when the Mayor asked him if he had anything to say for himself, Breads pointed at him and cried out: "That's the man I meant it for, and I would kill him now if I could." The Mayor, who in those days had the powers of a Judge of the High Court, pronounced sentence of death, and Breads was hanged. A close-fitting cage was made for his body, composed of iron bands connected with chains, with circular holes through which the legs dangled, and with its grim contents was set up beside the high road from Rye to Winchelsea as a warning to the sanguinary. The clothing of the corpse was disintegrated by the weather and flapped in the wind, crows and carrion fowl perched themselves on the bars of the cage and howked at the exposed flesh, and pieces of bone were broken off by wayfarers, for any fragment of a man who had been hanged was held to be a sovereign cure for the crippling rheumatisms and agues that were prevalent among the dwellers in the marsh. Perhaps even now in a remote farmstead may be found, kept as an ancestral relic, some relic of the sort with a vague legend attached to it of a great-grandfather who himself acquired and greatly prized it, and sat with it in his hand as he shook and stiffened.

Subsequently the course of the road beside which Breads swung in the gales was changed, and the cage, with such remnants as still remained in it, was affixed, as an interesting piece of municipal property to the wall of the Clare Chapel where Alan Grebell had been buried, and so for many years the empty eye-sockets of his murderer looked down on the white marble slab above his resting-place. There it remained till 1862, when the chapel was restored to its proper uses. The fire engine was transferred to quarters below the Town Hall, and the cage and its contents, now dwindled to a jawless skull, were placed in an angle of the staircase, where they stand to-day. The skull is of the most degenerate type: there is scarcely any forehead, the bone receding in a curve from just above the brows to the top of the head. If we further take into account the incredible recklessness with which

John Breads did his deed, his careless chucking away of his initialled knife, his pæans of triumph next morning at having, so he thought, revenged himself on the Mayor, there can be no doubt that to-day the sentence of the law would never have been carried out but that, after observation by the prison doctor, Breads would have been placed in the asylum at Broadmoor for criminal lunatics.

Beside the cage and its jawless contents, there is reputed to be another relic connected with the murder which now stands in the garden-room at Lamb House. This is a mahogany arm-chair, certainly of the eighteenth century with bottom and back and sides of cane, and the legend goes that it was in this chair that James Lamb found Alan Grebell still wearing the Mayoral cloak, when, troubled by his repeated dream, he went across to his house at daybreak for reassurance. He was given it, they say, as a memento of his brother-in-law and brought it to the then newly-built garden-room. The psychically disposed may be interested to know that, some ten years ago, a séance was held in this room, and that the medium, just before she went into trance, said: "There is a man in a cloak, sitting in that cane arm-chair." As far as could be ascertained she had never heard of the Grebell murder. . . .

Rye in those days, though fallen from its national splendours as a Cinque Port providing men and ships for the King's navy, maintained a national reputation for smuggling. The coastguards and excise officers must be evaded, but that was not very difficult. A fishing boat from the French coast met her English customer out at sea: English money and French brandy were exchanged, and the English boat returned to her ostensible occupation in territorial waters till on a dark night or when the sea-fog lay thick over the marsh she was rowed or punted up the river to the place appointed where a couple of men with ponies or donkeys were waiting. The kegs of brandy or the glass wicker-cased flagons of Hollands were carried up over the oozy river-bank and loaded into the panniers, and before day the goods would have been stowed in some big-cellared house in the town, and the fishing-boat be lying below Ypres Tower or Mermaid Street by the quayside, unloading her innocent cargo. Rye is astonishingly rich in small houses with large cellars, and you can still see where these cellars communicated with each other through iron doors that could be bolted on either side; four or five adjoining houses have this subterranean access. It is therefore a legitimate conjecture to suppose that, if some householder had reason to suspect that a police-raid might be made on his premises, he would arrange with a friendly neighbour to pass the contraband through the iron door, which was then bolted on the far side.

Smuggling was an exciting though hazardous game. The law of the land forbade it, and there were heavy fines if a householder was found with liquor in his cellar that did not bear the stamp of the Custom House. Much graver were the risks of the smuggler who had brought it ashore. If he was taken red-handed by the coastguards and resisted arrest or tried to escape they were free to fire on him, and if they killed him that was a regrettable accident. But smuggling was very lucrative; to defraud the revenue of the country does not appear as a dirty trick like cheating at cards and defrauding an individual.

Nowadays highly respectable ladies, who could be perfectly trusted if they found stray cash lying about in their friends' houses, conceal wads of lace and other taxable commodities on their persons when they cross the Channel. Also the evasion of income-tax calls forth high mental qualities. Astute and ingenious persons think out methods of avoiding what their consciences know to be the legitimate extortions of the Inland Revenue, and the myrmidons of the Chancellor of the Exchequer are as busy tightening up the provisions of the law as were the coastguards of Rye in watching suspicious fisher-boats two hundred years ago. The smugglers and their customers were of exactly the same species as the evaders of to-day and not a whit less respectable. Indeed it probably never occurred to the smuggler that his successful evasion of the duty on spirits deprived the exchequer of monies which must be made up by impositions on others, whereas the evader of income-tax, being better versed in the principles of finance, is well aware of it. And there is no comparison between the romance and picturesqueness of the two schools. In one case there is the manager's office, the ingenious assignment of capital, and all the solemn swindling hocus-pocus: in the other the fog-smothered marsh, the laden ponies traversing by-paths, the surreptitious conveyance of kegs to the houses of Town Councillors, and perhaps the exciting "Hunt the Hollands" through adjoining cellars. I prefer the smugglers. . . .

Far into the nineteenth century, their trading flourished, and it was only a few years ago that there died in Rye, at the respectable age of one hundred and two, an old fisherman who in his piping treble, between whiffs of his pipe, could recall a strange story of over ninety years ago, still fresh in his memory.

There was a family of fisher-folk living at the foot of Rye cliff, father and mother and a son in his early twenties, who loved the excitement of the game fully as much as the gains it brought him. Sometimes he brought the stuff to land on his father's boat, sometimes he received it from a boat coming up the river and conveyed it under cover of the marsh-mists to its purchaser in the town. But young John Verrall was now getting married and he had promised the girl's parents and her that thenceforth he would run no more of these risks. The wedding was fixed for to-morrow, the dinner following it was to be held in his father's house, and the evening before all was ready. The table was laid with the sugared wedding-cake and cold pies of poached game and mallards from the marsh, so that in the morning there would be nothing left to do but to heat up the soup, and draw the beer from the cask and the brandy from the keg. That night after dark had fallen there came a tap on the window, and John went out to see who was there. It was two young fellows, friends of his and hot smugglers, who were setting off with their donkeys to meet a fishing-boat that would slip up the river before the moon rose, and wouldn't John come with them for they expected a big cargo and would be glad of a third to help handle it. At the sight of them he longed for one more night of sport, for after to-morrow there would be no more such for him. His father and mother were already gone to bed and he put on his long wading boots and was off with his friends into the night, leaving the door on the latch.

The Captain of the Excise officers had long had his

eye on John Verrall; he knew he was a busy smuggler, but never yet had he or his men caught him at it. Abel was a savage sort of fellow, and sore at having been so often outwitted. To-night he had got word that a fishing boat, suspected of carrying contraband, was coming up the river, and he and four of his men were already out on the marsh. Crouching and creeping they watched it coming up, waiting for it to put into shore, for thus they could catch both the fishermen who brought the stuff in and those who received it. The wind had dropped and the tide was slackening, so it was easy to keep pace with it. Presently they saw it draw into the bank some half-mile below the town, and waiting for it were three men with donkeys. The night was not very dark for the moon was near rising, and as they closed in on them the lading of the beasts had begun. Abel blew his whistle and shouted out the order in the King's name that they should hold up their hands, and if any attempted to run he would fire on him. Two of them obeyed, but John Verrall thinking of his wedding next day, from which the bridegroom would assuredly be absent, as he would be appearing before the Bench of magistrates on the charge of receiving smuggled goods, took his chance. Fifty yards away a belt of thick mist hung over the marsh, and could he but reach it he would back himself to get clean away; for he knew the ground and the dykes and short cuts and bog holes as none of them did. He took to his heels and they were a nimble pair: once more the warning was called, but safety was near now and still he ran. Then came the word to fire, and he dropped, shot through the heart.

The light of a lantern revealed to Captain Abel who

the dead man was. He knew that he was to have been married next day from his father's house, and indeed John, in that gay insolent manner of his, had promised him some fine French brandy, if he would come to the dinner. Abel left the rest of his men in charge of the other prisoners, and with the rope that should have secured the kegs of brandy slung John over the back of one of the donkeys, and set off to Rye. He was just about to knock at the door of his father's house, but he tried the latch and found it unlocked. A flash of his lantern showed him the living-room with the table set for the wedding dinner next day. He thought to himself with a grin that it would be cruel to disturb the old folk from their night's rest with such news, and moving stealthily so as to be unheard, he carried the body in. That would be the bride's chair opposite the wedding cake, and she would be on the right of her groom, and he hoisted him on to the chair next it. The corpse had not stiffened yet, so the rope from the donkey came in handy, and he wound it underneath John's arms and round the back of the chair. "And his poor old mammy," said the old man, "came down next morning to sweep and make tidy, and there was John in his place at the dinner-table."

CHAPTER VII

THESE ancient yarns which I learned later seem relevant to my early days in Rye. Very soon the town took on for me, not only in the drowsy passivity between sleep and waking, a stable and solidified sense of home, and such picturesque pieces of its past embedded themselves in it, like fossilized shells in the native rock. You may live for a hundred years, like my old fisherman, in one place (if you are endowed with such extreme capacity for existence) without ever becoming part of it, but a few months sufficed to convince me that I was not only in Rye, but of it. To be there made me content: its cobbled ways and its marsh with its huge sky, as at sea, and in particular the house and the garden-room and the garden were making a ferment of their own in my veins, not because they were associated with any cherished and intimate experiences, but because they were themselves. This conviction, I hasten to add, was purely subjective. Rye and its social circles looked on me, I think, as one of those Londoners who so often take houses there for a few weeks or a few months and have their friends to stay with them because their town is so quaint and picturesque. They make sketches in the streets, obstructing the narrow pavements, or play golf on the far-famed links.

For my part I was quite content. I had not come to Rye for any reason except to be there. I am reasonably sociable, immensely valuing friends and appreciating acquaintances, and during my first six months there I made the discovery which much surprised me that I could be very happy all by myself, not speaking a word, for days together, to anyone but my small household. I had my writing to do, which occupied my mind and my hours; I enjoyed a spell at the upright piano which I hired from Hastings, as much as Brooks did, and daringly set myself to learn by heart the first book of Bach's forty-eight preludes and fugues. (Disillusionment set in very soon, like the steady fall of dusk, until it was black night.) I had no intention of becoming a hermit, but for the present I enjoyed being alone, and I vividly recall the sense of home-coming with which, returning from a long afternoon in the marsh, spying after birds, which now had become a very favourite pursuit with me, I twisted the knocker to enter my house again and heard it jangle as I closed the door, knowing that none would seek to enter till morn-ing. Sometimes I had seen the sea-fog creeping up from the coast, and by now the sound of lonely foghorns hoot-ing in the Channel enhanced the Lucretian glee of these contrasted solitudes, mine in the lamplight and the warmth, and the bleatings of a blinded ship longing to get home. Or if a south-west gale bellowed round the walls making the poplars wave and whistle, I blessed James Lamb for building so secure a house and chimneys in which the winds made such melodious riot.

The Vicar left his card one day but I was out, and once the son of an old friend of my father's asked me to tea. His wife had not come in at the appointed hour, and it was not permissible that tea should be brought up till she arrived. So we admired her budgerigar which flitted screaming about the room, and after we had talked very pleasantly for some while about Henry James, I went back to Lamb House and had tea there. This little incident pleased me immensely: somehow I felt it was Rye, the inner life of Rye. And what a setting, I thought, Rye and its cobbled streets and its gables and red brick, so profusely immortalized in the water-colour sketches of visitors, would make for some fantastic story! I could people it as I pleased, for I knew nothing of its inhabitants, apart from this pleasant talk I had had with one of them. As an external observer I had seen the ladies of Rye doing their shopping in the High Street every morning, carrying large market baskets, and bumping into each other in narrow doorways, and talking in a very animated manner. But that was no invasion of private life: I was as ignorant of them all as people as a man from Mars, and I vaguely began to meditate on some design. I outlined an elderly atrocious spinster and established her in Lamb House. She should be the centre of social life, abhorred and dominant, and she should sit like a great spider behind the curtains in the garden-room, spying on her friends, and I knew that her name must be Elizabeth Mapp. Rye should furnish the topography, so that no one who knew Rye could possibly be in doubt where the scene was laid, and I would call it Tilling because Rye has its river the Tillingham. . . . Perhaps another preposterous woman, Lucia of Riseholme, who already had a decent and devout following, and who was as dominant as Mapp, might come into contact with her some day, when I had got to know Mapp better. I began to invent a new set of characters who should revolve round these two women, fussy and eager and alert and preposterous. Of course, it would all be small beer, but one could get a head upon it of jealousies and malignities and devouring inquisitiveness. Like Moses on Pisgah I saw a wide prospect, a Promised Land, a Saga indefinitely unveiling itself. But one had to get a firm hold of Elizabeth Mapp first. Lucia I knew.

Arthur, meantime, after three years of misery, had begun to mend, but he was still far from real recovery. He had got on to firmer ground, but would he make further progress? He had stuck again: and in order to see whether a change from the nursing-home and the dismal intercourse of those who were in like case would do any good, he came down next winter for a month to Rye. He brought with him, as a companion, a curious invalidish Roman Catholic, once a friend of Hugh's and of Rolfe's, so that he could have somebody with him all day, at his beck and call, to walk or play draughts or chess and fill in the hours which otherwise—it was a symptom of his neurasthenia—he would have devoted to the contemplation of his own wretchedness. I had friends in Rye now (of whom neither the remotest sketch or caricature ever sullied the topographical accuracy of Tilling) and occasionally I asked someone to dine, and Arthur, after protesting that he could not face it, faced it without the least difficulty. A stranger could not possibly have known that there was anything wrong with him: he would have seen only a big handsome man, very courteous though rather grave, who talked pleasantly and well and was robust and hungry, and he would not have believed that within lay this load of joylessness. The chief cause of that was that he could not yet bring himself to get back to his writing, for writing was his passion, and without it the very source of happiness was dry. Then there were signs that the drought was breaking, though, as before, he clung to his malady in the tragic manner of neurasthenics. One day we had walked by the banks of the Rother, where the smugglers used to ply their trade, down to the sea: there were companies of dunlin and ringed plover on the ooze, and genuine red-shanks (not starlings) were calling. He was interested: he admired their flutings and their white-barred wings, and I knew that he was enjoying himself. Sure enough, when I came upstairs to the little green parlour for a game of chess before dinner, I found him established in his arm-chair with the writing-board in front of him, scribbling a few lines about red-shanks, which he read to me. But as we went to bed, I injudiciously congratulated him on this welcome sign, and that was a great mistake. He put down his bedroom candle again—electric light had not yet come to Rye—and very solemnly assured me that he was no better at all. . . . Then there came a further sign of recovery. Through these horrible years, he had had no independence, for he had to conform to the hours and the rules of the nursing-home, and had no desire to do otherwise. Now he began to want to control the day for himself, instead of letting others arrange it for him, and he took lodgings at Hastings for himself and his companion, and then went back to Magdalene for the Lent term. He was not able to do much, but he was handling life again. After the term was over, he came back to Rye for Easter and now the benevolent despotism was pushing through his apathy, like the vigorous new growth of spring. How often at Tremans had I seen that despotism at work! The strength of it lay in its geniality. We were alone together for some days, and when, day by day, he suggested some pleasant way of spending the afternoon, a bicycle-ride, a motor-drive combined with a walk, any counter-proposal at once seemed churlish and un-grateful: welcome, indeed, was the fact that he made any suggestion. Occasionally he told me that he had had a wretched night or a morning of barren heaviness, but it was clear that he was emerging steadily. Then he asked me if it would be quite convenient if he had a friend down to stay with us. I hailed this proposal, for I wanted to go away myself. So I said it was quite convenient, and proposed that when he arrived I should leave them. I think I expected him to protest, but he quite approved. He said he felt sure that a complete change of companion-ship would benefit him. The cordiality with which he fell in with my suggestion was a slight shock.

Off I went with a more like-minded friend of my own to the village of Blakeney on the north coast of Norfolk, to spend a fortnight in the observation of birds. At the foot of the village, separated only by a road submerged at spring-tides, lies the harbour, a great expanse, two miles wide, of shining water or, at low tide, of black mud and sand where the cockle-hunters dig. On the seaward side up to the entrance of the harbour stretch the long beaches of Blakeney Point, shingle and sand and dunes plumed with marram grass and acres of sea-lavender. Once I used to tramp all day after birds and little beasts, gun in hand; now, with far greater zest, my weapon was a field-glass. One saw a mixed company of waders and duck far off, and had to use the stealth of a stalker to get near enough to sort them out—and who knew what rare visitor might be among them? Or one advanced cautious and alert, through the sea-lavender, as once through turnips and undergrowth, to put up something and get a shot with the field-glass. Personal pleasure in the sport of killing had faded for me long ago, when one day I shot a hare. It lay quite still, paralysed, I suppose, but when I went to pick it up I found it was not dead. It looked at me from a soft brown eye, as if mutely wondering what I meant to do to it next. . . . Nowadays I found that I took far more pleasure in observing the wild ways of birds or beasts when alive than I had ever taken in killing them.

Blakeney Point and the marshes round Cley and Salthouse are the great hunting-grounds for bird-seekers from the time when the spring migrations begin to flow northwards till the birds which have bred in Scandinavia are coming south for the winter. You may, for instance, see companies of gold-crests flying straight in from the sea, ten or twenty together, for half the afternoon, dropping on the beach at the Point exhausted by their travel. The outspread stretch of their wings is scarcely four inches and yet here were these minute creatures, driven by an instinct which we cannot comprehend, following some air-route of their own, and arriving after an uninterrupted flight from the north of four hundred miles. Soon they began picking out their victuals from strands of seaweed, and by next day they had refreshed themselves after their journey and had dispersed over the English woodlands for the winter.

Late spring, when residents for the summer are arriving and when nesting and breeding are going on, is the far more frenzied business; terns, the sea-swallows of the Greeks, common terns, little terns, and Sandwich terns have their nesting colonies on the Point. Shrilly screaming and entirely fearless, they swoop at you and even strike you if you trespass among the nurseries, and one day I saw two Sandwich terns undauntedly attacking an Arctic skua and by sheer fury driving him off. They know his damnable nature: he is a highwayman, a thief and a cannibal immensely strong and swift on the wing. There is no fishing to be done along the water's edge when he is about. He does not fish for himself; others do his fishing for him, and when he sees a tern or a gull with his catch in his beak, he goes in fierce pursuit till the bird drops it, and then he swoops down and picks it up before it reaches the water. Far out on the sands when the tide is low there will be a company of great black-backed gulls sitting like bishops in convocation in white rochets and black hoods, but they are by no means episcopal, and with a stroke of the beak they will split the skull of a lamb or a sick sheep.. . . . One day there were three tall spoon-bills standing aloof and meditative on the flooded land near Cley; I wanted to see them on the wing, but could not get near enough to disturb their reverie.

The rare bearded-tits, the only English bird who never stirs from home, while all others make some migration, nest in the reed-beds. It is difficult to catch sight of them, for the yellowed reeds of last year among which they build are thick, and the bird's colouring protects it. But they can be located by their note: it is like the striking of two flints together or the metallic clack of a stone sent skimming over an ice-covered pond, and if the observer keeps very still they may emerge, and he will see the males with their smart black moustaches climbing up the smooth reed-stems and tobogganing down again. Rewarded, the watcher goes seawards; a bathe, a bask on the beach, lunch and perhaps a doze, and he wakes to find an elegant family of bar-tailed godwits, friendly and confident as robins, poking about for their dinner, close beside him. The tide is ebbing, and along the water's edge the endless procession of terns, unvexed to-day by any intruder, flap and poise and dive. Suddenly I perceived something I must have seen a hundred times before without noticing it, nor, as far as I know, does any bird-book record it. Common terns and little terns dive direct. The Sandwich tern twists in the air, as he drops, just a half circle. I bade my friend verify this. I do not know how long we watched, for there is no such thing as time on Blakeney Point, but we found no exception. What a day for a lover of sea and big skies and birds—a close-up of bearded-tits sliding down the reeds in the morning, the technique of diving Sandwich terns in the afternoon, and all day long the company of a friend! Towards evening the raucous cries of the gulls are still, the terns cease their chiding, and the only bird-sounds are the voices of the curlews whistling or giving out the liquid bubbling note which always connotes to me the fall of dusk on the lonely marshes, their huge emptiness and their ineffable magic. The call often goes on late into the night, and you may hear it also right in the heart of London when migrating flocks are passing northwards to their breeding places, and then London and its tumult melt into silence and the tide is low in Blakeney harbour.

It was Saturday night. The sky had clouded over, and far out at sea beyond Blakeney Point a thunderstorm was remotely flashing and booming like a distant naval battle.

As we sat on a bench facing the harbour after supper there joined us with secret tidings, a watcher in the employ of the society for the protection of wild birds. He had seen out at Salthouse that afternoon a bird that was new to him, a tall white wader, with streaks of black on its wings. He thought it might be an avocet. One had a remembrance of such a bird in the Walsingham collection of stuffed birds at the South Kensington Museum and it seemed to answer the description. Its most striking characteristic is its long beak curved upwards, as if Nature had wished it to find great difficulty in getting its food, for it cannot peck and stab downwards like every other known fowl. We consulted a manual. There was a picture of the avocet, and the text told us how just a hundred years ago there had been a breeding colony of them at Salthouse. Most of them had been shot for the sake of their plumage, and the remnant had deserted this unkindly home. So early next morning we drove out to Salthouse through drizzling rain, and after long spying found the tall wader with his plumage of ermine, feeding on the edge of the lagoon with a company of shelduck. We got sufficiently near to them to make the identification certain, and then the whole lot took flight. In the sand and ooze where they had been were the zig-zag scrabbling marks of the avocet's beak. It was strange that after the lapse of a hundred years a solitary bird had come back to the exact spot where his ancestors had had a colony. But, alas for the hopes that the bird would go back to his friends in Holland and tell them he had adventured to a quiet pleasant place oversea which suited him very well. He would give so good an account of it that perhaps others might join him next year and once more avocets might have bred at Salthouse. News travels like that among birds, for how else did the Serpentine become so thronged a winter home for black-headed gulls, when forty years ago there was not one to be found there? They tell each other of their experiences; they act on the knowledge thus communicated. A few days later some wretch with a gun who loved birds so much that he shot anything unusual, killed this rare and lovely visitor.

On these bird expeditions I usually stayed at small inns at Cley or Blakeney, with an occasional visit to Holkham or the houses of other friends. For the sake of study and record I would acquiesce in rare birds being occasionally shot, and at Holkham there was a collection that justified itself. For three generations the Lord Leicester of the day had built it up, never shooting a bird of which he had specimens, but only extending its completeness, and as a local record of Norfolk birds from the time of the great bustard up till to-day it is unique. Otherwise Holkham is a sanctuary for wild birds and none may be shot. One day a scarcely credible tragedy occurred in connection with this museum. Lord Leicester was out with his gun and saw, circling high above the lake where the Canadian goose breeds, a stork-like bird which, as it descended in its flight, he was sure he had never seen before at large or in his museum. When it came within range he killed it, and found that he was right. The bird turned out to be a Manchurian crane, whose migration had never hitherto been known to have extended westwards of Middle Europe. He had it stuffed and triumphantly set up in the bird-room. Not long afterwards Duchess Mary Bedford came over from Cley where, like me, she was bloodlessly observing birds: with the possible exception of Lord Grey of Fallodon, she was the best English ornithologist. She was shown the latest addition to the museum. "That's my tame Manchurian crane from Woburn," she said, and everybody's pleasure was spoiled.

This year when Arthur went back to Cambridge for the first time since his breakdown, he joined me here in the summer. A spring-tide with a violent winter gale from the north had made a breach in the breakwater on the coast, and the sea had poured through, flooding the fields outside Cley. Marsh birds and waders were quick to see what an admirable new territory this gave them, and ruffs and reeves appeared there. Arthur remembered, as a small boy, being shown ruffs in the plumage of mating time strutting before their ladies, and he wanted to see them again. We were fortunate that afternoon, and got a good close view of some birds, though not in their nuptial finery. But the sight delighted him; it linked itself up, I suppose, with the memory of a boyish excitement fifty years ago, and that evening he allowed for the first time that he had enjoyed himself.

His recovery was soon complete. As before, the curtains rattled back again, and the sun poured in. He resumed full work at Cambridge, his head was buzzing with plans for improvements and endowments at Magdalene, and he poured out the funds placed at his disposal for their accomplishment. In vacations he wanted to be entirely at Rye, and by a new lease which we took together jointly, our occupation of Lamb House was extended to ten months in the year. But since during term-time he could not be there, he very naturally wanted sole occupation for himself and his friends in his vacations. Straight from Cambridge after the end of a furiously occupied term, he flew to Lamb House, and occupied himself as furiously there. He hated solitude, and there was always with him some undergraduate or don from Magdalene, and he arranged the day according to the pattern which to his mind approached perfection. All the morning, strictly undisturbed, he wrote his letters or his diary. In the afternoon he and his friend drove or walked or bicycled, timed to be back for the sacred hours from tea till dinner. For a few days at Christmas and possibly at Easter, I stayed with him as his guest where lately I had been host, helping him as best I could, to get through the heavy days. But no longer were morning walks required, and games of chess or draughts to beguile the hours after tea, when most he had missed his beloved occupation, and now when I came in from the garden-room towards dinner-time, I found him in the little green parlour upstairs, with the writing-board across the arms of his chair, and the floor littered with scribbled sheets, incredulous that it was so late already, and beaming with literary accomplishment.

"I've been writing about our bicycle ride," he would say. "What's the name of that small mean church by the railway, like a cow sitting on its haunches? Yes, of course, Guldeford! And I've put off dinner till half-past eight. I know you like dining as late as possible. And you're going to have a bath, aren't you? so you won't be ready before that. . . . Oh yes: another thing. That small dead bird which must have killed itself against the telegraph wires: a dunlin, did you say? I think a bottle of Burgundy at dinner. Rich strong Burgundy. Would you ring the bell as you go? Half-past eight then." The pencil raced on in that firm clear hand-writing, and another sheet fluttered to the floor. . . . This exuberant extempore production never slackened: now it was an essay, now an article for a magazine, now the diary, the pages of which, bound in thin blue paper-covered volumes had passed the mark of three million words: now a fresh chapter of a novel. In the morning he came down very late, quailing, as in old days at Tremans, at the pile of letters by his plate which must be answered the same day, opening them with a silver stiletto of his own invention. He glanced through the morning paper with a rustle of swiftly turned leaves, then with his half-opened post withdrew into his parlour, appearing again at lunch huge and hungry and happy.

"An infernal morning," he said. "Twenty-seven letters and there are several more I must write before we go out. I think we'll motor to-day: I've ordered the car for half-past two. Let's be dropped somewhere out beyond Camber, and we'll walk to Lydd and be picked up there. Or shall we go to Burwash?"

"Yes, let us, and call on Kipling," I suggested. "He left a card here a few days ago."

"No. I can't pay calls. I should like to see him, but if I have to sit in a drawing-room and talk in the middle of the afternoon, I get dwams in my mind. Then we could come back by Bodiam Castle. I met Curzon the other day who bought it for the National Trust, and he seemed to feel it as a personal insult that I hadn't been to see it. And to-morrow I have to go up to London for a Fishmongers' Court. I never get a moment to myself.

I haven't touched my novel for two days, and I don't believe I shall finish it before I go back to Cambridge."

"Finish it?" I asked. "I thought you told me that you only began it after you got down here."

"I did, but it has gone very easily. The worst of it is that John Murray demurs to my publishing more than three books a year, and there are two more waiting. . . . Ah, about that ash-tree in the garden. I hope you'll give up all idea of having it cut down. I should very much regret it."

So we went to Burwash and back through Bodiam, and next morning he went off to London.

"How pleasant it has been," he said. "You'll be gone, I'm afraid, before I get back this evening. I am bringing Percy down with me for a few days."

CHAPTER VIII

I FOUND a letter from Brooks waiting for me in London. Our joint house, as I have mentioned, had been given up, and he had installed himself in the Villa Salvia. It was small, he said, much more of a cottage than a villa, but quite tolerable, though further from the town and the sea. Couldn't I come out for a few weeks? He would take a room for me in the new Hotel Tiberio, for he hadn't got a spare bedroom. And April was behaving angelically. The heat had come suddenly after a long cold winter, the spring flowers were rioting on the slopes of Solaro, and bathing had begun. In England, on the other hand, we were freezing under Arctic blasts, and had the Shropshire lad walked at Easter in the woodland ride, he would have found the cherry-tree hung with genuine snow. Home-sickness for the south overcame me, and I telegraphed that I was starting at once.

He met me on the quay of the Grande Marina on my arrival by the evening boat from Naples. It was some years since I had been here, our correspondence had dropped of late, and, as we drove up to the town, he told me that there had been many changes. The Vestals, Miss Kate and Miss Sadie Perry were dead, and Sayer's Symposium was shut up. Jerome, the Tiberian historian, was dead too; Norman Douglas was seen here no more, and Compton Mackenzie, though preserving his passion for islands, had left the blue seas for the grey and lived now at Jethou. Nearly as lamentable as these bereavements were the material changes on the island itself. Under the new Mussolini *régime* Capri was being smartened up and developed into a fashionable resort: a boulevard was planned, Italians flocked to the island for the summer months and bathed in elegant costumes. Motors had come; Morgano's café, where one used to sit in the evening, playing dominoes, with Donna Lucia dozing behind the counter, was thronged with folk from the hotels in dress-clothes who danced below an arc-lamp on the once dusky terrace. . . . But Brooks seemed in very good spirits, and to him, never leaving the island, the change had come gradually. We dined together at the hotel, and he arranged to call for me in the morning and go down to the sea for a bathe. Perhaps he wouldn't bathe himself for he had had a chill.

To me these changes seemed to have destroyed all the haphazard, distinctive charm of the place. More especially I found that living in a hotel full of strangers, with a liveried porter and a table d'hôte and a lift and a numbered room, was very different from having a sequestered house of one's own. One was a visitor, an alien, and with the sense of being a visitor, the spell of the island vanished. The bathing and basking were actually the same, and the walks over the cistus-covered hillside, but the genius of the island had fled before the Fascist. Brooks himself seemed at first unaltered, though his face was more ascetic and ecclesiastical: he might have been the model for some mitred adoring bishop in a "Nativity" by Bellini. There had been one great disappointment, for after years of hesitancy he had sent the Hérédia sonnets to a publisher, and the manuscript had been returned to him with thanks. The effect of that had been to convince him that they wanted more polishing, and he had been polishing again since their return, to their great advantage. He had lost not an atom of his faith in himself, nor in the quality of his work. Now he had embarked on the translation of a selection of Greek epigrams, and was devoting to them the same deluded and indolent industry. He read me some of them, his voice, charged with emotion, trumpeting out the ecstasy of the triumphant lover or falling to a whisper as it mourned for the untimely death of a beloved youth. Though I know nothing about French verse, I knew a good deal about Greek verse, and my heart sank at his elation. I could not understand it: he had an enthusiasm for his subject, a real appreciation of Greek, he had a just ear for the beauty of rhythm and melodious phrase, but all these had produced nothing but a careful translation devoid of any rendered magic. It seemed to me that he must have hypnotized himself by poring and polishing, as by gazing into a crystal, and saw there some image of beauty projected from his brain on to his script, which was invisible except to him. He described to me how he pondered over the equivalent of some jewelled Greek epithet (I forget what it was) and suddenly "starry-kirtled" had coined itself in his mind. What a red-letter day! Indeed, that was an apt word; it had the Hellenic stamp, but I had an uneasy feeling that Milton had struck it before. But where was the use of suggesting it? Brooks would probably have read through the whole of Milton to ascertain that, and have congratulated himself at the end on a fortnight of hard scholarly research. I had no doubt whatever that his taste in literature was sincere and ardent and that his critical faculty was fine, but he had no power of expressing them. Happily the gods in their mercy had withheld from him the perception of his own incompetence. I prayed that they would never grant him that disastrous boon.

The Villa Salvia was very small but sufficient for the comfortable housing of a single inhabitant. There was a kitchen, a minute dining-room next door, a bedroom and a sitting-room. A woman came up in the morning, cooked his midday dinner, dusted and set his bedroom in order and prepared his cold supper. The sitting-room was lined with classical literature, and on the top of the self-same ancient piano lay the dog-eared tattered volumes of Beethoven's sonatas not a passage of which could he either memorize or execute. Ten years ago the instrument had been of shrill canary-timbre, but age had taken the edge off its chirpings. Some notes stuck, a few chirped still, a few barked and some were nearly dumb: the whole was so out of tune that it sounded as if it was pitched to some barbarian scale. Brooks lamented that his finger-joints were growing stiff and not so agile as they used to be, but he still spent many busy, awkward hours of enjoyment at the keyboard, when literary inspiration deserted him. This confirmed my belief that he was self-hypnotized and heard not what his ears but his imagination conveyed to him.

We quickly slipped back into the old usage of desultory talk and unembarrassed silences, and bit by bit I formed a rather dismal impression of his history. He said he was a great deal alone. Few of his old friends who remained in the island cared to toil up the steep path to the Villa Salvia, but he did very well without them. They had grown tired of him, he supposed, and for his part he had no intention of thrusting himself in where he wasn't wanted. There had been absurd quarrels over trivial matters, such as in youth would have flared up and been forgotten or only remembered with amusement. But now, instead of flaring and burning themselves out, these offences retained a core of heat that could be blown into flame again. His very assurance that he did not mind being alone conveyed the sense that he was lonely, for constantly he recalled the sumptuous diversions of old days, when he wrote a Masque of Mithras which was performed one moonlit night in the Mithraic cave, himself impersonating Apollo with bare legs and a lyre. Or he spoke of the Villa Cercola, which we had shared, with its spacious rooms and sunny garden. The Villa Salvia, he said, was very cold in the winter and firing was a monstrous price. . . . Just then the woman who did for him came in to say that the supply of coke for the cooking stove would not last beyond to-morrow: should she order some more? He hesitated and then told her that he would see to it himself, and for the first time it occurred to me that he was hard-up.

Of one thing there was no doubt; one saw it in various small apathies and indifferences. That internal self-winding mainspring, which keeps a man ticking and chiming, was losing its coiled energy. For years now he had been living in a contracting milieu, and he acquiesced in its increasing narrowness and monotony, because he was incapable of effort. He needed the tonic of change, and I urged him to come back to stay in London with me, but he said that summer was beginning at Capri, and he hoped that a course of bathing and basking might cure this growing stiffness: besides he could not afford the journey. I told him that that could be managed, but he shook his head: to live in a town would suffocate him. Then would he come to Rye in the autumn when I resumed possession again? No, the rain and chilly winds of the north would be intolerable, and he had lost touch with England. . . . It was hopeless: nothing I could say stirred him from the path of least resistance.

On another day he would come down to the hotel in the most rosy mood. He was like a child; anything pleasant sufficed to make him happy to the obliteration of all else. It might be that the amiable Mrs. Andrews, one of the few old friends in the island who bothered herself any more about him, asked him and me to dinner, or perhaps he had satisfied his fastidious taste in the rendering of a Greek epigram of two lines, or a new pair of breeches had arrived from the tailor and fitted him (as I might see for myself) to perfection. In such moods he made plans for the future again instead of merely letting the days trickle past him. A site on the Via Tragara would soon be for sale, and he had been told that a building contractor was after it, for it would be a lovely position for a house. Of course there would be half a dozen lawsuits as to ownership: that was always the Italian way, but they would get settled. If I thought it was possible that I would come out here again and share a house with him, he would jump in, even before the house was built, with an offer to take an unfurnished lease of it. The owner would certainly accept a very moderate rent, rather than risk the house being left on his hands. I told him that with my joint lease of Lamb House I should find this quite impossible, but he said he would keep his eye open and let me know as soon as any chance presented itself. He came down to the Marina to see me off, and stood on the end of the pier in his impeccable breeches till the steamer gathered way.

Whether or no Brooks had any secret qualms about the future, or indeed the beginning of his literary career, I was now harbouring considerable misgivings about mine. I had been taking my own interest in the books on which I was so constantly engaged as a guarantee for their merits; they continued to sell in satisfactory numbers and I held that to be sufficient evidence of my prosperous progress. Perhaps my theory that Brooks was self-hypnotized about his work led me to wonder whether I was not self-hypnotized too. The thought, like a loud noise close to my ear, was sufficient to dissipate trance, and I took stock of my position. The upshot was that I realized that my literary career had come to a dead stop, or, more accurately, that it was moving, as in a back-water, slowly but perceptibly in the opposite direction. This retrogression, though I had not till now observed it myself, must have been obvious to anybody standing on the bank. How had it happened?

Thirty years ago, no less, I had scored without any effort beyond that of amusing myself a very big popular success. My first book—it was called *Dodo*—had sold enormously, it had furnished a theme for discussion in alert circles for many weeks, it had aroused serious as well as amused attention. Edmund Gosse—I never dared to remind him of it later—had told me that I had produced a work of high moral beauty, and that if I would "work, work and live," I should set my mark on English fiction.

I had worked with great industry, I had lived up to the lively measure of my capacity, but the mark was not quite so conspicuous as one might have wished. I saw now what a disaster that first success had been, for, backed by such critical encouragement, it made me think that all I had to do was to keep up my interest in life and dash off stories with ease and enjoyment. For a quantity of years I continued to do so, and earned the admiration of many readers and indeed of critics, but such as it was, it had certainly been fading. Imperceptibly to myself, I had long ago reached the point at which, unless I could observe more keenly and feel more deeply, I had come to the end of anything worth saying. My interest and pleasure in writing were unblunted, and though nobody can write to any purpose unless he enjoys it, such enjoyment in itself is no hall mark of value. I knew (and maintain) that I could express myself lucidly and agreeably, but I had been learning nothing. I had not been delving into myself or others, only turning over and over the patch of ground I had already prepared, and setting in it cuttings from my old plants. I observed with a certain acuteness, but not with insight. I made my people bustle about, indulge in what may be called "stock" experiences, talk with a rather brilliant plausibility, but, as a depressed perusal of some of my own volumes convinced me, they lacked the red corpuscle. I found other faults in these books, the chief of which was that I had often tried to conceal my own lack of emotion in situations that were intended to be moving, by daubing them over with sentimentality. I despised sentimentality in other writers. I looked upon it as a deliberate fake yet whenever I got in a difficulty I used it unblushingly myself.

Perhaps the most damning evidence against me was that I had quite forgotten what many of these books were about, and now that I read some of them again they roused not the faintest gleam of recollection. There is a story that Thackeray, years after he had written *Vanity Fair*, came across a copy of it, and found he had forgotten how good it was. My experience was precisely the opposite: I had forgotten how poor they were. They did not interest me, and I felt that I should very soon forget them again. Accordingly, I pronounced myself guilty, as regards a horrid large number of these. But in the case of some of these books, I pleaded not guilty and was willing to go into the witness box on oath, and be cross-examined. A novel called *Sheaves* was one, *The Luck of the Vails* was another; *The Climber* was a third, and a school story, *David Blaize*. Into these—there may have been one or two more which I have forgotten—I had put emotional imagination. That most of them were out of print did not concern me. I had chosen to be a writer, and on these occasions I had done my best.

At any rate I had now conducted an honest inquiry, humiliating but wholesome. Then I considered what was to be done next. Unless I decided to give up and dip in the ink no more (which I was unwilling to do, for it brought me pleasure and profit) I must start afresh. Looking at my case from outside, I had lost or was fast losing any claim to be called a serious novelist, and I was aware that it would be very difficult to regain that, for when readers or critics, whose opinion is worth having, have settled that an author is not worth their attention, they cross him off, and take no further interest in what he may subsequently write. He will have to do much better, in order to recover such position as he once had, than he did to attain it. Also this retrograde backwater movement had acquired momentum, and that must be checked before I could start again. After this succession of indolent outputs, I had to write and continue to write what I believed in. I did not feel that I had been selling my soul for lucre and a facile popularity, but rather that I had pawned it.

I did not arrive at these conclusions by any process of deliberate criminal investigation, though when they were complete they represented themselves as such, nor did they prevent me from pursuing my frivolous way with the preposterous adventures of Lucia and Miss Mapp, for there was nothing faked or sentimental about them, and I was not offering them as examples of serious fiction. They had no more to do with it than had a game of marbles. My failure to make my mark vexed me not only because a failure is always annoying, but because the attempt had, for all my industry, been such a lazy performance. I did not acquiesce in it, but I was sick of my own shadows, and I wanted realities. For the present I scrapped the idea of making a "come back" with fiction and turned to biography and memoirs. There, at any rate one had to do some honest work before one began writing at all.

I carried these egoistic explorations a little further. Wilfrid Ward, that candid and acute observer, once told me that I disliked thinking for myself. I so hotly repudiated that he hastened to explain that he meant something quite different. . . . But now I began to perceive that he meant exactly what he said, and very good sense it was. My mind was not really my own: I had, at any rate, filled it with furnishings that were not my own. In youth one can live very pleasantly thus, as in furnished lodgings, but in middle age such lendings must be turned out and replaced with home-made stuff. You cannot continue to live among ideas that do not belong to you. But there were cupboards—I seemed always to be turning out cupboards—full of things which did belong to me. I suppose I had bundled them away, when I let others furnish my house for me and they had dustily survived in the dark. Some had grown tarnished which were once bright: some were toys of youth with which I had once played, easily making myself believe the fantasies which I had woven round them, and there were truths which I had never faced, putting off the scrutiny of them from year to year, and falsities which I had cherished. These cupboards, when I opened them now, were cobwebbed with regrets, for things I had done or had not done and these, if I was hoping to make a habitable house, must instantly be swept away, for regrets, if allowed harbourage in the conscious mind, are like moth in curtains or carpets. They breed there and eat into its fibre. . . . Then there was the garden, attached to this house, to be weeded. The garden, so I figured it in this egoistic allegory, was the place of passivity and idleness, where the mind strolls about for refreshment, where it relaxes its employment on work or amusement, and where thought takes its ease. Primarily it is of the owner's planting, but in the way of gardens it soon gets out of hand if it is not looked after. Here there was much that must be uprooted and burned. It was overgrown with groundless fears and pessimisms which had no business to be there, and spoiled the quality of what one did. There were flowering shrubs which had promised well, but had been allowed to degenerate. Some might be pruned back and make fresh growth, others must be hacked out at once for they were full of dead wood and of woody buds which would never spread their petals: some sort of ambitions, I suppose, but they did not interest me any longer, or I saw that they were not compassable. And, like bind-weed, spreading its root-fibres underground and sprouting up in unexpected places with its cheap flowers and strangling stems, was the desire to be liked and admired. It is better business to like and to admire.

I did not tackle these cleaning-up processes with true missionary zeal, telling myself that I should be damned if they were not thoroughly done. I came into the house in the morning like a charwoman, for a little dusting and opening of the windows, and carted away some pieces of other people's furniture now and then. I came into the garden, like a job-gardener for an hour or two in the afternoon to weed and prune. For it is a mistake to take oneself too seriously. That only ends in self-consciousness which is just as deleterious a habit of mind as self-pity. No doubt it is an excellent thing to know oneself, but self-consciousness is a heavy price to pay for that knowledge. Indeed, perhaps the main reward of knowing oneself is the power to forget about oneself.

Once more, at Easter 1925, Arthur asked me to come down for a few days to Lamb House, at the end of which he would be going back to Cambridge for the May term. He, too, now looked upon Lamb House as a home, and we had been adding to its amenities. A Bechstein concert grand piano had been coaxed into the garden-room, curtains and carpets had been renewed and the central-heating was to be re-installed during his absence, via deep-laid trenches along the main garden path. We had passed these days on the invariable pattern which his benevolent despotism ordained for his guests. Our mornings were spent apart, our afternoons in his favourite forms of exercise, bicycling or motoring out into the country and being dropped and picked up again at some not too distant spot. Then after tea came the sacred solitary hours, and after dinner cards or chess or conversation till bedtime. There was never a host whom it was so delightful to please, or whose pleasure so genially diffused itself. On his last day, after writing till the last moment, he motored off to Ashford to catch a fast train for London, and so to Cambridge in time to dine in Hall. The car was piled high with suit-cases and dispatch-boxes and sticks and umbrellas which jerked gaily about as it bumped over the cobbles down West Street.

I was glad to be my own master again, however pleasant it had been to be his guest. For the next eight weeks of the Cambridge term the house would be mine, and after that I should see Rye no more till the October term took Arthur back to Cambridge again. I meant to spend these weeks without pattern for the days. Certainly I would not go for walks, unless there was some end in view, like spying out birds, for walking, owing to a very stiff hip-joint had become rather a painful process and only to be managed with a good deal of sitting down. My table in the garden-room was now piled with Hakluyt's *Voyages*, for, abandoning fiction, I was studying for a life of Francis Drake. By this time I had a good many friends in Rye, and I would ask them in to dinner and bridge, or, if I chose, I would be solitary and work, and in the afternoon, if this heat-spell continued, I would take sunbaths in the garden or sea-baths on the shore, and I would ask a friend down to stay with me, and we would both do exactly what we pleased. . . . So when Arthur had gone I pottered out into the garden and talked to Gabriel the gardener. Whether this was his Christian name or his surname I never knew nor inquired. (Probably Our Lady was equally incurious.) He is over eighty years old, long lean and upright with a pepper and salt beard stained with nicotine, full nine inches long from the extremity of his chin. He is not up to doing much work, and in cold weather he keeps indoors for he suffers from "me bronchitis." He has had an attack of it lately, and found great consolation in a glass of port with his dinner. Now that the weather has turned so hot he has come out to look after the garden again, busying himself with small jobs like planting out seedlings from the summer-garden and getting "his young man," a youth of about sixty, to do the heavier work. He disapproves of any change being made in the garden, which, like all proper gardeners, he considers his own, without his consent, but he allows me the produce, and is open to suggestions about flower-beds. Just lately a small corner of his garden was cut off, in order to give a plot of ground to an adjoining house belonging to the estate, which was being restored and rendered habitable. Gabriel had not been consulted about this and resented it. We went to look at the repairs and rebuilding, and he poured scorn on them.

"Call that a house?" he asked. "I wouldn't live in such

a house if I was paid for it. Where's the stairs going? Peuh! And then taking away a piece of me garden to make a backyard for it! The workmen come trampling about all over me strawberry-bed."

"But they're putting up a paling—" I began.

"Paling? And cut all the sun off me greenhouse."

"Not a bit. A paling there can't cut the sun off. The sun shines over the top of it."

"Well, perhaps it does, if you come to look at it," he conceded. "But I don't hold with these messings-about. . . . That oak-tree of yours is making wood wonderful. It'll be getting root-bound in its pot. Better plant it out. . . ."

The oak-tree requires a note. Four years ago on a November afternoon I was standing very still and gazing up into an oak-tree by Playden church, because I thought I had seen a great spotted woodpecker fly into it. I didn't know that the bird had ever been seen before round Rye, and as I stealthily adjusted my field-glass an acorn fell from the tree, and after hitting me on the face dropped *into my hand*. I clutched it and took it home. There could be no doubt that it was meant for me in some occult and special sense, and I wrapped it up in a bit of wet moss and laid it in Gabriel's greenhouse. I told him what I meant to do with it, and it took his fancy. When it sprouted we planted it in a flower-pot. It shot up, but crookedly, and Gabriel tied the infant stem to a stick and made it grow straight. Buds broke out on the side of the stem, but we rubbed these off, and now this four-year-old tree, eighteen inches high, has a good thick woody trunk, and a crown of leaf-bearing twigs at the top. It is a standard oak, like a standard rose. It is to be kept dwarfed in stature: all twigs growing upwards are drastically cut back, also those that extend too far horizontally. In the course of years (such is the design) it became a forest tree, thick-trunked and eighteen inches high. We turned it out of the flower-pot and planted it in a bed under the garden-room.

Gabriel approved of this because he had been consulted, but he was vexed about the new stove for central-heating which was being put in. Hitherto the pipes that warmed his greenhouse and the garden-room were not connected with those that warmed the house, which had a separate stove, so that in winter two stoves had to be kept burning (with coke at the price of some precious metal) to warm them both. So a bigger stove is being installed in the stoke-hole by the greenhouse with an iron ladder to lead down to the greater depth required in order to connect it up with the pipes in the house. Gabriel peered contemptuously into the pit, and said that he would never go down that nasty ladder to feed the stove. As he had not looked after the central heating for several years, I told him that nobody wanted him to. Gabriel's eyes twinkled, but he had plenty more criticisms. "Better have stuck to your old stove," he said, "you'll get no heat out of that rubbishy thing. And now I hear you're going to dig up me garden path. And where'll you put your coke?"

"In a bin close beside the stove at the bottom of the ladder instead of that shed of yours away across the garden which lets in the rain. It will be shovelled straight into the stove."

Gabriel sniffed and changed the subject.

"That was a fine tipple you sent me for me dinner," he said. "If my mother had reared me on port wine instead of her milk, I shouldn't have been weaned yet. And me lettuces are coming on beautiful. I'll cut you one for your dinner. Why, there's me tortoise. He buried himself by the potting-shed in November. Come out to see what the weather's like. I'll give him a drink, and put him on the lawn and he'll eat up your dandelions, for they always goes for what's yellow, but I don't want him near me lettuces."

"How do you give him a drink?" I asked.

"Pop him in a bucket of water for five minutes, and that'll last him a week. That's what they like, but no good to me."

He carried the refreshed tortoise to the far end of the lawn, then paused by a bed of fuchsias. One looked to me to be dying. Gabriel pinched its stem, pulled it up, shook it and rammed it into the earth again.

"That'll be all right now," he said. "Just wanted a nudge. . . . You're moving pretty stiff to-day. Hip, is it? They're nasty things. You rub your bottom with a raw onion and never mind the stink. It draws it out wonderful."

The sun was hot, but he scanned the sky doubtfully.

"Shouldn't wonder if we had a frost to-night," he said.

"The tortoise seems to think summer's come."

"Peuh! Don't you trust them insects. They've got no judgment."

Gabriel was wrong about the onion and the frost, but right about the fuchsia. He has the green finger with flowers, like a healer's touch, and his nudging certainly revived it. I spent unplanned, delightful days, taking the morning steam-tram out to the shore beyond the golf links, bathing, if the tide served, or if it was low, eating a packet of sandwiches among the dunes, and strolling along the firm sands where there were patches of small embedded shells, a mosaic of pink and lilac. Golf, alas, had become impossible, for owing to "that nasty thing" I could no longer make full shots, but sometimes I took a mashie and a putter from my locker in the club-house and practised approaching and putting, telling myself that my short game was improving enormously. I could still walk quite a decent way, if I thought it worth while to do so, and when a like-minded friend came to stay with me we had a grand day after birds. We motored to the shingle-beds, once below the sea, lying between Dungeness and Lydd, and donning "back-stays"—these are boards you tie over the soles of your shoes—we traversed a mile of loose stones, to those amazing ponds in the middle of this vast pebbly beach, where the black-headed gulls breed. There were mixed flights of duck to sort out, black scoters and shelduck and mallards and pintails, and I spotted a Norfolk plover on the scrape that serves her for her nest. There is something primeval about these odd birds, as if they were a link between reptiles and fowls, a large lizard-like yellow eye, a lizard's immobility, and then a vanishing. I would have sworn, as we shuffled stealthily on our back-stays towards the place, that I never took my eye off her; but she vanished, as by a conjuring trick, and nobody saw her go. A wonderful conjuring trick; she leaves her young, when hatched, in the nest, having apparently taught them to lie quite flat and remain motionless, and their protective colouring will render them practically invisible. . . . Then on towards Littlestone: a stretch of sand-dunes was the one breeding-place in the British Isles for the Kentish plover, and we saw several pairs. To-day their quarters are gay with florid gimcrack villas bordering on a beautiful concrete road. . . .

And often I was alone at Lamb House, and after dinner voyaged with Hakluyt, or discovered that I had forgotten yet another of the Preludes and Fugues.

CHAPTER IX

MAY fled by. Arthur wrote to me to say that a further large sum of money, £20,000, had been bestowed on him by his still unseen benefactress, and with that he could see accomplished all that he had planned to do for Magdalene.

He had always fought shy of any intimate friendship with women. They wanted, he thought, to improve one. But in this long correspondence he had grown entirely to trust her, and she had never threatened any such trespass. He regarded her, as he said in his diary, with "an unsuspicious love" such as he had only felt for two women, his mother, and Beth, the old family nurse. He was meaning to come down to Rye as soon as he could get away from Cambridge after the usual May week festivities—boat-races and balls and concerts, which fill the first fortnight of June. One morning I heard from the doctor who had seen him through those long years of misery, now quite forgotten, that he had an attack of pleurisy. There was nothing in the least serious, he joked about it himself. He hated this annual jubilation; so he concluded that if one was obliged to have pleurisy, May week was the very time for it. A week later, when he was out of bed, he had a sudden heart-attack, which might at any moment have been fatal, and for two days he could not be moved from the chair where he was sitting in his study. He knew that he was in imminent danger, but was quite undisturbed, and when the immediate peril was over, he observed to his doctor: "That was a near thing wasn't it?" Then he sent for one of the Fellows about some piece of college business, which had been left unsettled when he was taken ill. "We mustn't let them down," he said, and between them they completed it. He was got back to bed again, and then pneumonia developed. After his heart-attack, there was little resistance, and on a Sunday afternoon I got a telegram from Cambridge, which told me he was dangerously ill. I got there late that night, and found that he had said there was no reason that I should be sent for. He was lying in the stupor of half-consciousness, breathing fast and shallow, but he recognized me. "Why have you come?" he said. "I'm glad you've come."

Before many hours, all hope of his recovery had gone, and on Tuesday afternoon, his doctor told me that a friend of his had asked whether some stimulant should not be given him to bring him back into consciousness again. I knew what that meant. It was that grim and awful doctrine that when a man's soul is about to quit his body, some sort of final "chance" should be given it. Mrs. Charles Kingsley's seemed the truer view. She was thought to be dying, and her nurse asked her if she would like to see a clergyman. "A clergyman? she gasped. "When I'm dying? Why?" . . . I begged the doctor not to recall him. He was passing without struggle or any physical pain: what more could possibly be desired? He died at midnight on the same day on which my mother had died seven years before.

I felt no real sense of personal bereavement. It could

hardly have been otherwise, for except for those few days at Lamb House every year, we saw nothing of each other. Our ways of life, our diversions had little in common, and never, since we were boys had we spoken of things that intimately concerned us as we spoke of them to our friends. Close blood-relationship certainly implies dutiful instincts. A man who does not stick up for his kin nor is ready and eager to help if they are in trouble is wanting in normal decency, but it does not imply any warmth of friendship. His death left me with no relations nearer than cousins whom I scarcely knew.

I returned to Cambridge after his funeral, a few weeks later. There was no choice for the College as to what was to be the fate of the Old Lodge, which Arthur had made into a residence that so exactly suited him, and its brimming contents had to be disposed of. It covered a large area of ground within the precincts, and there was already a large and commodious official residence for the Master, which, during Arthur's ten years of office, had remained empty, for he preferred the house he had made for himself. The Old Lodge was far too big for any one set of Fellow's rooms, and indeed with its large hall, its labyrinthine structure, its dark northerly aspect, its accommodation for servants and guests it was utterly unsuited to the requirements of a scholastic bachelor, and no married man could possibly have lived in it. Moreover the ground was needed for the building of more sets of undergraduates' rooms which his endowments had made possible. Its destruction was no obliteration of him: he had done too much for the College to need any such personal monument of his making. Five courts, recreation rooms, scholarships and exhibitions, big buildings now in progress were his memorial, and to the College he had left all the capital yet unexpended which this benefactress whom he had never seen had showered on him.

He had left me, subject to certain bequests, the bewildering contents of the Old Lodge, and now that it was to be dismantled, once again, as at Tremans seven years before, I had to empty it, with no one's desires to consult except my own. I had then sent him quantities of family pieces, and now they confronted me again, mutely glittering in plate-chests and china cupboards. But who wanted with or without a sense of associative tenderness, a Crown Derby dinner service for thirty people, or a silver William IV urn, appalling in design and decoration, and large enough to supply boiling water for all their breakfasts next morning?

Some of the effects were easy to deal with. The house was crammed with books in ceiling-high bookcases, and these, after certain friends had made their choice of a dozen volumes or so, were to go *en bloc* to some University Institution. But Arthur had never been a bibliophil, and there remains in my mind the vivid image of Sir Edmund Gosse hunting, at first with zeal, and soon with the weariness of vanishing hope, for anything that could, as he said, give a quickened heart's-beat to a collector, which was what he wanted. He stood on ladders, he crouched on the ground, he went with sedulous care through a whole shelf-full of pamphlets in which there might lurk some unsuspected rarity, but in vain. Then there was Arthur's diary of nearly forty years: it had grown into a colossal document of 4,000,000 words.

He had left explicit directions that his friend Mr. Percy Lubbock, should he decide to accept the task, should read it, and, if he thought fit, publish a volume of extracts from it, which, of course, would be but a minute fragment of the whole. No other eye but his was to see it, and when his work was done, it was to pass into the possession of Magdalene, and remain there sealed up for fifty years after his death. When that time had expired the Fellows might deal with it as they liked. They could publish the whole or part or none: they could keep it or destroy it.

Mr. Lubbock accepted the bequest, and produced a volume of extracts with personal impressions of his own and an admirable thread of biography as guide to the reader. These selections (from which I have already quoted), reveal that aspect of Arthur's personality, of which there is not the smallest trace in those serene books, with their gentle, meditative musings, by which his readers knew him. In his diary, as the extracts show, he set forth his life as he was known to himself. It was a secret document in which he rendered himself with all the fidelity and frankness of which he was capable, a colossal self-portrait. As his editor points out a self-portrait is not necessarily a true portrait: a man may be deceived about himself, he may be blind to qualities of his own, whether failings or finenesses, which his friends are convinced he possesses. Or again if, as in this case, he is a master of incisive language, the mere pleasure of cracking the literary whip may cause him to over-emphasize the harshness and impatience of many recorded judgments. But allowing for that, such a self-portrait is both an authoritative and a final document; exaggeration and blindness, if they exist, are characteristic of the writer, and if he is naturally introspective, he knows more about his essential self than anyone else can.

No one who reads these extracts can fail to see the wisdom of the injunction that the entire document should be sealed up for fifty years. They are often fiercely critical and intolerant, and there can be no doubt that the feelings of many friends would have been justly hurt. He had, for instance, a long quarrel with his old friend Edmund Gosse, which was never made up beyond the point of renewed and polite intercourse. Arthur felt and spoke extremely bitterly about it, and these sentiments certainly found full expression in the diary. It would also have dismayed a company with whom he had been passing a convivial evening to learn how long-winded and empty-headed he sometimes found them when, in his diary, he corrosively surveyed them. Doubtless he held them really in high esteem and doubtless throughout the evening he had been the most genial and entertaining of them all, but when the feast was over and the lights expired, and, as so often, he lay long awake, there came to him the sense of the futility of it all.

Time renders picturesque, disclosures that would once have given pain, and in fifty years the justice of them will not matter a jot. All that will then concern the reader will be the vividness of this self-portrait. Arthur's clear-eyed introspection, his humour, his incisive clean-cut style seem to guarantee it.

There was yet another reason why for years to come only a discreet and intimate eye should see the whole. Below this picture of himself, as presented in these extracts, we have glimpses and hints, a line here a submerged tint there, of another aspect of his temperament. It lurked, deliberately imprisoned within his robust enjoyment of life, his tireless industry and perhaps lay at the root of his long depressions; a sense of deep-seated frustration, a consciousness that with all his friendships and eager interests he missed a more direct expression of himself. Reserve combined with fastidiousness, both of which were very characteristic of him, were perhaps responsible for this suppression. He shunned emotional experience.

Whether the diary will ever be published in full, it is impossible to say. It may easily prove to be a document of great psychological interest and of the quality which cannot date. To those who knew him only in casual conversation he was a first-rate talker; here he was talking to his most intimate self on the topics that at heart most engaged him. But since it was his habit to put down in it every day some account of his rides and rambles in the country, it must certainly contain a quantity of matter which is repeated, in all essentials, again and again. I say this advisedly, for among his unpublished manuscripts I found a volume and a half of typewritten pages which recorded the early days of the war of 1914 and his reflections on them. Though they cover a period of only six weeks, the repetitions are incessant. He wrote down, day by day, whatever impressed him without thought as to whether he had received and recorded the same impressions perhaps only a week before.

He had bequeathed to Magdalene the copyright of his published books, and to me all his unpublished manuscripts with the exception of the diary. In spite of the constant stream of his publications there were two shelves full of these, typewritten volumes slender or bulky bound in boards and patterned paper, essays, poems, stories and full-length novels. These must all be read, but it would take weeks to go through them, and I packed them up and sent them down to Rye. My immediate business was to clear the Old Lodge of all private papers and of such furnishings as I meant to keep before the sale which must precede its demolition.

During the fifteen years in which Arthur had lived in the Old Lodge, I had stayed there only for a couple of nights or so, and had never until now penetrated into the room where he kept his papers. Except for a small oasis for the table where his typist worked it was piled high with boxes containing manuscripts, a towering cliff of them from door to window. There were the boxes I had sent from Tremans, labelled "Archbishop's Correspondence" tumbling into them all sorts of ancient records which Arthur might wish to preserve. He had never referred to them since, and they bore the air of not having been opened, so I went through them. Then came a bale of letters to Arthur from Edmund Gosse, the communications of thirty-five years of close friendship. Gosse was in the house now, just concluding the hopeless quest of which I have spoken; and, as Arthur had enjoined that letters should go back to their writers if they desired them, I asked him his wishes. He was amazed at their bulk, he read one or two of the topmost, unable to make up his mind, but finally he said he did not want them and asked me to destroy them all. It was a pity, for, whether in friendship or fury (and here we should have had both) Gosse was among the best letter writers in the language, and, in consequence of his decision, there now appears in the admirable book of his *Life and Letters*, compiled by Sir Evan Charteris, no record of that long and close friendship nor of the estrangement. Letter-writing, indeed, suited Gosse's agile genius better than any other form of literature. He made decorative the most trivial happenings; he scattered wit and gaiety, or, when in a scolding humour, corrosive acids, as out of an elegant scent-bottle. Trouble had long been simmering before it boiled over. Gosse remonstrated with Arthur over the outpouring of his reflective books, and made unkindly mirth of them to mutual friends. Arthur, on his side, never welcomed criticism unless he asked for it, and found Gosse "huffy and affronted if he isn't deferred to and made much of."

So that box of letters went entire to the burning-ghaut; others had to be sifted, for among my father's miscellaneous papers, in wastes of correspondences over ecclesiastical questions, long obsolete, came small gems and treasures, such as a packet of letters from Queen Victoria. In one written from Florence (where he was going presently) she said she hoped he could get out there before she left. He must then have told her that he was engaged to preach somewhere and could not start earlier, for she wrote again saying that he could surely get somebody to preach instead of him, otherwise she would miss him. Another referred to the approaching marriage of Prince Albert Victor of Wales and Princess May of Teck, who, she thought, would set an example of a quiet and steady life "which, alas, is not the fashion in these days. . . ." Another from the Prince of Wales (Edward VII) written directly after the Tranby Croft scandal, was interesting, for he assured my father that he had a horror of gambling and would always discourage anyone who showed a tendency towards it. Gambling and intemperance, he thought, were the greatest curses in national life. There were gems also in the boxes of Arthur's own correspondence, for one suddenly came on a letter from Swinburne describing how he and Rossetti discovered a stack of copies of the first edition of Omar Khayyam, which had fallen flat when published, in a tray of penny books at Quaritch's, and how Rossetti, fired with enthusiasm, had gone back next day to buy more copies and found to his great indignation that the price had been put up to twopence. There was a letter from my father, somewhere in the 'eighties, which I read with amazement. Arthur had told him that Henry Irving had asked him to dine and that he had joyfully accepted. My father wrote him a long, kindly but very serious letter, saying that he ought to get out of it if he could, and if he could not he must never accept a similar invitation again. People would come to know that he was on friendly terms with actors and such persons, and it would damage him very much in the eyes of those whose opinion should be respected. . . . There were letters from Thomas Hardy: he had been made an Honorary Fellow of Magdalene, and highly appreciated this honour, and then once more I tossed over billows of unknown correspondents. Then came a packet of letters of very dangerous stuff, and one to be burnt unopened. There were other boxes that could be dealt with as summarily: some were labelled "College," and these could be sent straight to the President; some were labelled "MSS." and within I found galley proofs of his books and of Hugh's, and Hugh's sketch for the Life of St. Thomas of Canterbury, which he wrote in disastrous collaboration with Rolfe. Of the obscene and abusive letters that Rolfe showered upon him there was no trace. Arthur no doubt had destroyed them, but when, a few years later an enthusiastic coterie of explorers into Rolfe's works and days pushed forth into those sensational regions, bitter were the lamentations that such jewels were missing.

Morning and afternoon, with the clothes-basket going heavy to the furnace and returning hungry, I voyaged on not yet seeing land, till I felt that I was losing all power of discrimination as to what ought to be kept and what destroyed. When, day after day, that point of impotence had been arrived at, I hobbled out (for I was beginning to get very lame) along the backs past Trinity and Clare and through King's and so home again, in an aching weariness of body and the numb desolation of mind which my task induced. Sometimes I dined in Hall with the Fellows who were in residence or I fed alone in the half-dismantled Hall at the Old Lodge. Then came a spell of chilly days, and the little court full of giant hemlocks dripped with the rain, and the gutters gurgled, and the shrubs outside Arthur's sitting-room dropped their yellowing leaves. Now the books had gone from the shelves, and the contents of the boxes were sorted out; some had gone to the writers of these endless letters, and some to the College, and some I had sent off to Rye, but the most had gone to the fire. All was done and to-morrow the Old Lodge which had been the scene of such unceasing energy and hospitality would be empty and silent again waiting for the hammer of the auctioneer and the crowbar of the housebreaker.

CHAPTER X

MOST people of middle age are liable to rheumatic twinges, and though disquisitions on ailments are apt to be boring, I take that risk in the hope that my long experience (I celebrate the completion of twenty glorious years of crippling processes very soon) may divert or encourage other wayfarers on that dreary road.

These twinges much annoyed me, for I had been a skilled and active denizen of skating-rinks and golf links, and tennis courts, impervious to fatigue, and I regarded such threatened limitations as an offence against the liberty of the subject. So I hastened to consult an eminent general practitioner who after flexings and extensions solemnly bound a strip of adhesive plaster round the troublesome hip-joint, which came off in my bath. I knew he used suggestion with his patients, and concluded that this was an appeal to my mind. But my mind must have been in unreceptive mood: the treatment had no effect, and when next winter I went out to Pontresina for sun and skating, I found that I had to get on without the skating. It was annoying, but I said to myself that if this was all, there were plenty less strenuous activities left. Curling was a very pleasant winter sport, and there were slow and sedentary walks over the beaches of Blakeney and the marsh at Rye, watching birds.

It would be as tedious to follow the progress of this repulsive ailment as it was to suffer it. Like a clock of which the long pointer remains stationary till a minute is completed, it paused and then registered a perceptible advance. Activity diminished, and pain, which I abominate, increased. Firmly resolved to get rid of it, I scoured the medical cantonments of London. I went alike to notable regular physicians and to quacks. I returned to my friend of the sticking-plaster, who now advised tonics and a liberal consumption of oranges. He said there was no need to take an X-ray skiagraph, because he knew what it would show. Another gave me a course of atophan; another colonized my colon with hordes of the Bacillus Bulgaricus. When that region (such was the strategy) was securely held by this admirable Army Corps, they would march and manœuvre and inflict crushing defeats on the injurious bacilli of disease. I took great interest in this war. For two years I was a very diligent Colonial Minister, and kept adding brigades of Bacillus Bulgaricus to my garrisons, but they never seemed to win a single engagement. Another doctor injected something radio-active into my thigh; another some potion of dead bacilli into my arm. Another drove iodine into the hip by means of an electric current; another prescribed a course of iodine taken internally in increasing doses up to the maximum, and then in diminished doses, till I arrived at the precise point, in every sense, at which I had started. Another prescribed massage, another a system of physical exercises. I wallowed in brown mud, I drank the waters of Bath, I floated on the buoyant and saline streams of Droitwich, and had some healthy teeth extracted. I had a course of intensive X-ray alone in a room full of shining black pipes and buzzing mechanisms: it was like figuring in some nightmare picture by Syme,

Never in my life have I pursued a quest with such unfaltering devotion. The zeal of the Lords of Harley Street ate me up.

The quacks, if I may call them so without libel, were equally enterprising and empirical. I took herbal teas and sat in tepid baths. For a long time I wore a band of small crystals, which I take to have been glass, round my neck, and radio-active pads, which I take to have been flannel, over my hips, for both were now giving trouble. I carried a little tubular cardboard case, hermetically sealed and very heavy for its size, in my trouser pocket. One day I dropped it on the floor, the case was fractured and inside was a small bottle of quicksilver. I had a course —perhaps I ought to class this among scientific treatments —of Christian Science. The healer, a most charming fellow, gave me something by Mrs. Eddy to read, while he tuned in, as it were, by dipping into her text-book *Christian Science and the Key to the Scriptures*. He then closed his book and gave me mental treatment, that is to say he absorbed himself in the conviction that disease had not any real existence, with special application to me. I warned him that I was not yet a convert, but he said that did not matter; faithless folk, who had a false claim that they were ill, could be cured just as well as believers. This astonished me for I had understood that in the miracles of healing recorded in the Gospels the faith of the patient was a condition of his cure.

One evening, after the treatment had begun, he suddenly sprang up, remembering that he had not switched on the lights of his car, and ran downstairs. I am bound to say that this put me off. His concentration on the non-existence of evil, pain and disease seemed incomplete.

These treatments overlapped: I might be wearing my radio-active pads at Droitwich or my necklace at Bath. They all ran the same course, cradled in high optimism and gently expiring in complete failure. Doubtless this abridged catalogue of them gives the impression that I was a most credulous patient to spend so much time and money on régimes which my reasonable mind rejected as rubbish. But I wanted to get well, and was prepared to do anything, however preposterous, in search of this consummation. Indeed I think it would have been very foolish not to have been so foolish, for who could tell? From time to time these practitioners cheered me up by telling me that I was walking more easily, which was not the case, for when at last one of them suggested that an X-ray skiagraph should be taken, it showed osteo-arthritis in an advanced stage, and irreparable damage already done.

Rather a horrid moment, because now I knew that I could not be mended. Whether those unavailing physicians whom I had so sedulously consulted were very sanguine that their baths and their bacilli would cure me I have no idea, but perhaps their medicaments may have helped to retard the nasty processes which had been going on. There is no proof that they did, but no one can assert that they did not. So I resumed some of my pilgrimages not only on that chance, but because it maintains one's self-respect to put up some sort of a show against any affliction, instead of acquiescing in it. After a year or two more I got tired of them all and let my self-respect take care of itself.

But all reasonable activities (or such as I accounted reasonable) had vanished. Skating and curling and tennis were the first to go, golf followed, and the pursuit of birds, for walking hurt, and half a mile or so, with one stick (and, on less athletic mornings, two) was about my tether. But though all these pleasures were done with, I suffered no diminution of happiness, and learned to my great satisfaction that it has nothing to do with pleasures. One remained cheerful not because one was brave and high-minded, but because there was no reason for being otherwise. That was all to the good, for if I had known ten years ago the sorry figure I should be cutting to-day, I should have been very unhappy about it. But here I was not a whit the worse in that regard. Another encouraging discovery was that though I always have been and continue to be an arrant coward in the face of anticipated pain, I was learning to despise such pain as I had to put up with. I hated it, I regarded it as a foul nuisance, and it was a "score" to find oneself treating it as if it was of no importance. Severe pain, I hasten to add, would probably make me change my opinion very quickly.

I decided, after careful thought, not to grouse. The grouser, I observed, did not induce sympathy in his audience so much as boredom, and it is a mistake deliberately to bore your friends. Most of us do it quite enough while trying to be amusing. A further argument against grousing is that it often has an undesirable effect on the plaintiff, for his lamentations only render more vivid his consciousness of his maladies. Moreover, even if the grouser manages to elicit expressions of pity, these very expressions encourage his tendency to self-pity, and self-pity sickens the very sap of life.

But though I did not wantonly make myself a bore by grousing, I had become aware that in other respects I was becoming one. The presence of him who shuffles along on a stick, who cannot pick it up if he drops it, whose progress upstairs is a crab-like acrobatic feat and who can take no part in the mildest activities does not promote gaiety nor brighten the sunshine of social occasions. As long as he is among those whom he has reason to reckon as his friends, he will not be troubled by this slightly kill-joy consciousness. But if he has been gregarious, fond of crowds, he may feel, among many faces and the alert movements of acquaintances, that he is a tiny speck of tarnish on their silver hours, and will wonder if they are not suffering him rather than welcoming. Such mental twinges are of no more importance than those physical twinges which he has been learning to despise, but they can be disagreeable and they are unnecessary. He need not seek out the occasions which give rise to them, and his absence will cause no lamentations.

I had no intention of allowing this disquisition on arthritis to become so perilously like a homily; it seems to have twisted itself round in my hands as when one picks up a kitten that does not wish to be stroked. . . . So I turn to more exhilarating topics, and refer again to that agreeable moment, when the silence of Big Ben at 11 a.m. on Armistice Day 1918 inspired the finest historical writer of our times with a paragraph of immortal prose. I recall how on that day, two hours later, the wittiest man of our times, Mr. Harry Higgins, was lunching at the Garrick Club. He sat down in a vacant seat at the long table, and his neighbour, a stranger to him, opened conversation according to the friendly and informal custom of the club. He was exuberant on the happy event: on the awakening from the nightmare of the last four years with its air-raids, its lack of petrol for private motors, its rationed fare, its darkened streets, its dislocation of business and of recreation. No hunting, no racing, and so many caddies had joined up that one had to carry one's own clubs playing golf. Harry Higgins listened to this fine monologue very courteously, sympathetically nodding his head and eating his lunch. Owing to an operation in his throat, he could only speak in a whisper, and that whisper was worth waiting for. When there was a pause in this roulade of observations, he replied: "Yes, I was very glad to hear about the Armistice. It will be a great stimulus to recruiting."

That was characteristic of his wit, not only for its essential brevity, but for its complete unexpectedness, its apt incongruity. His technique, if we can apply that word to anything so spontaneous, was the exact opposite of Oscar Wilde's, who monopolized conversation. That monopoly was eagerly accorded him, for he talked superbly. But he talked too much to be called a wit in the conversational sense: he resembled floodlighting. Harry Higgins was more like a display of meteors, each brilliant, and each surprising, but intermittent and unassertive. Their quality neither dates nor deteriorates. . . .

He was for some years on the Board of the Opera Syndicate at Covent Garden. In this capacity he crossed the Atlantic to hear a tenor who had scored an immense success in New York in Wagnerian rôles. This paragon was singing Tristan on the night of Harry Higgins's arrival, and an American friend had bidden him to her box. She talked to him so continuously throughout the performance, that he could give no serious attention to the stage. At the end she asked him to come to her box again three nights hence, when the star would be singing Lohengrin. "Thanks very much," he said. "I shall be delighted. I've never heard you in Lohengrin. . . ." On another occasion he had a business interview with a fine vocalist whose talent as an artist was a little overshadowed by her genius for friendship. There was an idea of getting her to sing at Covent Garden, but when terms were discussed, she asked a price which seemed to him far in excess of her artistic merits. "But, my dear lady," he said. "We only want you to sing."

Again he and a friend (nameless for the moment) were engaged to lunch with a charming but severe hostess. The friend was late, and the hostess was much vexed with him. "There is nothing so rude and ill-bred as unpunctuality," she said to Harry. "One either has to wait or there is a vacant place. Upsetting everything." He put in a kindly word for the offender. "You mustn't be too hard on him," he whispered. "I expect he only wants to show you that he is no relation of Benson the watchmaker. . . ."

Apt and incongruous and impromptu also was his advice to a certain superb dame, whose house was a palace of liveried splendour. Her patriotism on the outbreak of war in 1914 had compelled her to harry her four tall able-bodied footmen into joining up, but her whole soul revolted at the degradation of being waited upon by parlour-maids. She consulted Harry Higgins about this wretched descent into the squalid habits of the middle class, for she felt she was making almost too costly an offering on the altar of patriotism. But what was she to do? "Quite simple," he said. "Just an advertisement in the *Morning Post*. 'A lady of title wants four ruptured footmen.' "

Of the same unexpected quality were the observations of my delightful friend Mary Crawshay. She was lunching with me once in Brompton Square. The dining-room looks out on to Brompton Parish Church and on to a large gravelled oblong which is packed with motors whenever a popular wedding is in process there. As we sat down I pointed out to her the great assembly of cars and told her what it betokened. But they were still there when we had finished, and Mary Crawshay said: "You must be wrong: it can't be a wedding. A wedding would have been over long ago. It must be a divorce. . . ." One morning during the war, there appeared in the *Daily Telegraph* a letter from the late Lord Lansdowne, to the effect that the Allies would be wise to make terms with the Central European Powers and bring the carnage to a close. The paper was brought to Mary Crawshay as she drank her cup of tea in bed, and she sprang to the telephone to ring up a friend. Yes: he had seen it, too. "Are we Lansdowne-hearted? No!" she cried.

Lady Tree scattered many such unpremeditated jewels about her path. A friend rang up to her on the morning Herbert Tree's knighthood was announced in the *Gazette*, though he had not yet received the ceremonial accolade. "Congratulations, Lady Tree," said this premature friend. "Oh, but you mustn't call me that yet," she answered, "though of course I am in the sight of God. . . ." And when, dining out with her hair dressed in some new modishness, her hostess said to her "How charmingly you've done your hair to-night, Maud," she replied,

"Sweet of you to call it *my* hair." Her husband, even before his accolade, was as quick as she, and instantaneousness is as essential to wit as brevity: staircases creak with the weight of the brilliance that becomes heavy as dough, if it has not leapt to the lips at the appropriate split second. I went once to his sumptuous presentation of *Julius Caesar*, and observed that on the day of his murder there stood in the forum a statue of Caligula, who was not born till some fifty years later. Tree asked me to go round to his dressing-room after the second act. His beautiful forum! What did I think of his beautiful forum? I pointed out this trivial anachronism, but not a split second passed before he answered, "Well, that only shows what wonderful people these old Romans were."

He was never at a loss, an unexpected emergency only quickened him. He and Oscar Wilde were spending the week-end in the same country-house. On Sunday morning Wilde was the last but one to appear at breakfast, Tree alone being absent. He told the company how a week or two ago the same thing had happened at another house, and how when Tree came down he looked worried, and said "I had a very curious dream last night." Wilde then recounted this strange dream. He had hardly finished, when the door opened and in came Tree. "I had a very curious dream last night," he said, and in a tense silence he began telling them exactly the same dream all over again: evidently it was his Sunday morning gambit. As he proceeded suppressed little giggles were heard, and people looked at their plates. The sight of Oscar Wilde roused latent associations in his mind, and an awful suspicion dawned on him. He broke off. "Oscar," he said, "I believe you've been telling them my curious dream on your own."

These were kindly lights, uncompetitive stars, shining because they were bright. Competitive talk can be a combative affair: I once witnessed an encounter of the sort between Mr. Joseph Choate, the American Ambassador and Sir Henry Irving. They were both very fine talkers, eloquent, witty and impressive and both were prepared, even eager, to provide memorable entertainment for the half-dozen men who, when the ladies withdrew after dinner, closed up to listen. That, I think, was the cause of the trouble, for neither of them would let the other have a look in. A dialogue between them would have been perhaps equally delightful, but that was far from the intention of either. Mr. Choate had hardly begun speaking of his old friend Oliver Wendell Holmes, when Irving chipped in with something about Mrs. Kemble and before he could tell us of that, Choate recalled something else which would doubtless have been highly interesting if we had been permitted to hear what it was. It was in fact an evening of "broken arcs" . . . But on another occasion Mr. Choate secured the undivided attention of a very exalted table, and, we may guess, would have been very glad to have let Sir Henry have it all.

Queen Victoria had asked him to dine and sleep at Windsor: there was no party, he and Lady Wolseley were the only guests apart from a few members of the household. The Queen was not in a chatty mood—perhaps it was for that reason that the Ambassador had not been placed next her. She spoke only to Princess Beatrice who sat beside her, and dinner proceeded at great speed and with periods of complete silence. The household exchanged a few low observations with each other but "it was a very whispery evening," said Lady Wolseley. The Ambassador, feeling no doubt that he must do something to make this little Royal party more of a success, leant forward across Princess Beatrice, and addressed the Queen.

"Queen Victoria!" he said, to call her attention.

Dead silence.

"Queen Victoria," he repeated. "I was just telling your daughter that she looks fine to-night."

The Queen acknowledged this gratifying remark by a small frozen bow towards the Ambassador. And not another word was said by anybody.

Puns, from time to time, have been listed in the equipment of witty conversationalists and great writers. Aristophanes abounded in them, so, too, did Shakespeare, who at one of the grimmest moments in *Macbeth* introduced a pun to enhance the horror of the spilt blood. Says Lady Macbeth:

> "and I
> Will gild the faces of the grooms withal,
> That it may prove their guilt."

Charles Lamb had a feeling for puns and he never said a wittier word than when, meeting a poaching-looking individual carrying a hare, he asked him, "My friend, is that your own hare or a wig?" In the 'eighties and 'nineties of last century there was a great Pun Age. Sir F. Burnand, editor of a weekly paper (which it is impossible to name in connection with puns), was the Archpriest, indeed, he was said to owe his knighthood to this inexhaustible facility. He was once challenged to make a pun on the word "pharmaceutical." "Nothing easier," he said. "I ask you this riddle: 'Why is a dispensing chemist cleverer than one who is engaged in scientific research?' Answer: 'Because he's a far more cute ickle chemist.' " . . . He once did me the honour to parody a very juvenile book of mine called *The Rubicon* in the paper which he edited. The parody was called "The Boobies gone," and as each character finished his rôle the parodist noted "So there was another Booby gone." Musical entertainments at the Gaiety were peppered with puns, introduced, not because they were apposite or relevant, but simply because they were puns. Somebody said, "I shall retire to my mansion," and Mr. George Grossmith junior, quick as thought, replied "Don't mansion it!" and the house rocked with laughter. Then, as is the fate of many forms of humour, puns ceased to be in demand, and in the conversation and literature of to-day they are not held in serious esteem.

Puns perhaps may be best defined as linguistic practical jokes and are certainly allied to the better known form of that class of humour. Practical jokes, like puns, have nothing intrinsically funny about them, but they make a strong appeal to that primitive instinct in man which is to observe their disconcerting effect on their victims. In the history of entertainment they are sporadic and epidemic. Even the Olympic-souled Pericles had to giggle at a prank of his nephew's, and it must please the most serious to read how Mark Antony gave a fishing-party, and arranged that divers should fasten large dead fish to Cleopatra's line as often as she submerged her bait. . . . The most unlikely people, we learn to our amazement, practised them. The Prince Consort, as a youth, attending a performance at the Opera House at Coburg threw several capsules containing sulphuretted hydrogen from his box among the occupants of the stalls who were driven, as by an outbreak of fire, from their seats by the intolerable smell. Or when his Cousin Linette came to a ball at his father's house, he filled the pockets of her cloak with soft cheese, in order to observe her dismay when she thrust her hands into them. No doubt he abandoned such crudities when he grew up, but both he and Queen Victoria immensely enjoyed the cognate jokes with which chance and circumstances regaled them, such as a footman tripping over the rumpled edge of a rug, or dropping a tray laden with glasses. Indeed Lord Granville, who was a most witty talker, said that when Minister in Waiting at Balmoral, he never bothered himself to tell them his best stories, because he found that if he pretended to pinch his finger in the door he roused a far more heartfelt mirth. In the mid-Victorian age practical jokes had a great vogue, for the Prince of Wales, inheriting the taste perhaps from his father, regarded them with the highest approval, and the world of gaiety and fashion was eager to follow so exalted a leader. His shooting parties at Sandringham produced the most ingenious and unexpected surprises for suitable guests. Apple-pie beds and booby traps abounded and sleeves of nightshirts firmly sewn together at the wrists.

Lord Charles Beresford was an adept at these inventions: one night he procured a cock from the poultry-yard, gave him a dope, and tethered him underneath the bed of a slightly pompous member of the House of Lords. Before morning the dope wore off, and the bird hailed the day with his usual lustiness. But Lord Charles was considered even by his admirers to have gone a little too far when he inserted among the sweetmeats for dessert at a friend's small smart dinner-party some tablets of a new French laxative called Tamar Indien. They were attractive and sparkling in appearance, and had a pleasant taste. . . . Then the epidemic wore itself out, and I do not think that there was another attack of it till the Bright Young People spread it again in 1919. They rang up the Fire Brigade from houses where they had been dining, and watched its arrival from the other side of the street. Or they sent anonymous letters to prigs and persons of propriety saying they knew their guilty secret, or they telephoned to social aspirants dinner-invitations from the most distinguished houses. But the epidemic soon died out again. There was a certain savagery about the Bright Young People that was altogether alien to the proper spirit, and their search for fun led to more than one tragic accident.

In spite of the eminent practitioners I have mentioned, I record my vote against all practical jokes deliberately devised. They should not be planned: they should be left to the blind fortuitous working of natural forces, and then I confess that like most other people (only they will not own up to it) the cave-man's mirth bubbles within me, and I should account myself a prig not to be amused. I like occasionally to see trivial embarrassments occurring, through nobody's devising, to dignified people. A Bishop's hat blowing off in a high wind (especially if the Bishop, as my father did, enjoys it too): a Mayor, as I was once privileged to behold, essaying to walk backwards upstairs in front of a Royal personage, and through stepping on his scarlet robe, suddenly sitting down on the step; or, as Thackeray recounted, the host at a dinner-party, intent on carving a duck, and causing the bird to leap from the dish, and deposit itself in the lap of the lady he had taken down to dinner—these little accidents, as I say, give me a secret joy. Even the sight of a man sitting down on the top-hat which he has put in his chair to keep his place, makes me quiver with laughter which I have not quite learned to suppress. It brings back to my mind a scene I once witnessed in which this incident was presented with such dramatic embellishments as the greatest of playwrights would be proud to have invented. . . . On a dark afternoon at Victoria Station, I had secured the last corner seat in a compartment for six persons. A moment afterwards there entered a large man in a top-hat who looked offended at there being no corner seat for him. He put his hat down on one of the two remaining seats, and went out again to the bookstall. While he was gone, another traveller came in, who, in the gloom, did not see the absentee's hat, and sat down heavily on it. He sprang up, and began to work out the situation with consummate art. He swiftly stroked the disordered nap on his sleeve, and deftly smoothed the cracks he had made in the fabric, watched by the gallery with the intensest interest. All my sympathy was with him, for the poor wretch was doing his best to repair the damage, and he must have been asking himself "Shall I get it done before the owner returns?" When he had finished his hurried valeting, he replaced the hat, and sitting down in the vacant seat effaced himself behind his paper. . . . That seemed like the curtain. Little did I guess how sublime a *dénouement* was to follow. Just before the train started, the owner returned. He forgot he had put his hat on his seat, and sat down on it himself. It was impossible for us, who had breathlessly watched this drama unfold, to help laughing, and he glared angrily round much vexed by our mirth. But we could not, without betraying the man whom Providence had so miraculously protected, explain the true reason why we laughed. One could not say "We are not, sir, laughing at your little mishap (though that was very funny, too) but because the gentleman sitting opposite you, and reading his paper so diligently, etc., etc."

Apt and incongruous, with the added spice of fortuitousness, was the remarkable experience of the retired Archdeacon who lived in Brighton. He was an elderly man with a long white beard, who did much good work among the poor, and went to mattins every morning in St. Michael's church. There was living in the same parish an elderly maiden lady, full of charitable works, who also worshipped every morning at the same church as the Archdeacon, and sat in the pew immediately in front of him. On Friday morning the Litany was always said at mattins, and it so happened that the lady, growing fatigued with such lengthy genuflection, raised herself from her knees, and sat quietly back in her pew. Presently she was aware of a tickling sensation on her neck, and at once concluded that some strands of her back hair had come down. She felt with her hand and found there was some loose hair there; so, with a few deft adjustments of hairpins, she secured them again. When the Litany was over, the Archdeacon attempted to rise from his knees and found that he was tethered to the lady in front, and could not move: she simultaneously felt that some mysterious force was pulling at the back of her neck. He was the first to perceive what had happened and in an indignant whisper he said to her: "You have pinned my beard into your back hair. Release it at once."

I like these surprises. They savour, it is true, of practical jokes, but their spontaneous, accidental quality lifts them high above the heavy deliberateness of things thought out. Dean Inge, in one of his suggestive articles, attributed the violent and grotesque colouring that adorns certain monkeys to a sense of humour on the part of the Creator. I do not know whether his theory can be brought into line with the doctrines of Darwinism, nor whether he would think it humorous if the Creator had given all Inges green tips to their noses as if they were about to play billiards with them. But it permits us to put the perception of the ludicrous among the higher attributes of fallen man. Accidents to top-hats and to the beards of Archdeacons may be meant to lead us higher.

Thus, anyhow, I interpret Dean Inge, and, on the subject of such alleviation to the woes of this vale of misery, I must quote another Dean, Dick Sheppard. He was constantly prostrated by illness, but whenever an ounce of energy returned, he spent a pound of it, and lived his life of perpetual self-sacrifice and devotion with an inimitable gaiety which sometimes puzzled his less discerning disciples. I once sent him a very frivolous book I had written, and his acknowledgment of it was exactly characteristic of him. "I wonder why people who say their prayers don't thank God for aspirin, Phillips's patent soles, E. F. Benson, Jane Austen and Charlie Chaplin and other real soul-filling things. . . . It does seem so silly that we should be expected to thank God because three coloured lads from Wanganui have been confirmed and not for real matters for rejoicing such as I have mentioned above."

CHAPTER XI

ELDERLY women, who think poorly of the reju-
venating effects of cosmetics, sometimes renew their
youth by recalling in volumes of attractive memoirs
the beautiful days when their unattainable charms set so
many young men a-sighing. Others do not need these
retrospective aids, for by some happy endowment of
nature they remain authentically young, and thus there
is no need to renew. My mother was one of these,
another whom I knew scarcely less well was the late Lady
Sandhurst. Age and she were incompatible terms.
Custom never staled the infinite consistency of her alertness or her childlike enjoyment. She had her share of
sorrows, but they never touched the receptiveness and
the elasticity which are the essential qualities of youth.

The surface of life never lost its brightness for her.
She found "treats" everywhere, small entrancing surprises; the conduct of the ducks on the Serpentine, when
she took her walk in Hyde Park; a barrel organ of the old
type, with one leg and a red-coated monkey sitting on
the top, huskily grinding out "The Lost Chord"; the
changing of the Guard at Buckingham Palace; the changing
of the traffic lights, then a new institution; the passing
of an aeroplane. She hurried up to London when, during
the war, a German bomb was dropped close behind her
house, and was immensely interested in the strange
manner in which some windows had been blown in and

others blown out. . . . "Such an *odd* bomb, my dear: I can't understand it"; and she made light of the horrid mess it had caused in her drawing-room. She had the genuine Jane Austen eye. Whether she directed it on barrel organs or bombs she saw with that uniquely humorous perception, and never omitted to turn its kindly but ironical searchlight on herself. One night her neighbour at dinner, who had been conversing with the lady on his left, whisked suddenly round on her and said: "You are sixty, aren't you?" . . . "I was rather surprised at such an unusual question," she told me later in the evening, "but I thought to myself, 'Where's the sense of an old woman like me minding about her age, so let's be honest! Besides he thinks me younger than I am.' So I said to him 'Well, I'm a little more than sixty!' The poor man was covered with confusion: he explained that he hadn't meant *that*. He had been talking to his neighbour of the difficulty of remembering the numbers of one's friends' houses, and he had been saying that he always knew. So to prove it, he asked me if I wasn't sixty; 60 Eaton Square. Do you think I ought to have guessed what he meant? But it's too late now."

Lord Sandhurst had been Governor of Bombay, and shortly before the war in 1914 he was appointed Lord Chamberlain to King George V. With her Jane Austen mind his wife was made and predestined for the rôle this gave her. She revelled, like a child, in palaces and pomp and ceremony, and, simultaneously she regarded such as the setting for a splendid charade, in which she was playing a part, with real tiaras and Koh-i-noors and her husband actually walking backwards before Majesties. It was as if she was performing in a dramatic version of Thackeray's

The Rose and the Ring, and yet when the pomp and ceremony was over it was still real, just as in the immortal
fairy story King Valoroso XXIV called from his dressing-
room next morning to his wife: "My dear, let us have
sausages for breakfast. Remember Prince Bulbo is with
us."

There was some great State function on her first visit
to Windsor, and when, exhausted with long standing
she tottered up to bed, she was thrilled to observe that
one of the blankets on her couch bore the crowned
monogram of George IV and another that of William IV.
"I got heated in the night," she told me, "and cast off these
two monarchs and slept with their niece." As Prince
Regent George IV was a great admirer of the works of
Jane Austen. He conveyed to her that he hoped she
would write a novel about the House of Hanover, and
said that he would give her all facilities for research. Had
these included a visit to bedrooms at Windsor, it would
have been a safe bet that she would have made a similar
discovery about blankets or what not, and have experienced
the same thrilled interest. . . . The Sandhursts were
lent Abergeldie for a month in several summers: it had
been King Edward VII's Highland residence when he was
Prince of Wales, and surely the shade of Jane Austen
rejoiced when Lady Sandhurst discovered in some great
cupboard in her bedroom an antique hip-bath with the
initials P.W. on it. And had Jane Austen lived at 60
Eaton Square, she would certainly have asked the garden-
committee to assign to her a small strip of flower-bed
opposite her house, to plant, at her own expense, as she
pleased. It would never have come to very much (nor
did it in the case of Lady Sandhurst), but she would

surely on one summer day have taken a friend to a high storey in her house to give him a better sight of the solitary geranium that had blossomed. And he, I hope, would have been sufficiently in tune with her to tell her that she must give a garden-party in its honour. Yet another Jane Austen touch. One night, dining at her house, I found myself, after the ladies had left us, sitting next a Duke. The work of mastication being over, he removed his false teeth and put them in his trouser pocket. I made haste to tell her and hear what Jane Austen would have made of that. "Perfect!" she said. "Only the bluest of bloods can do that without a loss of caste!"

Not physically robust, she had an immense store of quiet vitality and an invincible courage. Late in life, while staying in the Isle of Wight, she slipped while walking back to her bedroom from her bath, fracturing her thigh-bone close up to the hip-joint. In agonizing pain she made up her mind that she would not be a nuisance in a friend's house, and must be moved back to Eaton Square at once. She was certain of this also, that she was going to make a complete recovery and be not a whit the worse. It was a long business, for such a fracture, even in the young, is apt to prove a permanent disablement, but she never had a moment's doubt about herself. She made a festival of every stage of her recovery, of the day when she first shuffled across her room, of the day when she first hobbled out of doors with two sticks. I was staying with her in the country soon after these walks were prescribed, to be increased gradually in length. She came in almost weeping with pain and fatigue, lay down on a sofa for a while, and then proudly

said, "I got as far as the kitchen-garden. Isn't that grand?
. . . Next week perhaps to the front gate." And at
last the sticks could be left behind, and she walked the
length of the Serpentine again. To the original disaster
she never gave a thought: it was as if she had been born
with a broken leg and by a series of blessings showered
on her had gradually acquired the power of locomotion.

She was a daughter of Matthew Arnold, and by her
first marriage to a brother of Lord Kimberley's she had
one son, Roger Wodehouse; after Lord Sandhurst's death,
his brother Jim Mansfield lived with her. So every year
on her birthday she gave a dinner-party to the clans of
whom she was the connecting link and to a few close
friends, and not only was this party pure Jane Austen,
but Jane Austen herself in the person of our hostess was
giving it, because it was the proper and traditional thing
to do on her birthday. She was much concerned about
its success, and all the time she watched its progress
with the kindly, observant, authentic eye. The clans had
not very much in common, and I expect that few of
them met again till the next birthday came round, for
there were sudden recognitions, and an Arnold said to a
Wodehouse: "Yes, of course! Surely we met here last
year!" The style was Victorian: we went down to dinner
arm-in-arm, and the men talked to their partners on the
right till about the time that they had eaten their fish,
and then taking advantage of a pause they turned to the
lady on the left. Mrs. Humphry Ward, an Arnold
cousin, was invariably there, and first Jim Mansfield
devoted himself to her, and then Roger Wodehouse, a
high-church parson at Oxford took his turn. Afterwards,

when the men joined the ladies again upstairs we found them all sitting in a group together, but on our entry they opened out like a fan and the men inserted themselves in vacant places, and engaged in dialogues. I, being a literary gent, was generally instructed to insert myself next Mrs. Humphry Ward, but we could not talk about books because we had never read the same ones. These dialogues, as one glanced round, recalled sometimes the progress of luggage trains. They slowed down, and the conversationalists like trucks, gave out bumping sounds, "chunk, chunk, chunk," as they came to a standstill; then they got a move on again, and the couplings cheerfully resounded with "chink, chink, chink" as they started off again. Sometimes our hostess brought out, as stimulants, ancient family albums of photographs of Arnolds and Wodehouses and Mansfields, and identifications of members of the three clans as boys and girls took place. There were note-books of Matthew Arnold in which he had jotted down passages of books he had read which struck him, and Cousin Mary Ward and I marvelled at the scope of his reading. I think Lady Sandhurst was a little relieved sometimes when the butler said that the car for one of the guests had come, for the others would then soon see how late it was and ask for taxis, and tell her how much they had enjoyed it. But nobody had enjoyed it more than Jane Austen: she had been making notes all the time for some chapter in a book of hers which, alas, seems to be out of print.

Intermezzo on a dog

Walt Whitman protests somewhere that for the future he intends to live entirely with animals (cows I think he says) because they do not make him sick with talking about their souls. No one has loved the human race more than he, but coming across that illuminating passage, I felt I knew exactly what he meant and warmed to it. I did not see my way to living with a cow, but the house—I do not know how it happened—had long been dogless, and the fire kindled. So when my cook on holiday in Wales asked if she might bring home a black collie puppy I hailed the suggestion. When I returned to London one summer from the pickling fountains of Droitwich (where I had been thinking too much not about my soul but my body) he was carried upstairs to be introduced, for he had not yet learned how to negotiate such puzzling contrivances as staircases. At once and automatically he was Taffy, globular in figure with a black coat of short and curly puppy hair, a white shirt front and white tips to his paws. He had gay, inquiring brown eyes, and he set himself diligently to study the domestic etiquette of genteel houses.

From the first it was clear that we had got hold of a very intelligent young gentleman, and he very soon mastered domestic etiquette. But he manifested also odd signs of knowing things which he had never studied, and which it is difficult to refer to instinct. His father and mother both came from generations of working dogs, but Taffy had been brought up to London as soon as he no longer needed his mamma to feed him, and had never been out with the shepherd. But a very queer thing happened. One of his new friends was playing with him and teaching him to retrieve a piece of rolled-up paper which he threw about the room. Taffy missed seeing where it was thrown, and his instructor with a downward movement of his hand pointed to where it lay on the floor. That is the gesture a shepherd makes when he wants his dog to efface himself and wait for further orders, and Taffy instantly lay down with his head flat on his paws. Again, he was taken for a walk in Hyde Park, and there, careering about, he sighted some sheep feeding near by. He stopped with a paw up, and then made a wide circuit round them exactly as a trained dog would do. This is rather mysterious: it looks as if, through the generations of his working ancestors, he had inherited knowledge which was not instinctive with them, but was the result of education.

My house soon passed into his guardianship, and he had a cordial welcome for all visitors, upstairs or downstairs, whom his people brought in. But he required that guarantee, for he could not allow unvouched-for folk to enter, and a tradesman, accustomed to let himself in and go to the kitchen with his goods was met with furious barking. Taffy shed his short puppy-coat, and put up a sweeping black plume on his tail and plumes at the back of his forepaws, and round his neck a silky Elizabethan ruff. He took but little interest in other dogs, with one exception, and consecrated himself to the service of his adopted people. A young dog's brain should be kept alert and active, especially if he comes of a stock that is accustomed to think. He enjoys having tasks set him on which he must exercise his wits. He went out for a short early walk, and then accompanied the bearer of my breakfast-tray up to my bedroom, carrying the kitchen-book which contained my cook's suggestions for the meals of the day. This was discipline, for the kitchen-book was a slim paper-covered volume which seemed specially designed to be firmly grasped in the paws and torn to shreds. Having resisted this temptation as he mounted three flights of stairs Taffy jumped on to my bed and gave me the book. He carried it down to the kitchen again, and went out for his morning's shopping. At the butcher's he was sometimes entrusted with his own dinner, pieces of raw liver wrapped up in thick paper, and he carried it home running at the mouth with the anticipation of what should then follow. Later in the morning he heard a step coming down from upstairs, and at that he bundled up the kitchen stairs and waited by the door into the hall, for that step certainly meant a run in the garden of the square. The key to the garden with a wooden tab attached to it was kept in the sitting-room by the front-door, and it was his duty to carry this to the garden gate. Very soon he made the correct connection between the key and the garden and fetched the key himself. Sometimes it had been put for educational purposes, in some unusual place, and then he searched for it. Often there were small dogs in the garden, Pekinese particularly, but he took no notice of their yappings, except when they fussed him by running about under him. Then he lifted a leg and, having performed the contemptuous office on any small Oriental who chanced to be there, he trotted away.

There was exercise in the park in the afternoon, a little slumber, and then work began again. Taffy went out with one of his friends to fetch the evening paper from the vendor in the Brompton Road and carry it home. After a week or two he grasped the hang of this expedition, and of his own accord he trotted on ahead to the vendor and waited, very much pleased with himself, for his paper to be given him. That became the custom (for the man knew that somebody would follow with the price of Taffy's purchase) and Taffy got impatient if he was not served immediately and was known to snatch a paper which had just been handed to somebody else. Occasionally this expedition started too soon; and the last edition had not yet come in, and then he was given an old poster folded up. Otherwise he stood there barking, and impeded traffic. One evening on his way home he met the only dog in whom he felt the slightest interest, a large Alsatian lady of strong sex appeal; he dropped his paper on the pavement to have a few words with her, and the lady stood on it. Taffy made his decision without delay, for, as Queen Victoria wrote of John Brown "his sense of duty ever went before every feeling of self."[1] He pushed her off it and trotted home with it.

He attended lunch and dinner, lying on the floor and forbidden, under pain of expulsion, to call attention to himself and nudge guests with his nose. But there was a chair set for him next me, and if he thought that something smelt unusually pleasant, he might jump on to his chair and speak to me. Speaking was not barking, which was not allowed, but making a low melodious singing noise. (Melba said that his voice-production was the best she had ever heard. She sang to us afterwards herself, and her voice-production was very good, too!) One night I had not noticed that he was sitting on his chair and had spoken. With the idea of putting his paw on my arm to remind me, he put it by mistake into a dish that was being handed me. Everybody laughed, and Taffy

[1] *More Leaves from the Journal of a Life in the Highlands*, p. 223.

was quite aware that they were laughing at him. He jumped down from his chair, deeply offended.

A domestic problem that gave a little anxiety at first was his relations with my young black cat. Peter had come to live in the London house while Taffy was with his family down at Rye, and he did not approve of the advent of a dog who, while he was daintily lapping his milk of a morning, swallowed the whole of it in a few comprehensive licks, and chased the saucer about the floor with his tongue to make sure he had secured the last drop. Peter leaped on to the dresser and regarded this rude black robber with malignant eyes. For a while he had his meals served there out of reach, but presently he developed a *schwärm*. When Taffy was asleep he crept near him, sat down and watched him, and then put out a sheathed paw and touched him gently on the nose. Taffy opened an eye, saw who it was, and went to sleep again. Presently he began to like Peter: he was seen, as if rather ashamed of such a weakness, surreptitiously to lick Peter's face, he let Peter play with his ball, and before long, Peter cuddled up close to him as he lay on the floor. They were both black as night, and silky haired: it was impossible to see where dog stopped and cat began.

As soon as Taffy saw his other home at Rye, he fell for it: from the first moment it enchanted him. But he did not enchant the large marmalade-coloured cat who lived there. Sandy spat and scolded, and never in the eight years they were there together did they become friendly. Again and again they were on the verge of a scrap, but they got to understand that they must put up with each other as best they could. The garden particularly took

Taffy's fancy; he was quick to learn that the lawn and the path were his but not the flower-beds, and when he bit off a small bough from my miniature oak-tree he did it from the path. . . . His duties presented no fresh features, except that when he went shopping in the morning he carried a market basket, like the ladies of Rye: every evening he went to fetch the paper, which he brought to the garden-room. He understood that Sandy had a right to use the garden (and even sit in the flower-beds, since no one could prevent him) but other cats were not allowed. He galloped round in search of trespassers, and if he encountered Sandy he jumped over him. . . . The dogs of Rye liked him as little as he liked them: I think he gave himself airs as being a fashionable London dog on holiday. There was no fight, because he was not a fighter by nature and nobody felt inclined to be the aggressor against so large and powerful an adversary; but there were critical moments, when he and two or three others walked round in circles on tiptoe, very slowly and stiffly with various rituals for which I can offer no explanation. When dogs are behaving like that, any interference on the part of owners will almost certainly precipitate a row. Left to themselves they will probably solve the dangerous situation by these diplomatic exchanges and go on their ways without loss of prestige. . . .

There were expeditions to the sea. The sea proved not to be drinkable, but it was fringed with sand dunes among which on his first visit, he put up a rabbit. They were difficult country for hunting, for the steep slopes poured down avalanches of dry sand that smothered the feet, but the hope of some day finding another rabbit never left him. It was thirsty work under a summer sun, and so a bottle of proper water was carried by the expedition, and after Taffy had finished with the sand dunes, it was tilted into his mouth and he was very adroit in swallowing without spilling much. To get to the sea he had to travel by the steam-tram from Rye, which started on the far side of the River Rother, and if his afternoon walk lay in that direction, Taffy used to rush on ahead, get into a tram if there was one standing in the station, and wait for his friends. If they did not intend to go to the sea, it was disappointing after so pretty a piece of inductive reasoning to be hauled out. At tea-time the dining-room was reserved exclusively for Sandy, for that was his hour for drinking vast quantities of milk, and the presence of the blasted black dog filled him with such disgust that his appetite completely vanished. Punctually at ten every night, when drinks were brought out to the garden-room, Taffy made his last tour of the garden, barking loudly, so that any trespassing cat had plenty of time to get away, and with the sense of duty done, he retired to his rug in the pantry.

CHAPTER XII

MEANTIME I had been going through that enormous collection of typed unpublished manuscripts by Arthur which he had left me without any directions or even hints as to his wishes about them. For some years before his death he had been bringing out not less than three books every year, and there would have been more had not his publisher pointed out that this supply was up to the demand: simultaneously he was Master of the College, and next year to be Warden of the Fishmongers' Company. But even with such an outlet there was still this immense accumulation. About many of them there was no question: I do not suppose he meant ever to publish them himself. There was, for instance, a series of sermons he had preached in Magdalene Chapel: there were many lectures and addresses he had given. These lectures had been written at top speed; they neither contained, nor were meant to contain, any fresh or original aspect of their subject, and though at any speed it was impossible for him not to write with grace and charm, since that was the manner that was natural to him, they had served their purpose when he had delivered them. They were appreciations, pleasant to read, and they must have been extremely pleasant to listen to. Then there were two bulky volumes of ghost stories. Most of them had been written some years before his death, and there were no indications that he had ever thought about bringing them out. But a couple of them, sufficient to make a volume, seemed to me quite admirable. They were carefully worked out, they brewed that atmosphere of uneasiness and apprehension that at the proper moment culminates in horror. These I published.

There was a volume of poems: there again one had to determine what the author would have wished about them. Most of them dated from twenty years before when he had published several volumes of poetry himself. They had made no mark, and their reception had disappointed him. From that time he wrote no more poetry. He had not the lyrical urge which compels a man to use verse as the natural expression of himself. I concluded that these poems had been weeded out, though kept, by himself when he selected those which made up his last volume.

During the last eighteen months of his life Arthur had published two full-length novels, *Chris Gascoyne* and the *House of Menerdue*; another *The Canon* came out soon after his death. They had passed almost unnoticed. Among these unpublished works I found four more novels of the same *genre*. One of them, *Guy*, had clipped to it a letter from John Lane the publisher, to whom Arthur had sent it fourteen or fifteen years ago. Lane wrote that he would consent to publish it, but did not anticipate any sort of success for it; he would therefore offer no advance on royalties. A second letter from him showed that on the receipt of this Arthur had sent for the manuscript back. It seemed clear that he had not offered it elsewhere, or these letters from John Lane would not have been pinned to it, but that he had let it lie on his shelves, while he wrote more and yet more. Another of them had been completed within a month from the time he had begun it, and though one could imagine how an author whose mind was saturated with a theme long meditated over could gush forth in this abundance under strong emotional pressure, it was impossible to find sign of such in any of these novels. The pressure with him had been his own intense pleasure in writing. They had been an effortless pastime, an inexhaustible improvisation. As far as I could judge from the dates attached to some of these manuscripts, they had been put aside till a few months had elapsed since his latest publication, but meantime the incessant outpouring went on, and it was the book on which he had last been engaged that went to his publisher first; hence the great accumulation. Once or twice he drew off the flood water by publishing anonymously.

I made inquiries, and found that there was little interest in these manuscripts. Two books of his, the ghost stories and a novel, had appeared after his death and they had fallen flat. Fraternal piety dissuaded rather than encouraged me to repeat the experiment. I did not want, even if I had been able to find a publisher for them, to see them floating down the huge perennial flood of fiction without causing a ripple, and it looked as if he had abandoned many of them himself. Reluctantly, after reading them, I put them back on to their shelves.

There was another memorial to him, of which I was in charge, in the church at Rye, ready now to be unveiled, and in the inscription below it can be read the name of his dear benefactress whom he had never seen. This window in the south transept had been filled with

stained glass in the style of the windows in Chartres
Cathedral, mosaic glass with round medallions enclosed
in it. These are pictures, verse by verse, of the *Omnia
Opera*, the sun, moon and stars that praise the Lord,
the lightnings and seas and the green things upon the
earth, the whales that move in the waters and the beasts
and cattle. Among the fowls of the air I insisted on an
avocet in memory of the bird who flew with the shelduck
at Salthouse, and in the final medallion Arthur in his red
doctor's gown knelt at a fald-stool, with the court at
Magdalene for background. Lord Davidson, Archbishop
of Canterbury, came down to unveil it. He had retired
this year, at the age of eighty, after fifty years of marriage
and twenty-five of archiepiscopate. He was to receive
the Freedom of the Borough after the ceremony, and as
we lunched at Lamb House he made inquiry about the
privileges it conferred on him. First, by a statute never
repealed, he could not, as a Freeman of Rye, be arrested
in the streets of the Borough: "So if I get drunk," he asked
"on this delicious hock, will nobody take me up?" The
second privilege was that when the Mayor extended to
him the hand of Fellowship, he had the right to kiss the
Mayor, and he asked if the Mayor was a lady. . . . The
Mayoral procession with its huge silver maces came
to Lamb House to escort him to the church (little
did I think that before long on a similar scarlet occasion
I should be hobbling behind them, and should myself be
immune from arrest). The bells pealed, those bells that
had once been taken to Dieppe by the French on one of
their raids on Rye, and in his address the Archbishop
spoke of Arthur's love for the green things of the earth,
and the birds and beasts. . . .

I do not know of any modern glass that approaches it in jewellery of colour. Shortly after a friend of mine came to see it. I could not go with him to the church, but told him that the verger would direct him. He wrote to me saying that at first he thought the verger must have made a mistake, for the window which he pointed out was so evidently of ancient glass.

During these three years since Arthur's death I had received occasional news from Brooks at Capri. Yet it was scarcely news: it was chiefly a charmingly written record of the absence of news. Perhaps Dr. Axel Munthe had been up at Anacapri but Brooks had not seen him: perhaps an American friend had not been able to come to Europe with his yacht as he had intended. If he had, Brooks would have gone on a cruise with him to the Greek Islands, which he longed to do (though I doubt whether he could have brought himself to make such a move, when it actually confronted him). Perhaps the plumbago which he had planted against the wall of the Villa Salvia had not flowered; perhaps throughout the summer he had hardly been down to bathe; sun and sea tired rather than refreshed him. There were indications—one could hardly call them hints—that funds were low. I knew that he was grateful for help, and I rather liked the independent pride that cashed the cheques and yet treated them as if they were a *gaffe* on my part to which it was not tactful to allude. (I daresay he treated others in the same way, but that is no concern of mine.) He seemed to be content to be just a static point with the seasons drifting past him. That, I confess, irritated me, but where was the use of being irritated? I had long known that he was incapable of doing anything that involved effort. Then something stirred again. He had been reading D. H. Lawrence, and Lawrence became to him a beacon, a lighthouse casting a ray across the dreary waste of modern literature, unillumined since the days of Meredith or Walter Pater. Many of his friends were writers of some standing. Among them were the authors of such books as *Of Human Bondage*, and *South Wind* and *Sinister Street*, but he had taken only the mildest interest in these, turning the pages, and grunting a little and shutting them up. Under this stimulus, I suppose, he sent me amazing news. The Greek epigrams had been given their final polish, and he was sending them to a certain publisher whom—how long ago?—I had recommended when he had satisfied himself. This same letter spoke of his own health which was giving him trouble. He made little of it; he had been to see the local doctor whose drastic treatments gave him relief for the time; presently no doubt he would be quite restored.

I heard from him only once more. He said he had been very poorly, and suddenly he realized that these treatments had never touched the root of the trouble, whatever it was. He was going next week to Naples, to enter a clinic of a very eminent Italian doctor, where he would be X-rayed and observed. That was a dreadful worry: the cost of it, he said, would swallow up all the capital he had left, while, if an operation was advised he had no idea what he should do. But he hoped that they could patch him up, for in a month's time now the American friend would be here with his yacht, and would take him for the cruise among the Greek Islands. . . . The house on the Via Tragara, which he had told me about before, was practically finished. He had inquired as to the rent, and this seemed moderate, and he thought that they would probably accept less. Would I take it? Another winter in the bleak Villa Salvia would finish him off. And had I read *Lady Chatterley's Lover*? "A lyrical bed of roses with a broad trickle from a cess-pool running through it."

This letter was a shock. I had no idea that there was anything seriously wrong with his health, nor that he was on the brink of insolvency. I greatly admired the pluck with which he faced the apprehensions which must have been his, and the penury which he had to look forward to, even if they proved to be unfounded. I danced with exasperation at the calm proposal that I should take this new house in Capri for him to live in, because the Villa Salvia was so cold and he had nothing to live on. What it meant was that I should have to buy or furnish the house, spend a few months there, and for the whole year pay all the outgoings for him. It was a somewhat one-sided partnership. If he proposed that I should support him for the rest of his life, it was time to say so. . . . To continue to talk about sharing a house lacked candour. I wrote sending him some small sum to meet the immediate expenses in the clinic at Naples, and begged him to let me know his further news. I got no answer.

I learned the rest from the only friend he had left in Capri. There was no one else who bothered about him. He had gone over to Naples very cheerfully, and returned three days later. All that he had been told was that there was to be no operation. This friend went up to the Villa Salvia and found him evidently very ill. As she sat with him the post arrived, and it brought him a letter from the publishers to whom he had sent his translations. It told him that quite lately another volume of translations from Greek epigrams had appeared, and that in their opinion there would be no market for a similar book. They were therefore returning his manuscript to him. He died next day. No operation had been suggested because his case was inoperable: probably he did not know that. But the irony that ordained that his last contact with the world should be the knowledge that this little laboured book was on its way back to him seems gratuitously devilish. Perhaps he already lay shrouded in the shadow of death, and nothing really reached him. But that letter ought to have missed the post.

From any reasonable point of view his life had been a waste and a failure. But I am unreasonable and do not quite regard it as such. He was inexcusably indolent, he never took himself in hand, he dawdled and loitered year in year out. He never did a day's hard work, but translated his sonnets and his epigrams just as he fumbled at Beethoven's sonatas, appreciating his performance, enjoying the hideous result through a mist of self hypnosis. But he had fine perceptions, and a true sense of beauty and distinction. Somewhere beneath the ash of his laziness there burned the authentic fire. Literature was a passion with him, he disdained all that he considered second-rate, and perhaps the very fastidiousness of his taste was a bar rather than an aid to any sort of accomplishment. Browning tells us of the scholar who aimed at a million and missed it by a unit. Brooks aimed at a million and missed it by a million. But I respect that aim; it was sincere, and, though utterly barren in result, there was no sort of pose or sham about it. I daresay that if instead of aiming at a million, he had aimed at a unit, he would have missed that too, and in that case I should have found nothing to say about him that could warrant pen on paper, for a man who aims low and is eternally incompetent of hitting his mark, does not arouse either pity or interest. But to aim high, though with whatever futility and indolence, is a different matter.

I had by now managed to settle into that house of my mind of which I have previously spoken, having thrown away a great deal of the rubbish that encumbered it and of the furnishings which were not my own. What was left was scantier than I had anticipated, but, at any rate, it had a right to be there. Then there were toys which had to be replaced, for physically my activities were much restricted. Skates and golf clubs and tennis balls were no longer any use nor were field-glasses for the bloodless pursuit of birds. These had occupied not only many hours in my day but many niches in my mind, and the last things I meant to surrender were amusements, for without them life would be an intolerable business. There was the garden which would be a stand-by from spring to autumn, while for the dark months I had chess and the piano and bridge. Like poor Brooks I set high standards before me, and secretly in my fool's heart I meditated on the names of Alekhine and Harold Samuel and Culbertson. And I could enthusiastically collect almost anything except postage stamps, so I was for ever peering into the windows of the curiosity shops in which Rye is so rich, for undetected gems. The pleasure of collecting lies largely in the *chasse* and I scrutinized these windows with the minutest care, for if there was anything of distinction it would probably be some inconspicuous object which others had passed over. Prizes were rare (else they would not be prizes) but I came back one day with a silver "kitchen" pepper-pot of the time of Queen Anne, well marked, which stood modestly among little repoussé Dutch boxes; and on a day of days, with a Pentelic marble head of a statuette of the young Apollo, of the finest work of the fourth century: there it was dumbly beckoning from a shelf of modern Dresden china and forged Roman lamps. *Per contra*, I once returned hugging a brass ewer which, so the seductive vendor told me, was "very unique." It proved to be very unique indeed. An expert friend examined it for me, and demonstrated to me that it was made of three heterogeneous objects, deftly soldered together. The body was that of a hot-water jug, the handle was a curved bracket-support to a shelf, and the domed lid was a door handle sawn in half. I did not venture into brass again.

My other business, that of getting some sort of status again as a writer, was proving very difficult. The backwater into which my industrious laziness had drifted me, had carried me a long way, and by diligently reading some of the admired authors of the day I perceived how completely, as regards fiction, I had dropped out. Some I found hard to follow, and others, as regards style, had acquired lucidity by a blank disregard of euphony: they were full of jerks. To make your meaning clear, as everybody knows, though your meaning may be difficult to grasp, is an essential of decent prose, but I did not care so much about this jerkiness. I had always found an æsthetic pleasure in appreciating with the ear the sentences which the eye followed, and my ear was offended by the abrupt noises which it sensed below the print. I demand—for myself—that prose should have a certain intrinsic beauty of its own quite apart from the meaning it conveys. This beauty is quite consistent with the utmost lucidity and does not depend at all on decoration. The best example I know of it is the Gospels in the Authorised Version of the New Testament: their style reminds one of Holbein's portrait of the Duchess of Milan. To take a random passage, quite divorced, I must repeat, from the significance (to some) of its contents, I should choose this: "Come unto me all ye that labour and are heavy laden, and I will give you rest. Take my yoke upon you and learn of me, for I am meek and lowly in heart and ye shall find rest unto your souls." No one who has an ear for prose can fail to appreciate the perfection of that! And for economy and directness was there ever a story so well told as the parable of the Prodigal Son? Its subject has probably set many against it.

I am not a friend of the purple patch: in fact I dislike it exceedingly. It interrupts my pleasure in reading plain simple prose as much as these jerks. But I dislike it not because it is purple but because it is a patch. Prose of noble and sustained splendour is part of our great heritage of literature, and, in search of it, I go to the same volume from which I have quoted my example of lucid simplicity. In the Old Testament the books of Job and of the prophets furnish me with the most superb examples of that splendour. It therefore astonished me to find that others considered these to be tinsel from the Orient, and that, instead of the Old Testament being a corner-stone on which so much that is magnificent in the English tongue was founded, its influence had been extremely harmful and that a mistaken admiration for it had retarded the native and natural growth of the language towards its ultimate perfection. It was even quainter to find "The Bible" quoted as a single homogeneous source. Its contents are by many authors of varied styles and widely sundered ages.

I particularly studied the art of biography, for this now was the branch of literary work in which I intended to busy myself. Broadly speaking, the modern biographer seemed to conduct his dissections with the view primarily of exposing the littlenesses and defects of the character on whom he performed his marvellously skilful surgery: he must first be shown to be ludicrous. This was a natural and healthy reaction against the practice of Victorian biographers. To them death automatically transformed the eminent into miracles of wisdom and virtue, and in their hands they shed their humanity as a chrysalis sheds its shell. "De mortuis nil nisi bonum" was never a good formula for the biographer, but it had deteriorated into "De mortuis nil nisi bunkum," which was infinitely worse. Any fault or failing that made the memorialized ever so little lower than the angels was ruthlessly suppressed in the determination to produce a figure whose proper place was a stained-glass window. If he was of a miserly mind we were told that his playful little economies only endeared him to his friends: if he brutally swept aside anyone who stood in the way of his career, that he was a man of undeviating purpose: if he was a liar, that he had a glittering imagination. Sir Edmund Gosse, that witty and ardent biographer, applied these glowing colours far too excessively. In his reminiscences of R. L. Stevenson, he protested that he could not recall a single fault in the character of that very human personage; or in his life of Swinburne he told us that in one particular year the poet's health was more unsatisfactory than ever, which is a scarcely legitimate periphrasis for what he meant. Only in his book about his father did he exhibit that filial frankness which was soon to become so strong a characteristic of modern biography. But this reaction was now, perhaps, going to excessive lengths. Instead of suppressing a man's failings, the biographer made it his first care to suppress his fine qualities, or to present them in a ridiculous light, and to emphasize his faults to the point of falsity. No doubt this made more piquant reading, but the result was no less a caricature than the Victorian stained-glass window. Sons and daughters, remembering their young years, had unrivalled opportunities in this regard, and in place of the piety with which in Victorian days they had chiselled stainless marble monuments to their parents, they now scattered their deformed bones about the pit, and the Levitical prohibition against seething a kid in its mother's milk became an injunction on the kid to seethe its mother in filial corrosiveness. A touch of reticence, of reverence, was contrary to the whole spirit of the new Mosaic law.

Fiction, in the hands of new and distinguished authors, was undergoing a corresponding sea-change. It was pickled in brine, and over its pages moved pillars of salt, which Lot's wife observed without prejudice flying from the Cities of the Plain. It made its studies of morality in the monkey-house and followed its heroines to the water-closet. I was not shocked at these revelations, for I knew that such things happened, but I got tired of the fugal repetition of these subjects. I should have liked some of these authors, just for a change, to expose (even with a furtive air of betraying guilty secrets) fine impulses and high endeavour. The mirror which it is the function of Art to hold up to Nature, seemed to be always adjusted to reflect what lies below the belt: the heart and the brain (with the exception of the department of sexual urge) were outside the field of vision. I did not miss the message that this literature conveyed: it said, plainly enough, that sexual desire is as natural a craving as hunger or thirst, which everybody knew before. No doubt this boom in promiscuity was partly due to reaction, for an undue reticence had been Victorianly observed about sexual instincts as if they were inherently disgraceful, though when sanctified by the Voice that breathed o'er Eden, they became True Love. Now the reaction went too far: the faintest echo of the Voice that breathed o'er Eden spoiled everything. And the most unsatisfactory feature in these coitions was that the partners in them seemed to care for the act so much more than they cared for each other. They ceased to exist for each other when the desire was satisfied, and many of these stories, however daintily observed, had no more psychical significance than an account of a hungry man at his dinner. . . . There were of course many other authors who, already established, continued writing in their accustomed modes with their accustomed skill, but I was astonished to find through how monotonous a country the new fiction was passing, how lacking in wide prospects and far horizons. And I felt really sorry for these bloodless voluptuaries who got so little fun out of their amusements.

It was biography that occupied me most. I was not so antiquely-minded as to wish to go back to Victorian modes, but the delving for belittlement seemed to produce results which were equally wide of the truth. My chief danger, the foe by my fireside, was the facility with which I could write readably: that was a handicap rather than an asset, a temptation rather than a stimulus unless one had something definitely worth saying. My life of Drake had appeared and Edmund Gosse, far the most perceptive and best endowed of English critics had once again encouraged me when he wrote to tell me that novelists alone should be allowed to write biography. He meant, as he explained, that biography was primarily a study of character, and indeed I was far more concerned with what people were than what they did: to get as near as possible to the essential then was the ultimate aim. A man's achievements could be easily learned from the Dictionary of National Biography, but they were often a misleading clue, or, at any rate, did not lead to the centre. There were men of action, whose career had been one record of relentless success, but was only their façade. Lord Kitchener, for instance, all his life had gone from strength to strength, doing work in Egypt and South Africa which none but he could have handled, and finally he had saved England, in her hour of dark peril, raising, by sheer force of will an army of a million men, which was so much his own that it was known as Kitchener's Army. He might well have been thought to have embodied himself in what he had achieved. Yet he wrote to his best friend, one of the two human beings to whom he was not impenetrable, just before he embarked on the *Hampshire*: "I want to do better work before I get my release." Only he himself, the man that he *was*, knew what quality he had always missed in it, and that sentence was the key (though perhaps it was never turned in the lock) to the living-rooms behind the façade.

This, then, was the nature of my quest when I presently spent a year in the study of Charlotte Brontë. Already we knew more about the domestic circumstances of the three sisters and their brother than had been known about any family since the Flood, but apart from the mere setting of the scene, there was little reliable information about the actors.

Mrs. Gaskell was the first in the field. She was by no means an intimate friend of Charlotte's like Ellen Nussey. She wrote in the strictest Victorian tradition making her heroine, intellectually and morally, the pattern of perfection. She knew, for instance, that Charlotte had written the pitiful abject letters to Mr. Constantin Heger, for she quoted passages out of them, but omitted anything that bore on that: a heroine could not fall in love with another woman's husband. To emphasize the uncomplaining sufferings of her life she gave Charlotte for a father a man of almost maniacal brutality. Mr. Brontë slit into ribands his wife's new dress, he burned his children's new shoes, he fed them on starvation diet, and every evening fired against the church door the pistols he had loaded the night before. It was proved that these fables were invented by a servant who had been discharged from service at the Vicarage and when the book came out Mr. Brontë declared that he had not known he had an enemy in the world till his daughter's friend declared herself. Later in the book she gave so libellous an account of Branwell's relations with the mother of the boys to whom he was tutor—again to blacken the darkness and misery that surrounded Charlotte—that the threat of prosecution compelled her to withdraw it all with a public letter in the heading that she had no evidence.

Her successors in this service of passionate partisanship for Charlotte or Emily continued to falsify evidence or suppress it, or built on it theories that crumbled at a touch. I read everything that others had written about the family; I sifted and collated and compared, and I got so absorbed in this honest but unoriginal labour of exposing the errors in fact and inference into which my forerunners had fallen that when I came to read my typed manuscript I found I had arrived at nothing at which I had aimed. I had washed off some of the intolerable colouring which had been daubed on to the façade: I had demolished a good many of the fantastic and gimcrack edifices which had been run up round the lonely little parsonage, but where was the good of that unless on the cleared site I laid foundations that would stand more solid construction? So I scrapped all I had written and began again, not concerning myself with the work of others but only my own. Charlotte Brontë's novels were, of course, a fiery and vivid expression of herself and were, confessedly, autobiographical. But, as I studied her letters, it seemed to me that she both caricatured and idealized herself in her novels. It was in her letters that she revealed herself, her will of iron, and its pitiful surrenders, her own pitilessness with that minute trickle of infinite tenderness which ran through them. It was only thus that one could arrive anywhere near the truth about her, and I joyfully settled down to do an honest piece of work.

Beyond the west end of the garden there lay a small square plot of ground surrounded by brick walls. Henry James, years ago, had heard that a local builder was casting a constructive eye on it, and a house on the site would annihilate any privacy in his garden, for the occupants could command his lawn at point-blank range, as they took tea at the open windows. I have no idea how imminent the danger was, but the rumoured hint was enough, and he bought it. This was merely a defensive measure, and he had then leased it to a neighbour in Mermaid Street, allowing him to make an entrance into it from his side, and incorporate it in his garden. This neighbour had now died, and since it belonged to the Lamb House estate, I opened a hole in the wall between it and my garden to see if I could do anything with it. I never saw a more dejected spot. There was an aged pear-tree against one wall, there was a gnarled ampelopsis against another, and a discouraged buddleia languished in a sunless corner. The rest had degenerated into rubbish heaps, with a weed-ridden path curving aimlessly among overgrown and flowerless beds.

This ghost of a garden was framed on all sides by old brick walls, and there is no plot of ground that, thus encompassed, cannot be fashioned into a gem of a garden, however small. I carted away the rubbish heaps, I cut down the atrocious ampelopsis, and gathered bushels of snails from the wall behind it. I transplanted the buddleia, and dug deeply over the rest. On the south the top windows of houses in Watchbell Street overlooked me, but a high close-meshed trellis on the top of the wall pulled down their blinds for them. On all other sides the walls gave complete seclusion, and there I was with this small square space, which I could design as I willed. At once I saw what could be made of it, a secret garden, and withal an outdoor sitting-room of which no inch was visible from the surface of the earth. There should be broad flower-beds below three of the walls with paths of crazy pavement in front of them and crazy pavement close along the fourth wall which faced north, leading to a roofed shelter in the corner with two sides open to the garden. The square thus enclosed should be turfed and a round flower-bed cut in the centre of it. I would build a short pillar of old bricks in the middle of the flower-bed and place thereon a marble bust of the young Augustus (a replica of that in the British Museum) which I had lately bought in Rye because I could not bear to leave it in the shop.

It was autumn, the right time for laying grass and planting out the spring garden. The turf arrived on a cart, like pieces of brown Swiss roll with green jam, Augustus was placed on his pillar, and a *fond* of forget-me-nots planted round him with Darwin tulips star-scattered among them. In the other beds I planted the common flowers of spring, more tulips and daffodils and narcissi and scarlet anemones and wall-flowers with borders of aubrietia in front and summer perennials against the wall. The crazy pavement was laid down along the wall facing north with pockets in it for the clematises (Jackmanni and Miss Bateman) that hate the sun. In the corner I built the shelter, twelve feet square with tiled floor and wooden walls; open on two sides to the garden. Against the sunny walls I planted Mermaid roses, for I knew how the cream-coloured flowers and varnished leaves would look against the mellow brick. There was nothing of the slightest interest or rarity, for this garden was not intended to be one where the owner, with difficulty deciphering a metal label solemnly introduces the visitor to a minute mouse-coloured blossom, and tells him that never before has this species flowered in Sussex. . . . How I long, on such occasions, to stamp on the mouse, passionately exclaiming "And it shan't go on flowering in Sussex now. . . ."

As soon as there were signs of summer in the succeeding years I furnished my outdoor study, laying rugs on the tiled floor and hanging pictures on its two walls. By the side of my writing-table I put an oblong mirror, so that sitting at work, I could see the reflection of the garden framed in it. Out of doors the eye wanders, but by this device it is forced to concentrate on what is framed and the picture of the sunlit beds seen in the shadowed mirror glowed with an added brilliance. The luxuriance with which everything grew there was uncanny: a pool of unbroken blue surrounded Augustus, the aubrietias encroached on to the crazy pavement, and the web of wall-flower scent spread like gossamer over the beds. The Mermaid roses threw out long, sappy shoots against the wall, and the Jackmanni, covered with purple stars, shot up to the top of the trellis and entangled itself in the pear-tree. We had week after week of sunny days, and every morning I trundled down a small wheeled table, such as they use in hospitals for bedside dressings, laden with the books I wanted for my work, bolted the door that led from the other garden, sunbathed in the secluded heat, and wrote in the shelter.

Gabriel never saw the secret garden. He was eighty-six now and bedridden, smacking his lips still over his glass of port with his dinner, but dozing most of the day. Then came the time when he could no longer be looked after in the house where he lodged, for he required more nursing than could be given him there, and he was moved into the infirmary at the workhouse. Then a dismal little tragedy happened, wounding to the sentimentally inclined. His long beard could not be kept clean; the doctor said it must be cut off, and Gabriel cried.

Many quite unimaginative folk are conscious, in certain houses or in rooms in those houses, of a quality in the atmosphere which seems independent of the physical environment. It may be happy or unhappy, peaceful or troubled, it does not vary with their moods and it is as evident to some inner sense as the odour of wood-smoke from the winter fires of six months before. It clings to the place faint but persistent. The secret garden soon developed some such atmosphere quite unconnected, it would seem, with Augustus or the flower-beds with sun or cloud or with the associations that gathered in it. I enjoyed my sun-baths and the new version of Charlotte Brontë at which I was working and the frequent presence of friends. Francis Yeats-Brown sprawled on the grass busy with *Bengal Lancer*, and refreshed himself with Yoga postures and deep breathing: Dame Ethel Smyth recalled some strangely erroneous impressions she had formed about my father and mother for her sequel to her enthralling *Impressions That Remained*: Clare Sheridan came over from Brede Place, and we discussed reincarnation (for which doctrine I had no use): the place was impregnated with the commerce and conversation of many friends. But it was not they who made this atmosphere: it was as if something out of the past, some condition of life long vanished, was leaking through into the present, and at least half a dozen of these friends perceived it. Then—it is next to impossible to describe this—this atmosphere became more personal: there was somebody there. The presence was in no way perilous or malign, like the presences in the enchanted woods of Ware, nor was it friendly: it was entirely indifferent. Suddenly a curious thing happened. Whether or no it betokened a visible manifestation of the haunting presence, I have no idea.

One windless summer day two friends, of whom the Vicar of Rye was one, were lunching with me, and afterwards we strolled down to the secret garden. It was a brilliant, broiling day and we seated ourselves in a strip of shade close to the door in the wall which communicated with the other garden. This door was open: two of our chairs, the Vicar's and mine, faced it, the other had its back to it. . . . And I saw the figure of a man walk past this open doorway. He was dressed in black and he wore a cape the right wing of which, as he passed, he threw across his chest, over his left shoulder. His head was turned away and I did not see his face. The glimpse I got of him was very short, for two steps took him past the open doorway, and the wall behind the poplars hid him again. Simultaneously the Vicar jumped out of his chair, exclaiming: "Who on earth was that?" It was only a step to the open door, and there, beyond, the garden lay, basking in the sun and empty of any human presence. He told me what he had seen: it was exactly what I had seen, except that our visitor had worn hose, which I had not noticed.

Now the odd feature about this meaningless apparition is that the first time this visitor appeared he was seen simultaneously by two people whose impressions as to his general mien and his gesture with his cloak completely tallied with each other. There was no legend about such an appearance which could have predisposed either of them to have imagined that he saw anything at all, and the broad sunlight certainly did not lend itself to any conjuring up of a black moving figure. Not long afterwards it was seen again in broad daylight by the Vicar at the same spot; just a glimpse and then it vanished. I was with him but I saw nothing. Since then I think I have seen it once in the evening on the lawn near the garden-room, but it was dusk, and I may have construed some fleeting composition of light and shadow into the same figure.

Now ghost stories, which go back into the earliest folktales, are a branch of literature at which I have often tried my hand. By a selection of disturbing details it is not very difficult to induce in the reader an uneasy frame of mind which, carefully worked up, paves the way for terror. The narrator, I think, must succeed in frightening himself before he can hope to frighten his readers, and, as a matter of fact, this man in black had not occasioned me the smallest qualms. However I worked myself up and wrote my ghost story, describing how there developed an atmosphere of horror in my secret garden, how when I took Taffy there he cowered whining at my heels, how at night a faint stale luminance hovered over the enclosing walls, and so led up after due preparation for the appearance of the spectre. Then, for explanation, I described how I found in the archives at the Town Hall an account of the execution three hundred years ago of the then owner of that piece of land who had practised nameless infamies there, and how the skeletons of children, hideously maimed, were found below the bed over which Augustus reigned. I took a great deal of trouble over this piece, and having read it through I treated it as I had treated the first draft of Charlotte Brontë, and tore it up. What had actually happened (for I have no doubt whatever that the Vicar and I saw something that had no existence in the material world) made a far better ghost story than any embroidered version, and so I have here set it down unadorned and unexplained.

CHAPTER XIII

I WAS now more solidly and substantially at home in Rye than in any other of those delightful abiding-places outside London where my life had been passed. Addington in the holidays, Cambridge in term time, Capri in the summer months, Switzerland in winter, Tremans, as long as my mother lived, had all passed away, but Rye had so firmly pervaded me that I never even said to myself as I stepped out of the train, "Here we are at home again." London was beginning to transform itself into a most delightful hotel where many friends had lodgings too, but I had not got the true Cockney heart, like my friend Sir George Arthur, who loves London because it is London. He likes to be established there, he has told me, by August Bank Holiday. The months still called "The Season" are over, the parties and the dinings out and all the fuss have finished, and he can enjoy undiluted London in peace and quiet. But I had not that instinct and I found London in those months when it is called "empty" a dreary waste of sultry streets and closed houses with forlorn cats sitting on area steps. And I had ceased to be diverted by mere gregariousness. The elongated dinner-table no longer thrilled me *because* there were so many decorative people sitting round it, nor did I care to squeeze my way up a thronged staircase to emerge in a room packed beyond computation with friends and acquaintances and strangers. In such a crush

friends become acquaintances and talk with a roving eye
to see who else is there; and acquaintances, glued together
look round to find a friend, and strangers struggle to get
away from each other and find an acquaintance. And, as
I have mentioned before, a hobbler on a stick does not
add to general gaiety, and if such congregations do not
add to his own there can be no reason why he should
frequent them. I confess that I continued to like to be
asked.

I found that growing old was in itself quite a pleasant
process. All that was required of one was to keep
reasonably young and the years did the rest. I had expected that it would be a burdensome and joyless task,
but it resolved itself into a pastime. As energy diminished,
so did also the desires that called for it, and these diminu-
tions in supply and demand seemed to cancel against each
other as from the two sides of an equation, leaving the
resultant values still balanced. All through middle age,
had the chance been given me, I would have clutched at
the magic wand, and, violently waving it, have wished
myself back at the age of twenty, to live the years through
again. But now I did not covet such a chance, and had
it been granted me I should have thought twice before
I waved. I had learned some lessons, which, if one admits
any design in life, had served their purpose. I had also
greatly enjoyed myself, and I recognized that these enjoyments had by some process of psychical digestion passed
into my system and were part of me like my flesh and
bones. They "worked within": I could recall and relive
them far more vividly than disagreeable experiences. In
these respects it appeared to be a "score" to be getting
old: one seemed by some automatic process to be

eliminating past chagrins and retaining the pleasures. And the obligations attached to it were not onerous. People did not expect much from the venerable. Not to be sprightly and not to be cantankerous were certainly necessary. These were self-protective measures, to make oneself tolerable.

A friend and contemporary of mine came to stay for a couple of nights and we scrutinized the phenomena of age over the fire in the garden-room. A very large circle reveres him as a monument of transcendent good sense and assimilated experience, but he tells me that he is not in need of any advertisement and suggests "Henry" as a pseudonym.

"I get happier as I get older," he said, "just because I don't want so much, and am therefore not so frequently in a bad temper, if I don't get it. You surely must have noticed how much my temper has improved these last years. . . . And I take much more pleasure in little things in themselves, as when there's a clean smell of frost on an autumn morning. I don't say to myself: "It's going to be a fine day: how can I get the greatest enjoyment out of it?" Instead I sniff in the air and find it delicious. If it's pouring with rain when I wanted to be out all day, I don't curse it. I think how pleasant it will be to sit by the fire. . . . This cigarette: I used to smoke because there was a box of them handy. Now I wait till I want one and then enjoy it. Food, too. Like an ass I used not to think about food. Now I've become a gourmet. Why should it be supposed that the sight of a fine land-scape is an uplifting influence via the eye, or music via the ear, whereas the delight given to the palate by some exquisite flavour is labelled greedy? I put cooking among the most potent Christianizing influences. It causes the well-springs of charity and kindliness to gush forth. After that soufflé at dinner I could have washed a leper's feet, though I'm glad there wasn't one handy. All these appreciations are symptomatic of the wisdom that ought to come with age; the quiet cosy wisdom which is so comfortable."

"They sound materialistic," I said.

"They are materialistic. On the other hand, if I do want something, I don't take very much trouble to get it. If the grapes are too high, I won't risk a fall from a ladder to pick them."

"Consoling yourself with the reflection that they are sour?"

"No; rejoicing to believe that they are sweet. I perceive you understand nothing yet about the technique of growing old. I want to appreciate to the full everything that comes within easy reach. And there's time to taste things now instead of gobbling them up in such a hurry and grabbing at something else. That incessant desire to grab ages one frightfully: I'm delighted to say I've got over it. As to trying to be less cantankerous, which I admit was one of the pleasures of being young, that takes care of itself. It's too much trouble. Much better when one's old to be comfortable oneself and not mind if others are comfortable too."

"But I want to use all the energy I've got, if I happen to feel cantankerous. It's still a disgrace not to be rather tired every evening. And I feel that a day is wasted on which I haven't written a thousand words or so."

"Good gracious, what a number! Are they all good ones? But you enjoy it, don't you?" he asked.

"I don't enjoy it as much as I used. I take more trouble than ever. I tell myself that this time there will be a masterpiece. But I'm not quite as convinced of that as I used to be."

"Then it certainly won't be," he said. "You've got to believe in what you're doing to make a good job of it. You've always been your kindest critic, and it's not likely you'll change now. Drop it for a while, and see if the appetite returns. Try reading."

"The worst of reading is that I keep thinking how I should have written it and my attention wanders. And most new books aren't worth reading."

"But why read new books? The works of Jane Austen and a few tales from the *Decameron* keep you abreast of all that is worth having in modern literature. And better written."

"But I might lose my appetite for writing permanently if I stopped," I said. "And I like making money."

"Do you want it particularly?" he asked.

"No, but I like making it. I feel like the jolly miller when he hears his stones grinding."

"What do you do with it?" he asked.

"Give a little away, spend most of it, and save the remainder if there is any."

"The last is an awful habit. I have it badly myself," he said. "I tell myself that if I got appendicitis it would be a great expense, and I keep providing for it. Probably I've provided enough for a dozen appendixes. The thought of dying annoys me sometimes. I don't in the least want to die: I feel like the old lady who said: 'If I ever die, which God forbid!' I shall tell my executors to put on my tombstone that I lie here under protest.

But I'm extremely curious as to what is to happen next. That something will happen I have no doubt. I'm not going to be extinguished. The padre at my church preached the other day about us being souls under the altar. There'll be no exercise of free-will as far as I can see. That seems a dreadful waste of time. And very dull."

"But there won't be any time as far as you're concerned," I said.

"I know: but the human mind can't rid itself of the idea of time. Things will go on happening in the world after I've left it, I assure you, just as they did before I got here, incredible though it sounds. . . . But, if you come to think of it, the illusion that each of us matters tremendously was the only possible method by which God, having once given us free-will, could make us exert ourselves. Otherwise the clock would have had no mainspring. It would have stopped. . . . I wonder, by the way, if your writing has become a sort of superstition to you. You go on with it, perhaps, just as I used to bow to the new moon, not really believing in it. So I stopped bowing to it, and found it made no difference to me."

"But I've got to do something instead," I objected. "You don't bow to the moon very hard for several hours every day."

"Probably something else will turn up. Good heavens, how late it is. How you've been talking! I must go to mass to-morrow at eight. Will you ask your servant to call me at seven? No tea, but a couple of oranges. I shall go back to bed afterwards and have breakfast there if I may."

There were blinding torrents of rain next morning,

but Henry attends Mass every day whatever the weather, if there is a Catholic church within reasonable distance. He brought the local padre back to breakfast with him in his bedroom. They had a discussion, he told me, on some abstruse doctrinal point, but they abandoned it at once, when I sent *The Times* to his room, in favour of the crossword. "One can argue about the Holy Trinity any day," said Henry, "but the crossword has to be done to-day or never. . . ." The weather cleared, and we drove over to Dover and lunched with some friends, and called afterwards at Walmer Castle, the residence of the Lord Warden of the Cinque Ports. I had stayed there twenty years ago with Lord Beauchamp, and since then much had been done to render the castle worthier of its historical associations and less deficient in what we may delicately call plumbing. The Duke of Wellington's small bedroom had been restored to its original state. There was his camp bed in which he always slept and in a cupboard beside it the crockery tea-set with an "Etna" in which he made himself his early morning tea, his small deal wash-stand and his sponging tin. Somehow a prolonged study of his dispatches would not have brought one into such close touch with him. . . . I thought I remembered in a recess in the long gallery room facing the sea a brass plaque on the wall with an inscription recording how Lord Nelson and Pitt, then Lord Warden, had sat together on a seat just below it and discussed plans to meet the danger of French invasion. It proved to be actually in its original place, but the recess where it had been affixed had been cut off from the big room and turned into a bathroom for the adjoining bedroom. The attention of the plumber could not have been called to this plaque, for he had placed directly below it a water-closet, and one read how Nelson and Pitt had sat together here. . . . So we went home in great content, and Henry told me how he had once lost his faith in Christianity but fell asleep before he had finished. He half-woke just as we were passing along the side of a lake in a Kentish valley. A fish rose close to the edge of the water. "Trout. Grilled, don't you think?" said Henry very drowsily, as if talking in his sleep. Here, thought I, was an opportunity for a delicate and tactful surprise, and on getting home I told my cook to give us grilled trout for dinner, if she could procure them. There was never a greater failure: Henry must have been dreaming, and his dream came through the ivory gates through which, as the Greeks tell us, false dreams visit us. "Delicious fish," he said, "but trout should always be boiled." And I had meant so well.

An intermezzo, but it bore on future developments.

I did not take Henry's advice and drop writing for the sake of regaining appetite, but made myself busy again collecting all the information, private and public, that I could get about the Emperor William II of Germany, hoping to distil from it something of the essential nature of the man himself. It was a fascinating study, for presently I began to perceive that the bombast and bawling, which made him the firebrand of Europe, were not the sincere self-expression of a natural megalomaniac: they were the armour that he wore to protect himself, the smoke-screen by which he concealed himself. He had been born into the world with a disabling physical deformity. A powerless arm handicapped all the normal activities of boyhood. Other boys did with ease and exuberance what he had painfully to acquire, and there developed in him from his earliest years an inferiority complex. The effect of this pitiful condition on some natures is that they resign themselves, sullenly and bitterly, to the limitations of their disabilities. Others, refusing to acquiesce, doggedly fight their infirmities and hearten themselves up by bragging and self-assertiveness. He belonged to this latter class, and primarily his conscious aim was to break this complex for his own sake, and acquire confidence in himself. By the time he had grown to manhood this had become a habit, but it was never rooted in his nature. At bottom he was always full of fearfulness and misgiving: he collapsed always when his English grandmother took him in hand, for the pose of his own omnipotence could not stand up against her unassumed firmness. But the pose was a valuable instrument to the Prussian war-party, who exalted and encouraged his megalomania. Actually he hated and feared the idea of war, but his Field Marshals took his sabre-rattlings and his stupendous announcements that he was the chosen instrument of the Lord of Hosts at their face value, for it suited their own ends, and made him keep polishing up the shining armour which he had donned for his secret reassurance. His position, in fact, resembled that of Mr. Winkle in the *Pickwick Papers* who was always being put into false positions owing to the pose he had adopted of being an ardent sportsman, expected to ride and skate and shoot with skill and enthusiasm.

The Emperor also inherited many traits from his grandfather, the Prince Consort. He had his genuine love of art and music and the same general versatility, which dispensed with technical knowledge. The Prince Consort invented a process of fresco-painting which should have rendered fresco practically immortal, but which actually caused it to disappear with unusual rapidity. He invented a system of drainage, but in his calculations forgot the action of the law of gravity. Even so his grandson designed a battleship which would render the English dreadnoughts obsolete. It had only one defect, namely that when placed on the water it would instantly sink. He established a porcelain manufactory at Cadinen, but the clay, being coarse and full of iron could no more produce porcelain than it could produce gold-leaf. At his farm there he had some very fine cattle, and he made a brilliant plan to mate his cows with Indian buffaloes; these nuptials must inevitably produce gigantic beef and torrential milk. But the factor of sex appeal was wanting and the plan did not work. I liked these pot-shots that so lightly brushed aside all the limitations of natural laws. Perhaps the happiest moment of his life was when he fled from his defeated country, and safely passed the frontiers of Holland. Fear had always been his arch foe, and now there was nothing more to fear. He could live in peace, chopping wood for the Dutch stoves, and planting his rose-garden.

Surely a very picturesque figure, and one not sufficiently explored as an individual apart from his Imperial gestures. Though Potsdam was not so high in the scale of abiding human values as Haworth Parsonage, the inquiry into what the Emperor really *was* interested me immensely.

So once more the hospital table was loaded with books, and wheeled down on all sunny mornings to the secret garden, and sixpenny note-books crammed with references multiplied. But I did not look forward to the writing of this document: the *chasse*, as in the curiosity shops of Rye, had been absorbing to me, but I began to wonder—impious thought for a writer—whether anybody would care to know what I had brought back. This misgiving gained on me; it gave rise to another, and again I wondered whether Henry had not been very wise when he suggested that my need to write had become a superstition with me, in which I no longer believed, a false appetite denoting no real hunger. It might be better to treat it as such, and wait to see whether true hunger returned. I was quite aware how little my decision mattered to anybody but myself (or was that a threatening of inferiority complex?) and I had only my own comfort to consider.

Then one morning, out of the blue, my friend, Captain Dawes, the Town Clerk, rang me up. Could I see him? Rather important. He came, and he told me that the Town Council of Rye wished to know whether, if they elected me as Mayor for the ensuing year, I would accept the office. I expressed myself as being highly honoured by the suggestion. "Staggered" would have been a more precise expression, for it seemed too odd to be true. I might as well have been asked to be Speaker of the House of Commons or a station-master.

I knew at once that I was going to accept, and my mind so much resented my knowing that I knew it, that it poured forth a volley of reasons why it was quite impossible to do so. Municipal affairs were a sealed book to me, and I had not the slightest desire to open it. I had never been a member of the Town Council; I did not know who they were or what they did except impose rates and taxes, how then could I take a header into their experienced midst and emerge their Chairman? I was not prepared to live in Rye to the extent that would be necessary if I was Mayor. I was an author, and Mayoral duties would create a more incessant interruption to my work than I could afford. I should have to make speeches on official occasions, and to make a speech at all poisoned life to me for days beforehand. Then with high ingenuity my mind produced an even more subtle reason for refusing than these. I had written (and it would soon be published) another volume about my preposterous Lucia, in the course of which she would be elected Mayor of Tilling, and Tilling, as Rye knew very well, *was* Rye. Mallards, where Lucia lived, was a faithful delineation of Lamb House where I lived. Visitors to Rye quite often asked which was Lucia's house, and which Miss Mapp's. Surely it would be very unseemly that the man whom the Town Council were proposing to honour should presently publish a piece of farcical fiction in which the Mayor of Rye was the most prominent and ludicrous figure. I told the Town Clerk that the Council must know about this, and reconsider their proposal. . . . These reasons for declining the honour were all true as far as they went, but they did not go far. Nobody, for instance, could question my ignorance of municipal affairs, but I was not such an idiot as not to be able to learn about them. I was not, at the moment, prepared to be in Rye as regularly as Mayoral engagements would demand, but was that really a very unpleasant prospect? I was interested in my investigations into William II, but should I much mind interruptions to the task of writing, to which I was not looking forward? I was not like the

Victorian young lady who, when asked to play the piano, only needed a little pressing. I did not need to be pressed at all for I was perfectly well aware that I was going to be Mayor of Rye. What seemed finally to settle the matter was that my butcher told my cook that it would be a capital thing for Rye, and my cook told the out-going Mayor that it would be a capital thing for me, as it would take me away from my writing.

Then I had to find a Mayoress: this post, I must explain, is in the gift of the Mayor. Mayors' wives usually fill the office, but in this case there was no wife available, and an irregular union must be sought for. I approached, with some diffidence, my very old friend Mrs. Jacomb-Hood, who had a house in Rye and who was without rival among the ladies of Rye for decorativeness and a sense of duty, and begged her to live with me in municipal sin for the period of our municipal lives. She very charmingly consented, and I started on this unlooked for adventure.

I felt extremely pleased with myself when having been installed as the six hundred and forty-fifth of my dynasty, I was invested in a crimson robe trimmed with fur, a double gold chain round my neck and a new cocked hat trimmed with gold on my head. I walked behind the maces from the Town Hall to the George Hotel, from the balcony of which, when my guests had refreshed themselves, I and other Councillors threw bagfuls of pennies to be scrambled for, according to immemorial custom, by the children of Rye assembled in the street below. These pennies used once to be heated so that the donors might enjoy the medieval amusement of seeing the children burn their fingers when they picked them up, thus combining a mild sadism with an inexpensive charity. I liked pomp and ceremony and the due observance of ancient tradition, and being prayed for in church on Sunday morning without the disadvantage of being seriously ill. From my seat by the organ the sermon was not very audible, and I fell into the habit of gazing with a vague designing eye on the unstained glass of the west window. It was a noble example of the decorated period, beautifully proportioned, with five lights and with florid and graceful tracery above. I imagined the two outer lights filled with mosaic glass and medallions, similar to those in the south transept window and framing some central scene which should include the islands of glass among the tracery. One could fill them with tongues of fire descending on the twelve apostles at Pentecost, but that might be mistaken for fire descending on the cities of the plain. . . . Blue must be the prevailing colour, masses of blue, the turquoise blue of the Morning Glory which now sprawled over the entrance to the secret garden, the blue of a clear sky in winter. . . .

The week started with my presiding over the Borough Bench at 10 a.m. on Monday morning. That was not new work, as I was already a Justice of the Peace, but when Lord Morris wrote a letter to *The Times* to say that we country magistrates were a farcical body, idiotic by nature and wholly ignorant of law, I felt that I had to answer him with the same publicity, and invited him to visit Rye and commit some petty larceny in order to ascertain for himself that we would handle him in a very competent and correct fashion. . . . There were Council meetings, at which I cultivated a suave but firm demeanour which was very foreign to my nature, and finance meetings and committees of boards for housing and highways, and fire brigade and water supply and hospitals and burials and elementary schools. All such organizations I had hitherto looked upon as natural phenomena pursuing their courses with the ordained placidity of the stars, but I found that they were far from being placid in their origins, for they emerged from a welter of arguments and contrary opinions. There were many meetings for the local celebration of King George V's Jubilee in the summer, and we settled to raise as much money as we could, and spend it all on providing an ephemeral festival for children. There were other suggestions: a swimming-bath, the upkeep of which would be a heavy permanent charge on the rates unless a mania for bathing all the year round seized our citizens; and a lady with an eye for the picturesque proposed that every man, woman and child in Rye should dress in a costume of not less than a hundred years ago, and wear it for three days in-doors and out at work or play. She thought this would be "a very gracious and fragrant thing to do." So no doubt it would, but the expense of providing five thousand antique costumes was felt to be fatal to it, not to men-tion the inconvenience to the gardener of digging his beds in doublet and hose or to the golfer of driving in chain armour. So we ordained a non-stop festival for children, starting at a reasonably early hour with the presentation of commemorative mugs and finishing thirteen hours later with fireworks. Even apart from such extras it would be absurd to call these duties onerous, but they gave me interests, hitherto quite outside my accustomed orbit, to think about. It had never included the spend-ing of time or trouble on the welfare of the community.

I had worked hard at my profession, but in my leisure (which was as abundant as I chose to make it) I had never taken up any form of social service. I do not pretend that the desire to repair this omission had prompted me, but I told myself, when a Council meeting occurred on a day when I should have liked to be somewhere else, that I was making an offering to the cause of civilization. We debated on slum-clearance or water supply or the drainage system, or speed limit for motor-cars through built-up areas, so when debate got wordy or wasteful of time or slightly acrimonious I told myself I was a civilizing influence. As for the Mayoral salary for the year, I managed to dispose of it in just under three weeks. It was not liable to Income Tax and that gave me a pleasant sense of having scored off the Commissioners of Inland Revenue.

Sometimes I secretly and insincerely moaned over what I called these "incessant interruptions" to my work; and sometimes I thought that I was terribly tied at Rye, having to be there for a part of every month in the year. But I was aware that these incessant interruptions were actually rekindling my interest in writing again, and I hurried back from Council or Committee meetings to the garden-room and the hospital-table piled high with books, longing to get to the Emperor William again. I recaptured the fading illusion that my work mattered to anybody except myself. As for London, it regained much of its glamour because I could no longer be there whenever I chose. Slipping back into its cheerful friendly tranquillity after the stir of business in Rye, it became a little backwaterish, a little provincial. After all, was it not the centre of Suburbia?

A second year of office followed on the first and during it there befell a very grievous domestic tragedy. Taffy was now seven years old and young for his age, but during that spring he grew suddenly old. He went to see his vet, who could find nothing amiss. He was in good spirits, he carried his market-basket proudly down the High Street of a morning and fetched the evening paper, and pranced round the garden before bed-time. But he got tired very easily, and there were no more expeditions to the sea, and when he encountered the dogs of Rye there were no more dangerous exchanges of compliments. His appetite failed, and though his dining-room chair was always ready for him he never sat on it. His coat was still glossy, but it bagged on him for he grew very thin. There were more medical consultations, but the faculty could not help him. One evening, carrying the paper, he tried to get up the stairs of the garden-room where he delivered it, but he could not manage them. He put it down, barking to show he had done his duty, and crept back into the house again. The June weather was very hot, and all day he lay for coolness on a rug in the hall, very polite, with a languid thump of his tail for his friends, and he did not seem to be in pain. When the sun was off the garden he shambled out there to lie on the lawn, but one evening he could not find strength to walk, and he was carried out on his rug. He sat up for a moment and looked about, then lay down panting a little and stretched his legs out and moved no more.

That summer came one of those solemn and traditional functions which date from the time when the Cinque Ports were perhaps the most important national organization for the defence of the realm. Lord Willingdon had been appointed Lord Warden to succeed Lord Reading, and the Court of Shepway assembled at Dover, as it had done on such occasions since the thirteenth century, for his installation. Mayors of the Cinque Ports and Antient Towns and Limbs of the Cinque Ports, fourteen in number, accompanied by their maces and mace-bearers and their Town Clerks and Recorders drove up through streets lined with troops to St. Mary's Chapel at Dover Castle. There the Archbishop of Canterbury conducted the service, and at the conclusion of it solemnly blessed our new Lord Warden. Then the procession returned to hold the Court of Shepway in a huge marquee in the grounds of Dover College. I had been elected Speaker of the Cinque Ports that morning and it was my duty to ask him, according to the medieval ritual, if he would observe "the Franchises, the Liberties, the Customs and the Usages of the Ports." I was glad that he promised to do so, for there were no instructions in the records of this ancient office as to how the Speaker should proceed, if he refused.

Once more in the autumn of 1936 the Council asked me to continue at my post for a third year. It was not often now that I left Rye for more than a week or two and this winter was not one when I much wished myself elsewhere. There were many days of pellucid blue and brightness, and the knowledge, conveyed in the weather report on the wireless, that in London there was a choking fog, with trains running hours late, and no visible visibility gave them a peculiar preciousness. . . . On the shortest day of the year with the noon sun at its lowest, there was still a patch of brightness in the secret garden, and I dragged a deck-chair to the corner of the crazy pavement and sat there for half an hour. It was Christmas in four days, and I have an affection for its traditional usages. The spruce-fir which had furnished my Christmas-tree last year and had since been bedded out in the garden had grown, but it was not too tall to stand on the sideboard in the dining-room again, hung with dazzling objects, balls of lustre and peacocks with tails of spun glass and red wax tapers and tufts of uninflammable cotton-wool for snow. A few friends, old in friendship, would be my party, and crackers would be pulled and whistles blown and paper caps worn. . . . Just opposite my windless seat in the patch of sunshine was the pear-tree I have spoken of before. The bare branches enclosed islands of blue sky, some small, some large, irregularly shaped, as if in the tracery of a decorated window, and there passed through them, dipping and poising in his flight, a seagull, dazzling white in his winter plumage. Instantly the design for which I had been searching so long through inaudible sermons flashed upon me. In each of the blue islands in the tracery of the west window there should be an angel swooping downwards, and the top half of the three centre lights should be blue sky full of descending angels who alighted on the roof of the stable at Bethlehem. Within on one side knelt the ox and the ass, in the centre was the Virgin and Child, and on the other side Joseph the Carpenter kneeling also, with his saw in his hand. From below on the left, across a Fra Angelico meadow of flowers approached the Kings of the East, on the right the shepherds. The two side lights that framed the central scene must be full of angels, too. They required thinking out, but the central picture was clear.

I went back to the garden-room, blessing the seagull, and filled sheets of paper with sketches. I cannot draw, but I could indicate what somebody else would draw, and I outlined the five lights of the window and the islands of glass in the tracery above. These I filled with angels: some looked like moths and some like aeroplanes, all plunging downwards. In the heights, as suited the distance and the smaller islands, they were little, and they grew bigger as they approached the stable of the Nativity. They alighted on the roof, feeling with their feet, as birds do, before they perch, and once perched they opened their mouths and sang. The design grew more elaborate with each new sketch, but not better drawn.

The next step was to think out subjects for the medallions in the outer lights. Angels from the Old Testament must be shown on one side and angels from the New Testament, in corresponding subjects, on the other. An angel, for instance, appeared to Abraham when he was about to sacrifice his only son Isaac, and an angel appeared in the garden at Gethsemane to the only Son on the eve of His sacrifice of Himself.

I have been in a hurry all my life when I wanted to do something or to get something done, and it was not many days before my friend Mr. Hogan, who had designed the window in the south transept came down from London about the new project. He grinned at my moths and aeroplanes, and my mis-shapen shepherds and Kings, but he took my design seriously and we went to the church to see how it would work in the window itself. Yes: blue, blue, right down to the roof of the stable with a flock of angels converging from above on to the central point of the Mother and Child, and to the same centre point from below converged the shepherds and the Kings. He said that it "composed" very well, and was I thinking about taking up window-designing when I ceased to be Mayor? A few weeks later came his coloured drawing: it was just what I had seen but could not draw, and I had only one further suggestion. Could not the leading shepherd have with him, as he knelt in the flowering meadow, a large black collie? I sent him a snapshot of Taffy, who had turned his head away from the camera, just when he should have been looking into it: so now he was looking where the shepherds and the Kings looked. Taffy was not a great church-goer in his mortal pilgrimage: in fact he had only been in the church once. It was having its spring cleaning, and, the north door being set wide, he had walked in to see what was going on, and was instantly driven out by an indignant charwoman with her broom. But he is secure there now until a German bomb expels him once more.

King George V had died in January of this year 1936: I find that in my diary of that date I had made an entry about the new King: "He must eventually, and indeed probably before a year is out, choose between the Throne and this Lady." He abdicated in the following December, choosing the Lady. His abdication caused the profoundest regret to millions of his subjects, for, as a young man he had been a Fairy Prince in their eyes. The date fixed for the Coronation in May 1937 was adhered to, though another would be crowned in his stead. So while Mr. Hogan was making angels of my moths and aeroplanes, the solicitors of the Cinque Ports, the Town Clerks of Dover and Rye, were instructing me, as Speaker, on the engaging history of the privileges and duties which fell to the Mayors of the Cinque Ports and Antient Towns and Limbs for this occasion. Those in office during the year must through the medium of the Lord Warden state their claim to be summoned to attend the King on his Coronation in Westminster Abbey, and, if this is granted, they automatically become Barons of the Cinque Ports. This very distinguished title, I hasten to add, does not carry with it a seat in the House of Lords: its bearer's career and honours begin and end on Coronation Day, when he wears a dazzling traditional costume procured at his own expense, a scarlet cloak heavily braided with gold, a brocaded waistcoat, black breeches and white stockings.

The history of these Barons is equally picturesque. From Tudor times up till the Coronation of George IV it was their duty to carry a canopy over the heads of the newly crowned King as he walked from Westminster Abbey to Westminster Hall where the Coronation Banquet took place. But at the Coronation of George IV the performance of their duties was hampered by most surprising difficulties. The King was determined that Queen Caroline should not enter the Abbey and be crowned, and he was terribly frightened that she would find a way through the troops who closed all approaches by land, while a bevy of prize-fighters were stationed on the riverside to prevent her gaining access by water. There was much popular sympathy for her, for the King's divorce proceedings against her had failed, and therefore being still his legally wedded wife she had every right to be crowned with him. He got through the Coronation safely, and now he was in a great hurry to get into Westminster Hall for the banquet, and finish with the ceremonies before any conjugal invasion happened. The Barons, loaded as they were with the canopy, found it very arduous work to keep up with him. The day was very hot, and the Baron on the King's right had been furnished, in addition to his ceremonial burden, with two embroidered bags, one of which was empty when the procession started, the other full of clean handkerchiefs, for the King was very fat and perspired profusely during his agitating walk, and it was this Baron's duty constantly to take from the Royal hand the handkerchief with which he had mopped his face and give him a dry one. This manœuvre necessitated his taking one hand from the pole of the canopy which he carried and fumbling in the embroidered bags, and it caused the canopy to wobble in an alarming manner. The King, already in a state of nervous tension at the idea of Caroline's possible appearance, was afraid that it would collapse on him. He may also have known that, at the Coronation of King James II, when Samuel Pepys was one of the bearers of the canopy, this actually did happen. He therefore stepped out from its dangerous shelter, and sped on ahead. The loyal Barons whose office it was to hold it over his anointed head quickened their pace, but the King was determined to keep clear of it, and broke into a shuffling trot, as if he was some gross bejewelled moth avoiding capture in a net of cloth of gold carried by scarlet-robed entomologists.

It cannot have been a dignified spectacle, and when the Barons made their application to carry the canopy at the coronation of William IV it was refused, though indeed it was not they who had been to blame. It was further alleged against them that they cut pieces off the canopy and carried them away as mementoes.

At the Coronation of Queen Victoria there was no banquet in Westminster Hall. Instead a substantial breakfast was provided for Ambassadors and high Government officials in the Jerusalem Chamber before the ceremony, and a cold collation was served in St. Edward's Chapel directly after the crowning for the Queen, the Peers who bore the Regalia and her ladies and train-bearers. It was a slight shock to the girl who had been brought up by her mother to hold in the deepest reverence the hallowed offices of the Faith of which she was the Defender, to find the Altar spread with sandwiches and bottles of wine, and her oracle, Lord Melbourne, seems to have misunderstood the nature of her scruples when she called his attention to this, for sipping a glass of wine, he genially replied that the Dean and Chapter of Westminster were responsible for these arrangements, and when the clergy were in charge of a ceremony there was always plenty to eat and drink. . . . In these circumstances there was no use for a canopy since the Queen would not go to Westminster Hall, and when the Barons applied for their privilege, they were invited to stand in the Abbey, carrying banners, outside the Choir screen, but any closer or canopied attendance on their Sovereign was not granted. This snub, followed on that administered to them by King William roused the Cinque Port spirit. The haughty Barons all refused Her Majesty's invitation and the Coronation was shorn of the splendour of their presences.

A lapse of sixty years enabled their successors to get over the insult to their order, and they made their loyal and dutiful application again for the Coronation of King Edward VII. · Once more there was no canopy—had the

bearers perhaps carried it all away in small pieces?—
but now they accepted the invitation to stand with their
banners outside the Choir screen, and thus, as at Runny-
mede, the distressing quarrel between the King and his
Barons was reconciled. King George V renewed this
privilege and the Barons were confirmed in their right
to be present at the Coronation carrying banners. Now
what was I to do? Truly I had no wish to snub my
Sovereign as my predecessor at the Coronation of Queen
Victoria had done, but owing to my infirmities I was
quite incapable of standing for many hours in Westminster
Abbey, carrying a banner, however historical the occasion, and I created a precedent of my own about Corona-
tions. I asked my deputy Mayor to take my place, and,
as he gladly consented, I thereby conferred my automatic
Barony on him. Can any historian produce for me
another instance of a commoner conferring a Barony on
anyone of his own will and pleasure, and carrying it
through unchallenged? I swankily told my friend Baron
Cartier de Marchienne, the Belgian Ambassador, that
I had decided not to go to the Coronation but to give
my place to someone else and to celebrate it down at
Rye, and he not knowing the hidden splendour of this
decision, frivolously replied: "You are quite right: you
prefer to be a big toad in a small pond to being a small
toad in a big pond." That pleased me very much, for I
am sure that nobody else ever heard His Excellency make
a mistake in English. He meant "frog" not "toad." Toads
do not live in ponds however small or large.

The west window of Rye church was now nearly
finished, and in July the bells, recalled from Dieppe,

welcomed Archbishop Lang who came down to unveil it, as his predecessor Archbishop Davidson had unveiled the window in the south transept. On this occasion Lord Willingdon, our new Lord Warden, first visited his Cinque Port, and now the Mayoral procession to the church formed up outside Lamb House without the Mayor for he was within with his distinguished guests. Though the month was July the subject of the window, as yet veiled, pervaded the service. There were Christmas hymns and the Lord Warden read the lesson telling how there were shepherds abiding in the field keeping watch over their flocks by night. The window was in memory of my father and mother, and the Archbishop in his address spoke of him and the guiding principle of his life, Christ Incarnate, and of her whose lambent presence made perpetual stimulus and illumination. He walked to the west end of the church, and pulled the cord that released the sheet over the window, and the sky was full of singing angels, and the kings and the shepherds and their black dog had come to adore.

There was yet one more Cinque Port function for me before my three years of office were over. In the autumn the ancient ceremony of "Brotherhood and Guestling" which for the last six hundred years has met periodically to discuss the business of the Ports, was held at New Romney. Again the Mayors and maces assembled, with the Barons in their Coronation robes, and passed in procession down the main street of Romney to the Norman church. There was a public service first and then the profane crowd was ejected and the doors of the church locked, lest anyone should steal in and hear the secret deliberations of the Cinque Ports. A curtain was drawn across the Sanctuary and the Mayors and Barons sat themselves in a half-circle of noble Chippendale chairs: Major Teichmann Derville, Mayor of Romney, now become Speaker, presided. The business was not controversial. There were no discussions, as in the old days, as to the quota of ships and crews that Hythe, or Winchelsea should provide for the defence of the realm, and indeed all the matters that could be controversial had previously been gone into by their Worships' advisers and settled, so that they had only to propose and second and vote. Petitions were presented by Gillingham and Eastbourne setting forth their claims to be affiliated to the Cinque Ports, but their Worships, previously instructed that these would not hold water, rejected them. A vote of money, not specified, was passed for the framing of an address from the Cinque Ports to King George V on the occasion of his Jubilee to be hung in Walmer Castle. There was a vote of thanks to the Parson for his admirable sermon, and their Worships decided to print it. There may have been a few more similar enactments, but I have forgotten them, and the Brotherhood's labours were done.

Many folk will consider such a solemnity superfluous and ridiculous. "Why," they will ask, "should a score of elderly men dress up, as for charades, drive from long distances to New Romney, in order to sit in a church for the passing of resolutions already determined, and after a substantial lunch with speeches to follow, motor back, flushed and drowsy, to their scattered homes?" But such people have no historical sense. Our placid meeting had six centuries of tradition behind it, dating from the days when the deliberations of the Brotherhood and Guestling were of the same national import as the Navy Estimates. It is bound up in the history of England and I should be sorry to see this illuminated page torn out. If we scrapped every observance which is not of practical import to-day, why should we endure to be startled by squibs if we walk abroad on the evening of November 5, because three centuries ago Guy Fawkes did not succeed in blowing up the Houses of Parliament? Or why should the King be crowned with all pomp at Westminster if it has been already clearly established that he is the legitimate successor to the late Sovereign? Forms and celebrations, as well as films, keep history alive.

So, after three years of office, I was back in Lamb House again, free to spend my time as I chose. I had a good appetite for my own prospects; they wore a friendly aspect, and still the masterpiece beckoned, and still I pursued. Was it a will-o'-the-wisp? Such a notion never entered my head, or I should not have pursued it. Two great honours immediately awaited me, for I was elected an Honorary Fellow of Magdalene, and the Town Council conferred on me the Freedom of the Borough. In both of these I was adopted into a very distinguished company for the two previous holders of this Fellowship were Thomas Hardy and Rudyard Kipling, and the last Freeman of Rye was Archbishop Davidson. So there was one last piece of ancient ceremony for me in the Town Hall. I paid two pennies, coin of the realm, to the Town Clerk for his trouble in drawing up my Charter of Freedom, and the Mayor extending the hand of Fellowship told me that I had the right to kiss him. Then he handed me the gift of the Council, a silver model of the first armed frigate launched in the British Navy in the time of Henry VIII, the *Rose Marie*. She had fifteen guns, and in the crows' nests of her three masts stood sailors, and on deck her Captain, and her sails were bellied with the wind. I read that to be a friendly wind and the pointed guns to be firing a salute.

INDEX

INDEX

INDEX

Frazer, Mrs., 114
Frederick, Empress, 82

Gabriel the gardener, 188–91, 256
Gaiety Theatre, 217
Garrowby, 84–5
Gaskell, Mrs., 74, 251–2
George I, King: at Lamb House, 146–8
George IV, King, 225, 281, 282
George V, King, 274, 280, 284, 286
Ghost stories, 85, 258–9
Gladstone, W. E., 54
Golf, 4–5, 44, 45, 52, 56
Gorki, Maxim, 109
Gospels, the, 246
Gosse, Sir Edmund, 25, 181, 197, 199, 201–2, 247–8, 250; letters to Arthur Benson, 201
Gourlay, Nettie, 13, 14, 15, 17, 32
Granville, Lord, 218
Grebell, Alan, 149–54
Grey of Fallodon, Lord, 171
Grossmith, Mr. George, 217
Grosvenor family, 136
Grosvenor, Miss Victoria, 136

Hakluyt, 187, 193
Halifax, Lord (2nd Viscount), 17, 81–4
Halifax, Lord (3rd Viscount), 17, 82
Hardy, Thomas, 203, 287
Hare, Augustus, 27
Hare, Sir John, 57
Hare, Lady, 57
Harris, Frank, *Contemporary Portraits*, x
Heger, Constantin, 251
Henley, W. E., 3
Hickleton, 74
Higgins, Mr. Henry, 210–13
Hoar-Cross, 83
Hogan, Mr., 279, 280

Holkham, 170

Income-tax evasion, 156
Inge, Dean, 222
Irving, Sir Henry, 203, 215

Jacomb-Hood, Mrs., 272
James, Henry, 1–6; and Lamb House, xi, xii, 1, 145, 253; his habit of *viva voce* composition, 2, 142; literary style, 3–4, 126–7; enigmatical prose, 110–11; characteristics of, 3–6, 97, 127; death, 141, 142
    Other references, 77, 146, 147, 162; his comments on E. F. Benson's *Dodo*, 1–2; Burne-Jones portrait of, 65; *The Wings of a Dove*, 3
James II, King, 282
Jerome, Mr. (American vice-consul), 109–10, 175

Kenmare, Lord and Lady, 88
Kensitites, the, 83, 84
Kingsley, Mrs. Charles, 195
Kipling, Rudyard, 62, 63, 173, 287
    At the End of the Passage, 62
Kitchener, Lord, 250–1

Lamb, Charles, 216
Lamb, George, 147–8
Lamb, James, 147, 148–54, 161
Lamb, Martha, 147, 149
Lamb House, xii, 6, 142 *et seq.*, 186 *et seq.*; Henry James and, xi, xii, 1, 145, 253; E. F. Benson and, 142 *et seq.*; leased jointly with Arthur Benson, 171–2, 186–7; the oak-tree, 189; outdoor study, 253, 254; secret garden, 253–9; the apparition, 257–9

INDEX

INDEX

INDEX

THE HOGARTH PRESS

This is a paperback list for today's readers – but it holds to a tradition of adventurous and original publishing set by Leonard and Virginia Woolf when they founded The Hogarth Press in 1917 and started their first paperback series in 1924.

Some of the books are light-hearted, some serious, and include Fiction, Lives and Letters, Travel, Critics, Poetry, History and Hogarth Crime and Gaslight Crime.

A list of our books already published, together with some of our forthcoming titles, follows. If you would like more information about Hogarth Press books, write to us for a catalogue:

30 Bedford Square, London WC1B 3RP

Please send a large stamped addressed envelope

HOGARTH LIVES AND LETTERS

E.F. Benson
Paying Guests

New Introduction Stephen Pile

Bolton Spa is infamous for its nauseating brine and parsimonious boarding-houses. Exceptional is the Wentworth. Every summer this luxurious establishment is full of paying guests come to sample the waters and happy family atmosphere. But life in the house is far from a rest-cure. Acrimony and arthritis are the order of the day: battles are fought with pedometer, walking stick and paintbrush, at the bridge table, the town concert and afternoon tea. The trials and tribulations of the Wentworth will be relished in drawing-rooms throughout the land for years to come.

E.F. Benson
As We Were

New Introduction by T.J. Binyon

E.F. Benson's eye roves back to those nostalgic days of pincushions and paperweights, of 'Floral Lotto' and soulful renditions of *The Lost Chord*. Starting from the top – with a trenchant picture of Queen Victoria – he unfolds the extreme oddities of his own family and of the people he encountered in their vast social circle. Gladstone tells us how to pack a sponge bag, Tennyson talks of braces, Whistler challenges Moore to a duel – writers and artists share the stage with famous beauties and doughty dowagers in these unparalleled memoirs of late Victorian and early Edwardian England.

T. C. Worsley
Flannelled Fool

A Slice of A Life in the Thirties

New Introduction by Alan Ross

This is the story of one young man's rude awakening from the innocence of a prolonged childhood (where hitting a six had been his wildest dream) into the turbulence of contemporary Europe – the rise of fascism in Italy and Germany, the purge of homosexuals, turmoil in Spain, and scandal at home. Like J. R. Ackerley's *My Father and Myself*, *Flannelled Fool* is remarkable for its rueful self-awareness, its hilarious anecdotes, its mirror to a whole generation. Long recognized as a classic portrait of youth in the Thirties – rushing with all its illusions and self-confidence into the crisis ahead – this haunting memoir is frank, funny and unforgettable.